ON THE
SAME PAGE

A Novel

N. D. Galland

wm

WILLIAM MORROW
An Imprint of HarperCollins*Publishers*

P.S.™ is a trademark of HarperCollins Publishers.

ON THE SAME PAGE. Copyright © 2019 by Nicole Galland. All rights reserved. Printed in the United States of America. No part of this book may be used or reproduced in any manner whatsoever without written permission except in the case of brief quotations embodied in critical articles and reviews. For information, address HarperCollins Publishers, 195 Broadway, New York, NY 10007.

HarperCollins books may be purchased for educational, business, or sales promotional use. For information, please email the Special Markets Department at SPsales@harpercollins.com.

FIRST EDITION

Designed by Diahann Sturge

Text break ornaments © Tribalium / Shutterstock, Inc.

Library of Congress Cataloging-in-Publication Data

Names: Galland, Nicole, author.
Title: On the same page : a novel / N. D. Galland.
Description: First edition. | New York, NY : William Morrow Paperbacks, [2019]
Identifiers: LCCN 2018018493 | ISBN 9780062672858 (paperback)
Subjects: | BISAC: FICTION / Humorous. | FICTION / Contemporary Women.
Classification: LCC PS3607.A4154 O5 2019 | DDC 813/.6—dc23 LC record available at https://lccn.loc.gov/2018018493

ISBN 978-0-06-267285-8

19 20 21 22 23 LSC 10 9 8 7 6 5 4 3 2 1

For Kate Feiffer, who is so often on the same page with me

I
JANUARY

JOANNA HAD THE DECK TO HERSELF, BUNDLED FIVE LAY-
ers thick to keep out the damp. The saltwater of the sound, teal-
gray under a hazy sky, wafted the scent of her childhood across the
bow. The movement of the boat soothed her. She remembered her
grandmother's dining room in Edgartown, with its undulating set
of floorboards intended to remind some returning whaling captain
of this precise sensation after years away from home.

She had been years away from home, herself. Not at sea, but on
the mainland, which was just as far away. She was returning now
to calamity.

From the bow of the ferry, it was hard not to love the Island for
itself, even in the clammy gray air. Even if you dreaded what its human population might have in store for you once you arrive. The
bluffs of West Chop, the lazy stretch of the North Shore unfurl-
ing up-Island toward the Aquinnah lighthouse. It wasn't a dramatic
landscape, just the cobbled moraine of a dying glacier. Perhaps it

was not even beautiful. But Joanna could never view it without feeling a primal attachment. That is why she rarely came home to visit.

The ferry turned to starboard at the channel entrance buoy and steamed southwest into the harbor, entering the sheltered water between the Chops. A helicopter slowly crossed her line of sight, droning inland. Helicopters. She wondered if Hank had been medevaced to Boston. She paced across the breadth of the foredeck from starboard to port, past the bright orange life-saver ring, and stared at the bland brick building facing the harbor from East Chop. The hospital. She didn't know if Hank was still in there, or if he was even still alive. She didn't know whom to call to ask. Feeling anxious and impotent staring at it, she trudged inside to the lunchroom.

Under the fluorescent lights, the scant array of passengers looked depressed and nauseated. Most people sat ignoring a large television screen showing an infomercial. In the past, it had been Fox News. It always seemed ironic, that the primary means of reaching a liberal mecca included forced exposure to illiberal media. Perhaps it had been the Steamship Authority's idea of a hazing, she thought. Too unsettled to listen to what these new talking heads were saying, she turned her attention to the closest Formica table with nobody at it, near the coffee dispensers.

There were copies of both Island newspapers on this table, lying slightly askew as if forgotten by a distracted traveler. One was a slender, old-fashioned broadsheet, much larger than the *New York Times*, the sort of paper an Edwardian butler would iron for his master before serving it at breakfast. Its elegant masthead featured decorative scrolls and some invented coat of arms, and was crowned by a poetic quote, which changed each issue. This issue's, appropriate to the season, was from *Twelfth Night*: "When that I was and a little tiny boy, With hey, ho, the wind and the rain, A foolish thing was but a toy, For the rain it raineth every day—William Shakespeare."

The second paper was smaller and thicker, stuffed with advertising supplements, splashed with color, bedecked with peppy weather icons and taglines for articles waiting inside.

Each paper sported a photo above the fold. The larger paper— the *Newes*—featured a large black-and-white shot of smiling teenagers standing hand in hand, in medieval costumes, on the lip of a stage. The depth of field created an almost three-dimensional effect, the foreground and background figures artfully blurred, those in the middle distance sharp and luminous under stage lights. "CAMELOT enchants at the newly refurbished Performing Arts Center," the headline announced.

The smaller paper—the *Journal*—had a sans serif headline that read: "Vineyard youth lead state in marijuana use." There was a gripping color photo of a back door at the high school, featuring a DEA officer with arms akimbo staring toward the camera at three teenage boys with their backs to the viewer.

Some things would never change. Those weeklies had defined themselves by their differences since the day, back in Joanna's childhood, that some disaffected Newesies had rebelled and huffed themselves halfway across the Island to launch the *Journal*. If Hank didn't survive his injuries, he'd want an obit only in the *Journal*. The *Newes* would cloak him in the pastel hues of an old-school Island sage, while the *Journal* would celebrate his rabble-rousing.

The purser's Yankee accent, over the ferry's speaker system, was distorted and gruff. "All vehicle drivers and passengers, please return to your vehicles on the freight deck. All walk-off passengers will disembark from exit number four on the starboard side of the vessel, mezzanine deck. Please refrain from standing on the staircase while the vessel is docking. Thank you for traveling with the Steamship Authority. Vineyard Haven." She could almost recite it in time, and despite her intention to resist childhood comforts, its familiarity soothed her like a rough seafaring nursery rhyme.

As always, the ferry jerked fitting into the slip, everyone by the passenger-exit door swaying with the movement as if genetically conditioned to expect it. Once the ferry docked, the gangway was hooked up, and some two dozen of them, a drab school of minnows with faces averted against the drizzle, tramped down the ramp to the paved dockside. She squinted into the afternoon dim, looking for Celia.

Celia was about Joanna's height, but a little broader everywhere—hips, breasts, hair, laugh, personality. Celia was the one who'd called to say Joanna's uncle Hank fell off his roof in the winter storm. She was the one who'd looked up the earliest bus from Manhattan to Woods Hole, and which boat it met. She had not said the words "I'll pick you up at the ferry," but Joanna knew she'd be there.

And she was. Wearing her black wool ushanka hat with the earflaps pulled down, and a long down jacket with peace symbols quilted onto it, Celia was the most fashion-forward neo-hippie-chick on the Island. She waved wearing black wool mittens, and

Joanna, seeing her, began to run. They fell into each other's offered bear hugs.

Without preamble Celia said, "He's gonna be okay, kiddo, he broke his leg in some horrible way, and a bunch of organs are bruised, but otherwise he's okay."

Joanna exhaled a short, fierce sob and then pulled herself back together. "Celia. Thanks so much for—"

She waved this away. "Where's your luggage?" and as Joanna was saying, "On the cart," she added, "He's out cold on morphine so they told me to just take you straight home, you can see him tomorrow morning," and was already steering her toward the luggage cart.

"Thanks," Joanna said, suddenly exhausted. It was not the calamity she'd ruminated on for the past eight hours. She had assumed a broken neck at least. A broken leg was no big deal, especially for a retiree . . . surely? Plaster him up in a cast and he'd be fine. The adrenaline from hysterically rushing home suddenly failed her. She probably hadn't needed to come. It was shameful, but she was almost relieved not to go straight to the hospital.

"I stopped by and put the heat up," Celia added, pulling the sole piece of luggage off the metal cart. "There's plenty of firewood but I figured he wouldn't begrudge you some propane. And I've got groceries in the car for you because God knows what he's got in the fridge."

"You are an exceptional human being."

"Oh, c'mon, you'd do the same for me. Is that all you brought, kiddo? I take more than that when I'm going on a cruise for a week, and all I need on a cruise is my bathing suit."

She shrugged. "I've learned to pack light."

"All right," Celia said jovially. "Let's go." She pulled Joanna's wheelie behind her as if Joanna were a toddler who couldn't have managed it on her own, and Joanna followed, feeling the wet seeping into the seams of her suede city boots. Celia came from one of those happy families, the ones Tolstoy said were all alike, and for thirty years she had shared the emotional largesse with Joanna.

Minutes later, they turned up Lambert's Cove Road, a wiggling semicircular loop off State Road, providing access to the North Shore. Many of the seasonal rich and famous had their houses off of it—musicians, politicians, actors, writers, people famous for reasons it was hard to put a finger on. They passed the mailbox of Joanna's second cousin, who had no money but had inherited a family parcel of land and lived in what was hardly more than a shanty, down a mile-long dirt driveway that she shared with a famous chef, a fashion designer, and a pig farmer whom they'd been in second grade with. Tashmoo lapped gently a few dozen yards from her front door, sapphire-blue and smelling of marsh sand. Joanna had spent every childhood November scalloping knee-deep in her briny waters.

Farther up-Island—farther west—the road wound cheerily alongside ancient, lichen-covered stone walls, the scrawny oaks and dense underbrush occasionally yielding to picturesque vistas that were not safe for a driver to look at because there was the next turn already. Near the up-Island end of Lambert's Cove Road, they turned left onto the dirt driveway of Joanna's childhood home, with deep wheel ruts and dead tufts of grass in the middle strip poking up through the sodden snow. Pebbles pinged the undercarriage and they were jolted about, even in the insulated comfort of Celia's Forester.

Hank had built this house almost single-handedly, even though he wasn't a trained carpenter. Or plumber, or electrician, or tile layer, or painter, or roofer. It had no architectural charms at all, but Joanna had been raised here and it felt homey. Even the apron of random crap around the driveway was comfortably familiar. One summer, Joanna had lost a boyfriend who had been mightily enthralled with her until she brought him here. As he drove into the yard, he'd gazed upon both half-disassembled Jeeps, and the five half-disassembled grills; upon the enormous collection of fishing gear literally falling out of the garage doorway; upon the messy pile of metal-mesh crab and lobster traps; at the toddler-size mound of compost . . . He'd smiled wanly and said, as if it were a joke, "Gee, Anna, I didn't realize you came from white trash." And she had nothing to say in response to that, so she said nothing. He did not ask to meet her grown-ups. She never saw him again. Years later she learned he had become a Wall Street tycoon, with a summer house less than a mile distant from Hank's.

All of the junk she remembered was still there, and more besides. A couple of dress-making dummies, a three-foot pile of rusting cast-iron skillets, many heaps of empty planting boxes, unfamiliar lawn furniture. But it was all indistinct through the gathering sleet. They hurried into the house, which was never locked. Celia had turned the heat up high, and it was toasty inside. As they shed coats and boots, two cats greeted them with noises of complaint.

"I fed them," Celia said. "They're lying, ignore them. I let the chickens out this morning too, but make sure they have water."

She had carried Joanna's wheelie into the overstuffed mudroom and now pulled it directly across the carpeted plywood floor of the living room, to the door of Joanna's childhood bedroom on the far side. The floor in here was a few large sheets of particleboard, painted dark green, with braided rugs thrown over it. The bed was still a mattress and box spring on the floor—Joanna's choice, as a girl. She had suspended a sheet over it, nailing it into the popcorn ceiling, and pretended for several months that she was living in a tent, in solidarity with the dispossessed Native Americans. Or something.

"Want me to help you make up the bed, kiddo?" Celia asked, after she'd brought in the bag of groceries.

"I can do it," Joanna said. "You've already done so much."

When she was alone, she checked the refrigerator and saw that Celia's "groceries" included a pot of homemade chicken soup, with a stickie note commanding, *Eat some of this tonight, Joanna. No, seriously, eat some.* She smiled, grateful for the mothering. She put it on the stove, sliced and toasted some bread, and glanced around the familiar space. Five mounds of papers—"piles" would be too respectful a word—almost buried Hank's computer. Bills, bank statements, viral internet memes he wanted to read to visitors, newsletters from the ACLU, the National Libertarian Party, the VFW. Both newspapers on the table, of course. Hank tracked how they talked about West Tisbury politics, so that he could write her long rants about which paper was being biased (usually, according to him, it was the *Newes*). It all smelled of Aging Male Person, and of course Cat. Today was too cold and wet, but tomorrow she would open all the windows and air the place out. She'd probably end up staying a few days once he was home, just to make sure he could get around on his crutches. It was Tuesday. She would be back in New York by the weekend.

As the soup was heating, she grabbed a chipped bowl from the cabinet above the washing machine and set it on the countertop. A pot of vegetable waste, intended for the chickens, sat by the sink. She looked out over the expansive front yard, full of winter rye that Hank would be plowing under in a few months, leaving furrows in the earth that would fill with mud that smelled like sour milk. She'd forgotten how many smells there were associated with her childhood.

So here she was, back home, on the resort paradise isle of Martha's Vineyard.

She'd been home less than three hours when Everett called from the *Journal* and asked her to come in.

"You don't miss a trick," she said. "I'm headed to the hospital in the morning. I'll stop in on my way home."

Then she remembered she hadn't called Brian.

After a decade of her renting tiny studios in the outer boroughs, she'd gotten cold feet when her sweet, redheaded IT-geek boyfriend asked her to move in with him to an apartment on Central Park West that he'd just bought. *Bought!* On *Central Park.* Two weeks ago he'd surprised her with the revelation that they could now co-habitate; she had surprised them both with the revelation that she wasn't sure she wanted to. Brian, the most agreeable human being in North America, was confused, wondering how he'd miscalculated so badly when he'd offered Joanna everything he believed she wanted: a prewar building with a doorman, stability, walking distance from both green space and shops, proximity to eight million other people when he disappeared into his introverted geek/maker zone, stability, a pet Yorkie, her favorite café close enough to frequent in her slippers, pleasant sex, and stability.

"I'm not sure I'm ready for that much stability," she'd said at the time, over coffee in their favorite bakery in Carroll Gardens. She was trying to joke.

"All you ever talk about is needing stability," he'd countered, bemused, watching her fiddle with her espresso spoon. "Let's find a way for you to be more comfortable with this."

He'd suggested—in a reasonable, friendly tone—that they take a few days apart so that Joanna "could sort out what you think the hang-up is," and then they would meet and talk it through. Not one neuron in Brian's brain believed she would reject him, given time. It was human to have doubts; it was human to get over them.

She knew she wanted to be with him—at least, she thought she did—but she couldn't stop embracing opportunities to avoid "The Talk." The first time they were supposed to meet, she'd leapt at a sudden now-or-never chance to fly to Austin to interview an emerging music producer. Two days later, she'd postponed again because she'd conveniently had a touch of food poisoning.

The re-rescheduled talk was supposed to be this evening.

He answered on the second ring, and chuckled sadly once she'd explained where she was and why, and how long she'd need to stay here. "You're getting *really* good at delaying this," he said.

THE NEXT MORNING she woke under flannel sheets and musty wool blankets. One of the cats was pressing its cool wet nose against her ear and purring loudly for breakfast.

"Subtle," she grumbled. "Did Hank train you, or did you train him?"

She made herself some eggs. Then she shrugged herself into her wool coat and started to head outside, thought better of it, shrugged out of that coat, and wrapped up in an old down jacket she found in the mudroom, whose rips were patched with duct tape. She slipped her feet into an old pair of Uggs under the bench. She went out squinting into the unexpected sunshine carrying vegetable scraps, tossed the scraps through a window in the chicken wire, made sure the water wasn't frozen, and opened the door of the coop. Inside here it was warm and stuffy and smelled like cracked corn and dirty down comforters. She felt like Goliath. The hens muttered among themselves in disgruntlement as they hopped off the roosts or out of the nesting boxes. They all went straight out to the yard for the scraps, grumpy as every generation of chickens Hank had ever raised. She checked the boxes for eggs, but there were only three. The ladies didn't lay much in the long nights. How disconcerting that she even remembered that; she thought New York had erased her rural life. That had been the plan.

She went back inside, put the eggs away, and took a quick shower. Three tiles at about head-height, loose since friends at her junior prom after-party played Bathing While Drunk in the bathtub, were still loose. The grout between them, which had always been in danger of flaking away, was finally gone. There were probably a bazillion generations of mold spores reproducing promiscuously in the damp dark within.

She dressed in yesterday's travel clothes, bundled up in her aunt Jen's ancient nylon down coat, a step up from the one with duct-tape patches. She shoved her hair into a knitted cap, found the keys to Hank's green pickup truck under a pile of mismatched gloves in the coatroom.

It was a Wednesday in January, so there was no traffic anywhere as she drove past the Tashmoo Overlook, then through the brief stretch of Tisbury's commercial zone of auto mechanics, grocery stores, and office buildings. She skirted the archetypal-New-England-small-town Main Street of Vineyard Haven and zipped down through Five Corners onto Beach Road, the causeway between the harbor and the Lagoon. Today was a brisk beauty: bright blue sky, darker blue harbor, the Lagoon a muted mirror of the harbor. The new ferry pushed through the gentle swells, headed back to the mainland, passing a couple of masochistic pleasure boats. She sped over the drawbridge to the brick behemoth.

Martha's Vineyard Hospital was the largest repository of local artwork on the Island. Its corridors were lined with donations from scores of local artists, both year-rounders and summer people:

photographs of life here a hundred years ago; uncountable seascapes and rural landscapes and harbors; abstracts; ancient marine charts. Joanna's theory was that the hospital had been made as inviting as possible so that people would actually use it. New Englanders did not go in much for admitting they needed help. Celia, on the other hand, posited that since a huge percentage of summer visitors somehow ended up there—usually thanks to Lyme disease or moped accidents—the artwork was to make up for lost opportunities to sightsee.

Two of the nurses looked familiar to her from high school chorus. They both wore wedding bands, and she wondered in passing what the odds were that a local kid could grow up to find both a good year-round job and a good year-round partner here. It had never occurred to her to even aim for that. She felt slightly sucker-punched by her own lack of imagination.

No, she didn't mean that. She meant she was lucky to have escaped being caught in that trap.

"He just woke up," said one of the nurses in a firmly cheerful voice, following her into the room. "He's fine, and he can go home later today."

Hank looked hideous under the recessed fluorescents, hooked up to various machines that disturbed her too much to look at directly. He'd clearly been in need of a shave before he went up on the roof—there was about five days' growth of beard. His hair looked styled for a punk rock performance, and his skin tone, where there were no bruises, was sallow. One leg, draped discreetly with a sheet, was elevated on three white pillows and the ankle swaddled in some kind of sheath. It was unnerving to see that tugboat of a man so vulnerable.

"Howdy, cowboy," Joanna said. "You get bucked off a mustang?"

He took a moment to register that she was not a hallucination. Then his lips twisted toward an almost perfectly straight diagonal slant, as they always did when he was trying to disguise his pleasure with sarcasm. "Oh, God. Who brought you back here?" he asked. His tone was soft. The drip beside the bed had morphine.

"Celia."

"Damn gossip."

"Were you planning to keep this a *secret*?"

"I didn't want them to make you come running back from New York. Don't you have a job?"

"Freelance," she said cheerfully. "I don't have to punch the clock."

"Don't you have a *life*?" he said.

"Freelance," she said again, in a more insistent tone because it wasn't entirely true. "My life fits in my suitcase, and there's this awesome new thing called the internet that lets me stay in touch with everyone." She wasn't sure he knew about Brian. They'd been dating less than a year.

"Don't you have plants to water?"

"It's all under control," she said, although it wasn't. Celia had called at 3 A.M., so Joanna had assumed it was to report an imminent death. She'd caught a 4 A.M. Greyhound to Boston that was delayed for hours in the death throes of a nor'easter before it transferred her to a bus for the Cape. Before she'd left New York, she'd had the presence of mind to clean the bathroom, chuck the garbage, and make the bed. But she hadn't thought about her plants or her mail. She wasn't even sure what she'd packed. "I'm here until you're back on your feet," she said.

"That's going to be at least another week," he said ruefully.

More like two, she thought, now that she'd seen him, but she said nothing.

He was dopey enough that further conversation was useless, so she waited until a woman hardly older than she was, a doctor in purple scrubs, came in through the open door and asked if Joanna was family, and would she like to know what was going on with him. This was how she came to know of Henry Holmes's Complete Medical History.

It wasn't just a low-energy pilon fracture and a slew of bruised organs. He'd been having sundry health crises for years, which she'd never heard about because he was a Yankee Male. High blood pressure, dizzy spells, heart murmur, breathing problems, pneumonia, three bouts of Lyme disease, once with babesiosis, which had hospitalized him . . . That was three years ago and she'd never even heard about it, although she'd seen him since. She managed to keep her surprise from the doctor, lest the doctor stop telling her things.

"Will you be taking him home?"

"Yes," she said, feeling a fraud because the doctor seemed to think they actually lived together. "You better tell me what I need to know, because he will play down whatever you tell him."

The doctor nodded. "Of course. We'll be sending him home

with prescriptions for painkillers and blood-clot prevention medication. He'll need to elevate his leg and ankle for the next five to ten days to minimize swelling. He should just get up for about thirty minutes at a time for meals and to avoid blood clots, and to use the bathroom and have a sponge bath, otherwise he needs to be on the bed, torso flat on the bed, and the right foot raised up on two or three pillows."

That was far more than she had anticipated for a broken leg, but it was better than planning his funeral. She tried to estimate how many gallons of chowder she'd have time to make while she endured Hank's ranting about the doctor's orders when he got home. There would certainly be ranting. Would it be better, or worse, if she hid the rum?

"Make sure he does basic stuff like wiggle his toes now and then," the doctor was continuing, "that will also help with the edema. You'll need to drive him to any appointments and help to make sure he doesn't trip or anything until he gets used to the crutches and the boot."

"He won't have a cast?"

The doctor shook her head. "Luckily the surgeon got to him quickly for the ORIF. That means he's full of plates and screws, and when you take the insult of the injury and add to that the insult of the surgery, you don't want to put on a cast. The boot is better; he can take it off to shower eventually, and check skin tone and swelling. But he can't do any weight-bearing for six to twelve weeks."

"*Oh,*" Joanna said, sounding more dismayed than she wanted to. "How long before he's, like, totally back to normal?"

"He should be at ninety percent improvement in six to twelve months," she said, nodding to make sure Joanna understood how great this news was.

"Oh!" Joanna said, unable to hide her alarm.

The doctor looked confused, then smiled reassuringly. "You don't have to play nurse for that long," she said. "He definitely needs someone around for three or four weeks, because he'll be on prescription pain meds, but he'll have started physical therapy by then, and after twelve weeks he shouldn't even need the boot anymore."

She smiled tightly through a claustrophobic wave of panic. "So I should plan to be around for a while."

"Well, the first few days, we'll be sending a visiting nurse to help out, especially with the sponge bath and stuff—you're not his wife, are you?"

"Ick," Joanna said without thinking. "Sorry, that was rude," she added, in response to the doctor's quizzical expression. "He's my uncle. He raised me."

"Right, so you probably don't want to give him a sponge bath, that's what the visiting nurse is for. But otherwise, unless there are complications, he won't need you around by, where are we now, mid-January? Assuming no complications, then by early March, you should be off-duty."

There could be no such thing as "no complications" with Hank the patient. Joanna felt edgy: she had left behind her successfully transplanted life on an hour's notice, and now she was on a rock in the Atlantic Ocean in midwinter, to take care of a vinegary crank who would not want her to tell him what to do. She'd have to find a subletter. She'd have to ask her upstairs neighbor, who kept her spare key, to water the plants and check her mail since generous Brian, even at his most wanderlustful, was never one to cruise the subway out to Queens. Where was her extra mail key? Did she have her research notes for the article she was polishing for *Upstate* magazine? Was she going to miss her college roommate's birthday? What should she do about Brian and his invitation and The Talk they had to have?

"I'll be back later today," she assured Hank, pretending none of these things were on her mind. She pecked him on his forehead and headed out.

BACK OVER THE drawbridge, under a glaring-pale winter sun. A few seagulls were scoping the rocks along the causeway and skimming over the boatyards and empty docks, their shadows pulling long even in late morning. This stretch of road was dreaded in summer, almost constantly backed up from Five Corners halfway to the bridge; now she was the only car in sight. She turned into a cramped dirt lot near the shipyard. She barely registered the familiar harborside miscellany of her childhood: a clatter of overturned, weathered dinghies, frazzled ends of great hempen lines, battered buoy-floats. A trio of retired marine pilings, still bound by heavy nylon ropes, lay horizontal as a traffic barrier. She parked by these, being careful not to block other cars, and walked through a stiffening breeze that smelled faintly of sea air and diesel fumes. She was headed for the cedar-shingled building of the *Journal* offices.

This building had housed a health food store once, and a cluster of offices decades before that, but its inner layout had been gutted and inside it now functioned like a barn for scriveners. Low-walled cubicles circled a big open space around a wooden conference table. Up a set of unfinished wooden steps was another worktable in another open space. Off of this were private offices for the publisher and the managing editor. An old family friend, Everett, was that managing editor, although he wore a number of other hats too.

She introduced herself to the smiling young woman seated behind a sanded-pine counter, who gestured Joanna to go on upstairs unescorted. She was thrown by the laissez-faire attitude; in New York she could never go anywhere inside any office unless she showed ID and then let herself be shepherded. Upstairs, two young women sat at the central table working at laptops, with intense expressions on their faces—one looked displeased, the other delighted. Neither of them registered her presence. The muted taps of fingers on keyboards were the only sound besides the soft drone of premillennial heating.

There were two office doors, and only one was open. A man of about seventy years sat behind an old barn door resting on metal trestles. Artisanal office furniture was trendy in New York, and expensive; but this, Joanna knew, was not artisanal, it was probably recycled or donated. The total cost would have been at most twenty dollars for some bracing.

A computer was sitting like a shunned orphan on a smaller table in the corner. Everett—shortish, stocky, and gruffly avuncular, somewhere between a human Yorkshire terrier and the Lorax—sat on an old wooden chair, deep in thought.

She said his name as she walked in, and he perked up.

"Joanna Howes!" he said with mock formality, then stood and crossed the spartan room to hug her. "My favorite New Yorker. How's things in the city? If you want a break from Hank duty while you're here, how about some local reporting?"

She'd been expecting this—why else would he ask her to come to his office? Having Everett as her boss again would feel like regression. She was supposed to go home to New York and pitch to *The New Yorker*. But she'd be here awhile, and hackneyed as it sounded, the rent wouldn't wait. "Sure," she said. "Love to. What do you have in mind?"

"It's freelance," said Everett, returning to his seat. "Of course. I can't put you on staff since you're only here temporarily."

"I better be here temporarily," she said. "Have you seen his leg?"

"Not yet, but I heard. That's what he gets for trying to fix his own roof at seventy."

"In a storm," she amended. "He's lucky he's alive. I'm sticking around until he's self-sufficient."

"He's an ornery old bastard and he'll be walking again in a month, Anna."

"He better not. He's going to push himself too hard and reinjure it, we both know that."

"Well, we don't put people on salary unless they're staying put. We both know you're not staying put."

"This is true."

"I'll pay you per piece—and we're understaffed at the moment so there will be plenty of work while you're here. I mean, I can put you on half—"

"How can you be understaffed in winter, if all your writers are year-rounders and there's nothing going on?"

"Now is when they all go on vacation," said Everett patiently, as if that should have been obvious. Which it should have been, were she thinking like an Islander. "Or get the flu or fly to Cuba for cheap medical care or go into rehab or have their annual nervous breakdown. But there's still commission meetings and school sports and the Steamship Authority and the housing problem. And the opioid crisis isn't going away either, but I won't put you on that since you don't have a real news background. No offense."

"Actually I'm glad you realize that."

"I love your features," he said, as if in compensation. "That profile you did of Nina Brown—"

"Thanks," she said. She flashed the weary smile of somebody accustomed to compliments for primarily one thing. The Nina Brown piece had come out five years earlier, for the online mag *Impeccable*. Brown overdosed five hours after the interview, so the profile was never going to go out of date. Half the planet had read it by now, indifferent to how old it was. It had included a strangely mesmerizing passage on Brown's opinion of various breakfast cereals, about which she had waxed kinesthetically for ten minutes. That bit went viral for about a week—"rock star's favorite cereal" meme—and the article had become Joanna's calling card without her making the effort. Because of it, she'd gotten enough freelance assignments to quit her copyediting job and pay her Outer Boroughs of New York City Lifestyle bills without really feeling like she was doing anything useful.

She was too shy to be a serious investigative reporter. But her quirky upbringing had wired her to adapt, chameleon-like, to other people, so put her in a room alone with almost any willing subject— celebrity, convict, politician, cult leader, activist, billionaire, geek, poet—and she could coax them into showing their most engaging selves. Being in the same room with them was key, though, so that meant she was off the clock as long as she was stuck on Martha's Vineyard in winter doing Hank Patrol.

"How many stories a week can I file?" she asked Everett now, staring across his desk at him. "How much can I make? I came home too suddenly to find a subletter, so even if I'm staying at Hank's, I've got to make rent in New York for February."

The door was open and the young women outside, although they weren't listening, could hear them clearly, so Everett took a moment to think, then pulled a small notepad from his vest pocket and wrote a figure on it. He turned the pad to face her. She read the figure. It wasn't enough. She made a wry face.

"I can get you some guest posts on the arts blog, and the community blog, if that helps. And I can put you on some of the weekly beats for now, but only until my regulars get back. Do you want me to do that? I could put you on an hourly payroll for that, if you like."

She almost said yes, then reconsidered. "If I'm freelance, I can write for other papers, right?" she said. "If I need more cash?"

He frowned. "Theoretically, I guess. But the *Newes* won't hire anyone who's freelance for us. They have a formal policy against it. I think it's even posted somewhere in the newsroom."

"That's stupid," she said crossly.

A small shrug. "Well, it fits their zeitgeist. One reason I left there."

"What if I just don't mention to them that I'm freelancing here?"

"We read each other's papers, Anna, they'll see your byline."

"How 'bout I just do pieces for you without a byline?"

He gave her an overly patient look. "We don't do that except for news briefs and editorials, and I'm not going to change policy to accommodate a freelancer trying to game the other paper's system." A beat as he considered her grimace. "I promise to give you as much work as possible. I'm glad you're here, Anna. It will be a treat to work with you again."

"I feel the same way," she said quickly, and meant it. Then the afterthought: "And it's okay that I'm related to almost everyone I'll be reporting on? Or grew up with them or was their lab partner in school or something?"

He shrugged expansively. "Hazard of a small-town paper. If you ever feel like you're too close to a subject, let me know and I'll figure out a way to take you off the story."

"That probably won't happen, honestly. I haven't lived here since high school, and Hank's not going to get up to anything."

"Let's see about that," said Everett with a chuckle. "I've known that guy my whole life and I've never seen him not get up to anything. Give him my best, I'll swing by the hospital to say hi. How much longer is he in for?"

"He'll be out this afternoon," she said. "Come by the house tonight and distract him so he doesn't climb the walls with boredom. Maybe a Scrabble game, you'll beat him pretty easily while he's doped up."

Everett smiled affectionately. "He'll find something interesting to do. He always does."

"Yeah," she said. "That's what I'm afraid of."

Everyone called Hank her uncle, but genealogically he was Joanna's maternal first cousin by marriage. The family made up about a tenth of the Vineyard population, counting third cousins twice removed, ex-aunts-in-law, and half uncles. This had ensured a needed safety net when each of her very young parents, in quick succession, proved insufficient at parenting and each in turn left the Vineyard. (Mother = uppers, father = booze. Both went away to rehab and never returned. Joanna did not blame them; recidivism ran high in small, depressed communities.) The West Tisbury Elementary School had been the only stable thing in her life, and the family members who were paying attention agreed it should remain so, even though both sets of grandparents lived in Edgartown. So after a series of short-term in-family fostering, her mother's eldest niece Jen (who was actually a few years older than her mother—don't think too much about this, it was just one of those families) stepped in and announced she was taking care of little Annie. This meant by association, her husband, Hank, would be doing likewise.

Joanna lived with Jen and Hank until she graduated from high school and continued to make them her home base when she went off to college, and then grad school, and then real life. Jen had died of a brain aneurysm about five years back. That was horrible. Joanna still went home to Hank's, on those rare occasions she went home at all. Hank and Joanna—both without any immediate family nearby, despite droves of extended kin—adopted each other for life.

Most people weren't quite sure how Hank and Joanna were related. Such ad hoc parenting was not strange on the Island, so there was no stigma and only passing, benign curiosity. The folks she grew up with knew that Hank was her somehow-parent and didn't sweat the details. On the other hand, many friends he'd made since he was widowed had no idea who she was.

Some of the enemies he'd made, it turned out, didn't know who she was either.

CELIA HELPED HER fetch Hank from the hospital. The pickup was too high for him to navigate in and out of, but her Forester was a workable height. He was a little zonked on painkillers as they were transferring him from the wheelchair to the car in the shadow of the hospital's high front portico that chill afternoon. Mostly, he seemed mortified about being dependent.

"Well, that's just *great*, being taken care of by a couple of *girls*," he said to the nurse overseeing his discharge. She was one of those Joanna had gone to school with.

"We're in our thirties," said Celia.

"You'll always be girls to me," he said. "Is that the title of a song? That would make a terrific song title."

"Can't think of it," Joanna said shortly, hitching him over her shoulder as she helped him transfer to the passenger seat.

"I think it should be a song," he said, dreamy and cheerful. "Anna, you're a writer, write a song about that."

"About a senior citizen who calls grown women girls? Who would the audience be for that, do you think?" she said, securing the seat belt across his belly.

"Come on, kiddo," said Celia, grinning. "Give him a break. He's drunk on morphine."

"That's right," said Hank happily. "I'm drunk on morphine. You could write a song about that too. Has anyone ever written a song about being drunk on morphine?"

His smile was so dopey, Joanna smiled back. "I'm not a song-writer," she said.

"Well, maybe you should be," he said. "Y'know, Carly Simon didn't write most of the songs she got famous for singing, did you know that? Other people wrote them. You haven't heard of those people, but they made a lot of money too. Hey, it's cold out here! Maybe if you wrote songs . . ."

"I'm terrible at rhyming," she said, adjusting the seat belt for him.

"Not every song has to rhyme," Hank argued in a dreamy tone. "Is there a rule saying that a song has to rhyme? I don't think so."

"Okay, fine, I'll write some songs," she said irritably, and closed the door. She could hear Celia laughing at them.

She rode in the backseat, holding Hank's bag of medications, in-structions for care, and the remains of the clothes he had been wear-ing when he'd toppled off the roof. She'd brought him clean jeans and a flannel shirt to wear. At least, she hoped they were clean, since they'd been folded in a drawer of his dresser, rather than on the floor or his bedside chair, like 90 percent of his wardrobe.

Celia drove them up the wooded turns of Lambert's Cove, and then the muddy trenches of their driveway, with dispatch. With some effort, they toted Hank into the house, where they parked him on the sofa with a small table to keep drinks and food and the TV remote. They did a spot check of accessibility—towels, pillows, snacks, cups. The cats were fascinated and horrified, and then bored. Most of the first week, Joanna would be playing nursemaid, but they both assumed he'd find some way to get into trouble, so at least if things were close at hand, he wouldn't try to wander about too much.

Once he was settled, Celia, in layers of paisley sweaters, all of which celebrated her cleavage, sat herself down on the coffee table to be level with him. "Okay, now, Hank," she said, cheery. She reached into the pocket of her outermost sweater and pulled out an amber bottle with a rubber top. "This is a tincture of valerian."

"Valerian?" he hooted. "What's that?" An impish grin, made grotesque by the bruises. "Is it a magic potion?"

"Sort of," she said. "It'll help you sleep. Once the morphine's out of your system, you might get agitated. This will help you calm down. If you start getting antsy, it will take the edge off."

"That's great, I need to take the edge off!" he said, and examined the bottle, squinting slightly. "Thanks. Valerian. That's cool." He glanced back up at her. "You sure it's not some kind of *Game of Thrones* potion?" And he giggled.

THE NEXT MORNING, Joanna called Brian to update him ("So you're telling me we're still in limbo? That's not actually news, sweetheart, we were already in limbo") and then began her dual vocation as Hank-minder and *Journal* pinch hitter. That first week, she wrote (particularly badly) about an intramural junior high basketball game, and also (not quite so badly, but nothing to crow about) an issue with the transfer station—that is, the dump—in Edgartown. She wrote a profile of a new minister coming in to the UU church, which let her trot out her interviewing skills. She tossed off a review of *Yellow Satin* at the Film Center, because the usual reviewer hadn't had a chance to view it, and she'd seen it on the mainland hours before she got Celia's call about Hank.

When she drew up her invoice for the *Journal,* she realized if she made that amount per week, then by the following month she either would be living on her savings or losing her apartment. Jobs of any sort were scant in a summer resort in mid-January. If she had been a mental health worker, they'd have lassoed her into service at Community Services. Otherwise, slim pickings. Anyhow, she wasn't going to be staying here, she was going back to New York to almost-certainly-not-break-up with Brian.

"I'm going to need to freelance for the *Newes* as well," she informed Everett after attending her first editorial staff meeting. She said it in a stage whisper, since they were in his office and the door was never closed.

"They won't use you," he said immediately.

"Well, I'm going to ask anyhow."

He grimaced. "So try. I can't stop you, but I don't like it."

"I know that. I'm sorry, I wouldn't do it if I could see some other way."

He gave her a sternly avuncular look. "You have to promise me you will not take ideas I've thrown at you, and write them for the *Newes*. Or use sources that you generated while you were here."

"No, of course not! I'll write as much as I can for you, the more the better. It's just, if there's not enough . . ."

He shrugged, and settled back in his chair. "Anyhow, they won't use you."

"Remember I used to write for them? In high school?"

"Of course I remember that, I was your boss," he said. "You did the restaurant reviews. Before we realized that doing restaurant reviews was a stupid idea because the restaurants stopped advertising if they didn't like what you said about them."

"So I'm still in their system, right? The bookkeeping system or whatever?"

He shrugged and leaned forward, resting his elbows on the desk and fiddling with his amber plastic reading glasses. "That was fifteen or twenty years ago, and I haven't worked there for more than a decade, so I have no idea. Anyhow, it doesn't matter—if you've got a byline in this paper, they won't hire you to write for them. But I've got another assignment for you, if you need cash."

"You know I do."

"There's a big ZBA meeting tonight in West Tisbury. Cover it for us."

She grimaced. Hank had served on nearly every board in town—appointed or elected—but the Zoning Board of Appeals was his recurrent favorite because—Joanna felt—it allowed him to play petty dictator, allowing or forbidding deviations from the established old-school norm. It was an appointed post, so he tended to cycle in and out at regular intervals, leaving the impression that he had been on the board unceasingly since 1972. Therefore, she knew a little about how the ZBA worked, not because she read the paper but because, with her aunt Jen, she'd had to listen to him vent after each meeting, and then help Jen calm him down. But that had been a child's-eye view, intrinsically associated with the tone of sarcasm and the smell of beer.

"I have no idea how to cover a ZBA meeting. Can I just take notes?"

"Anna. No. You're not a stenographer."

"All that bureaucratic legalistic language wrecks my head. I will screw something up."

"Look holistically at what you learn, and decide what the story is, and tell us why we should care. Okay? Make it lively and brisk and informal. And, eh . . ." Seeing her anxiety not diminishing, he plunged ahead with a Country Journalism Lecture: "Remember it ain't the *New York Times*. You don't need to impress upon the reader how smart or important you are. You want to come across as *familiar* with things—geography, people, political situations—"

"I know squat about the political situation, Everett, that's the—"

"So take your best shot at figuring out what matters," he said. "But don't listen to them—the ZBA officers, I mean. We don't care what they find interesting. We care about what our readers find interesting. Show it to me, I'll do a heavy edit so you can see what to emphasize going forward. Okay? You'll get the hang of it. We'll be leading with the helicopter."

"See that's what I mean—what helicopter? I'm going into this blind."

"Look it up in the archives. Rich summer guy wants to use a helicopter as a personal shuttle right from his property. Which by the way is next to Beechwood Point, protected wetlands. The building inspector gave him a cease and desist right after Christmas and he ignored it. He sent an appeal to the ZBA, wants a variance."

"What's a variance?"

He looked dismayed. "Did you or did you not grow up under Hank Holmes's roof? It's, you know, a *variance*. He appealed back at the start of the month so, in case you *really* don't remember growing up under Hank Holmes's roof, the ZBA advertised a public hearing for tonight. That starts at five fifteen at the Town Hall, and after the hearing, they'll vote on the appeal. Don't look like a deer in the headlights, Anna, just sit with the *Newes* guy—James Sherman, I think it's his beat. 'Kay?"

"Eh . . . but . . . isn't James the enemy? Aren't we supposed to hate him?"

Everett looked curiously at her. "Well, if you want to get technical, yes, but you used to work alongside him, so just give him a nice smile and I'm sure he won't hurt you. The *Newes* team is the genteel one, it wouldn't be like one of them to get nasty."

"So nasty is *our* job?"

"Nah, but we're a little scrappier."

"Roger," she said.

"So, write something up, and I'll edit it, and then you'll know what you're doing. Got it?"

"Got it," she said.

"And be confident about it. Remember: the reporter is always in control because he gets to have the final word."

SHE LEFT THE *Journal* office early so that she could tend to Hank before heading out again for the ZBA meeting. The vague shadows were already lengthening, the roads beginning to darken even without a canopy of leaves to darken them. Already she was bored with how bleak and gray everything was here this time of year. The English language lacked variants enough for the word *gray*. *Leaden, gloomy, somber, dull, steel, ashen, grim, cloudy, overcast, dismal.* Only, if you put them all together it created the impression of a riot of colorlessness, something decadent in its own right, like the English moors or a storm at sea. The gray of a Vineyard winter did not deserve such a comparison. It hadn't as much energy. You'd have to take just one word at a time and slowly, slowly, dribble each one, solitary, across the whole of a week, or a month, or a season.

That's what she was, once again, driving home through. And home was barely more welcoming. Hank was mellower than the worst of her childhood five o'clock memories of him, because he was on painkillers. But he was not a good patient.

She felt for him. He had been a "strapping youth," once, and the best kind of Yankee—a blue-collar Renaissance man, jack-of-all-trades and master of whichever one he happened to be doing at the moment. Fisherman, carpenter, lumberjack, part-time inventor and entrepreneur, farmer, back to being a fisherman, maker of artisanal objets d'art repurposed from found objects. His hands were excellent for practical things, like welding and sanding and gutting fish and shucking oysters. Things it was hard to do while doped, lying horizontally for twenty hours of the day with a leg propped up on pillows.

Joanna came in, greeted him, and turned the flame on high beneath the smallest pot on the stove, which had just enough water to fill a thermos with tea. The thermos had been her big expenditure since landing here.

"And what gossip has Everett assigned to you this week?" he asked, as she was turning on the oven. That oven needed cleaning badly, like everything else in the house. He'd been a widower for five years now, and the scruff was becoming entrenched. Even the cats, who had been Jen's more than his, were growing scruffy.

"I'm covering the ZBA meeting tonight," she said, pulling the remains of a turkey lasagna out of the refrigerator and thinking—fleetingly—about the chicken bastilla Brian was headed for at a friend's dinner party. The weight of the casserole dish had been stabilizing a jar of pickled mushrooms and a large block of cheese, and both required some assistance to keep from tumbling. She missed her organized, clean, nearly empty mini-fridge in Queens.

"Oh, Christ," he said. "The helicopter pad's on the docket, isn't it?" His voice was dripping with distaste. "Helen mentioned it. You don't even need to go, I can tell you right now they're going to reject it. As they should. Those damn summer people and their outrageous sense of entitlement."

"Everett said you know the guy who—"

Hank laughed. "Smith. Yeah. We've been . . . introduced. We've exchanged a few words in public. I have given him plenty of reasons not to like me very much." He sounded pleased about this.

"How unusual for you," she said.

Hank laughed the inelegant but sly guffaw that made him lovable, no matter how truculent he was.

"So you either get a super-early dinner or you wait until I'm back," she said, returning to point.

"It'll take five minutes," said Hank. "I'll wait until you're back. Eating alone with myself is even more depressing than eating alone with you."

"Wow, high praise," she said. She turned the oven off, picked up the lasagna again.

"That came out wrong," he said, more amused than apologetic.

She opened the door to the fridge and tried to sort out how to fit the lasagna back in given the new configuration. "Do you want anything to hold you over until I get back?"

"I could use a beer," he said.

"How about something solid." She rested the dish as best she could on a bag of wan-looking romaine lettuce, closed the door, and returned to the stove.

"If I had a rock I could throw it at the television."

"I'll take that as a no," she said, tossing a tea bag into the thermos and carefully pouring in the water. "Hey, I saw some honey in the pantry, I'm going to open—"

"Don't open that!" he said vehemently, glancing back over his shoulder at her. "Don't touch it. That's a special gift. That's from

Paul's first hive. It's local and unfiltered and very special. It has the honeycomb still in it." He returned his attention to the television.

"Are you saving it for a special occasion?" she asked. "The jar is so covered in dust, you can hardly see the contents."

"Honey doesn't spoil," he said, in a defensive tone, as if to the television.

"I know that, but it's not like it improves with age either," she said. "What are you saving it for?"

"It doesn't matter, I don't want you to open it."

"Fine," she said. "Is there any other honey in the house?"

"No," he said. "I don't like honey."

"Then why are you holding on to *that* honey?" she demanded, trying to tamp down her exasperation.

"Because it's mine," he said. "But tell you what, I'll leave it to you in my will."

"Oh my God," she muttered, screwing the top on the thermos. "I'll just buy a jar from Paul."

"He doesn't sell it commercially," said Hank.

"Then I'll *ask* him for a jar," Joanna said.

"The bees aren't producing any honey this time of year," he said triumphantly.

"But honey doesn't spoil," she said, imitating his tone. "He can give me some from the same batch as the stuff that is gathering cobwebs in our pantry. Then you can have your honey and I can have my honey and we will label them and nobody touches each other's honey, and we'll all be happy, okay?" she said, more exasperated than she wanted to be. *Senior citizen*, she rebuked herself. *Broken leg.*

He laughed the Hank Laugh again. "All right," he said. "And since I don't eat honey, I'll have mine after you no longer have yours, so that makes me the winner."

"Hank, you're already the winner," she said. "Look who you get as your primary caretaker." She bowed, ironically, but he was still looking toward the television.

"Yeah, Anderson Cooper," he said.

"I thought you liked Christiane Amanpour."

"Not since she cut her hair," he said.

THE OLD MANSARD-ROOFED building that functioned as the Town Hall had once been the elementary school. That was before Joanna's time, but scores of her family had passed through it. For years after it was converted, and clearly in her memory, one upstairs room was kept, museum-like, as it had been on the last school day: the rows of lift-lid student desks, the dusty chalkboard with broken chalk still in the tray, the out-of-tune piano, the cloakroom, the American flag. A slate tablet on the wall had listed students' names in colored chalk to mark which multiplication tables each had memorized.

That was long gone, though. The Town Hall had been renovated and expanded, and now all board meetings took place in what had been that classroom. Now it was painted sage-green, carpeted, and wainscoted. It was accessed from the second-floor common area through broad double doors. The large windows were still there from the old days—or rather their energy-efficient descendants were—but now on the walls, in lieu of slate multiplication tables, hung survey maps of the town, and an oil painting of a stone wall by one of the town's celebrated homegrown artists, who decades earlier had been a student in that classroom.

There were so many people gathered to witness this particular ZBA meeting that nearly a score spilled out over the threshold into the common space, rumbling to each other. Hank would have been here, were he allowed to stay upright for more than thirty minutes at a stretch.

She excused herself as she brushed by two men at the back of the crowd. She blanked on names, but she knew them: the owner of one of the Menemsha fish markets, all wool and canvas and an air of melancholy, leaning his shoulder against the wall, and Celia's boss at the bakery, a short, potbellied, avuncular flirt in a blue flannel shirt. As Joanna passed them, she heard them talking about that idiot Holmes who fell off the roof trying to adjust his satellite dish during a snowstorm. The story had already morphed into a wisecrack. Despite herself, she slowed and turned her head in their direction.

"Hey, Anna," said the fisherman, casually, as if they ran into each other every day and he had not just been mocking her injured uncle. "We were just talking about Hank there. How's he doing?"

"Does he need a care package?" asked the baker with a puckish smile. She knew, from some hazy memory, that he meant a bag of pot.

"I'll ask," she said, although Hank only tended to self-medicate with alcohol and Jeffrey Toobin. "Thanks. He's doing fine."

As she continued toward the boardroom, each gave her a New

England wave: two fingers raised briefly and laconically from whatever height their hand happened to be.

"Hey, Anna!" said a cheery redheaded woman she nearly walked into. Joanna recognized her as the vet who'd tended her childhood pets, including her long-gone Nubian goat. "How's the baby?"

She smiled politely. "You're thinking of my cousin Lisa."

The vet laughed, pressed her fingers over her brows. "Of course. You always looked alike. Well, when you were ten you did." She laughed again and shrugged. "Anyhow, hope you're well, nice to see you."

She kept walking, swiveling around legs and purses and backpacks. The crowd smelled of damp wool and a more prosaic scent, a musky, musty human scent. Everett had said a press seat would be held for her, so she politely nudged her way through the bottleneck in the doorway.

Along one side of a wooden table, the four ZBA officers sat facing into the small room. Two men and two women, all wore varieties of the local winter uniform of flannel shirts, jeans, and work boots. She knew from her childhood civics catechisms that four ZBA officers made up a quorum, but the board was supposed to have five. Like many town committees, they were no doubt scrambling for membership.

Behind the audience lurked the public access camera and its operator, a volunteer for MOCC—Martha's Own Cable Channel. In the front row, the back of his head in view of the camera, was a sixtyish Jimmy Stewart doppelgänger. This was James Sherman, her counterpart from the *Newes*. Beside him was the sole remaining empty chair. She moved with her jerky pivoting gait toward it.

She remembered the lanky, bespectacled James Sherman vaguely from her adolescence. He had been a reporter for the *Newes* when she'd interned there writing the doomed restaurant reviews. He'd been pleasantly aloof when he was around, and he'd done a few other things to make ends meet, including working at the boatyard doing some specialized boat-mending task she couldn't place now, something that sixty years ago might have been a full-time calling, but wasn't anymore. She settled into the padded chair beside him and held up her backpack shyly as if to justify her presence.

"I'm filling in for Susan," she said, lowering the pack to the floor.

He looked suspicious, but then recognized her, and grinned. "Joanna Howes?" he said. "Are you back on the rock?" Then a look of understanding: "Oh, to help out Hank."

"Yeah."

"Sorry to hear about that. Damn, he was lucky," said James. He made a show of moving his own bag to make room for hers. "That could have been so much worse. And he's lucky to have you here. How long you down for?"

"Long as he needs me." She settled in beside him and reached into her backpack.

"So, wait, hang on. I thought you had a glamorous international career interviewing famous people. You're writing for the *Journal*?"

"Just temporarily while I'm helping Hank. I'm a little out of my depth with town government, though."

He made a dismissive expression. "It's just the *Journal*—no offense, but c'mon, it's an advertising rag."

The *Journal* was not an advertising rag. The *Journal* was a scrappy everyman-style paper created by disgruntled former *Newes* workers who felt the *Newes* had abrogated its responsibilities to working-class Islanders (who made up the majority of year-rounders) in favor of an elegantly romanticized perception designed to cater to genteel summer residents. Most of the original *Journal* founders had moved on to other projects off-Island, or reinvented themselves into something nonjournalistic. But. Big but. She'd grown up aware of the animus between the two papers.

Hank preferred the *Journal*, of course, while Jen and Joanna had been drawn to the art and poetry that regularly graced the pages of the *Newes*. Joanna had been rhapsodic when she was offered the restaurant-reviewing gig there in high school, an internship Hank and Jen had argued about for an hour before she'd been allowed to accept it. Once on the job, she remembered Everett—who had been the *Newes'* community editor, and thus her boss—dissing the unprofessional snarky tone of the *Journal*. The same paper he now ran.

"I mean, it's a pretty *good* rag," James was continuing, "but it's a rag."

"You realize that's an insult," Joanna said. "I mean, it's a pretty *good* insult, but it's an—"

"It's a statement of fact," said James calmly. "The *Journal* succeeds if it has enough ads. The *Newes* succeeds if it has enough subscribers. They're not even the same species."

"If you say so," she muttered. She settled the laptop on her lap and opened it, turned it on, tried to shake off her emergent pique.

"I think it's fine to have a little outlet like that on the island," he continued, placidly, as if she had no connection to the paper he was dissing. "Helps people appreciate the quality they're getting with the *Newes*. Plus, it keeps everyone on their toes, you know?"

She recalled the elegant old homestead that housed the *Newes*, and the affectation of disused manual typewriters (not even electric!) collecting dust beside the sleek Macs that had replaced them. It was, indeed, an elegant paper. Her pique was superseded by nostalgia. "Actually, I wish I could freelance for both papers," she said. "Then maybe there'd be enough work to pay the bills."

"Hm," he said, cleaning his glasses with the hem of his sage flannel shirt. "Too bad the *Journal* has a policy against that."

She grimaced. "It's not the *Journal*'s policy, it's the *Newes*' policy."

He grimaced back. "I'm pretty sure it's the *Journal*'s."

"That's not what the *Journal* says." She pulled her phone out of her coat pocket, rested it against the laptop screen, and launched the voice-memo app.

"Why would the *Newes* care?" puzzled James, almost to himself. "We get first pick of writers because we've been around longer and we have the reputation. And I'm sure we pay better. We're not going to lose someone we want to the *Journal*, so why would we be precious about it? The *Journal* doesn't want to lose people to the *Newes* because people want to write for the *Newes* more." Noticing a hurt look on her face, he added, "Even you! You interned with us all those years back, not with the *Journal*."

"I don't think the *Journal* had internships back then."

"See, that's what I mean," he said, comfortably. "We've been around longer, we've got it down, we just do our thing. I bet you're only working for the *Journal* because Everett called you, right? If the current *Newes* editor knew you and called you at the same time, you'd be working for us now, you know it and I know it. The *Journal* is an upstart, and there's nothing wrong with that, even if it *is* totally preoccupied with a crass commercial agenda—but Everett's the one making things complicated and trying to start a competition for writers."

"I don't care who started it. I just want to write things and get paid for them."

"Amen, sister," he said, and then the hearing began.

When she was a girl and Jen had to work late, Hank—who had a more flexible schedule than Jen did, especially in winter—would get stuck watching Joanna, so she'd been brought to more than a few such board meetings. Despite her discomfort about trying to pass as a newshound, there was something cozily familiar about this room.

The plump, gray-haired chair of the ZBA, Helen Javier, was dressed in the requisite layers of flannel and denim, but her rubber boots sported a paisley design and she radiated such an earth-mothering energy that, had she been wearing a wreath of flowers in her hair, one might have asked if they were growing there by the roots. Joanna had known her since toddlerhood and had always adored her, occasionally fantasizing that somehow she might be Helen's changeling offspring.

"Hello, Anna! Thanks for coming home from the big city to take care of that damn fool," she said, then turned vaguely in the direction of the camera. "We'll start the hearing by reading correspondence on the helipad, and then the plaintiff will state his case, then we'll open it up to public comment." Shifting her gaze now to the densely packed audience: "When it's your turn to speak, we ask you to say who you are before speaking."

Spread before her on the table was an array of notes and letters. Most of these were printed copies of emails, a couple were typed on textured stationery, and two were handwritten on lined notebook paper, one neat and one scrawled. Helen pushed some of the papers toward the other officers and they each took turns reading aloud. Joanna typed and watched at the same time.

"To the ZBA"—this in an email—"My family has lived seasonally on the North Shore for three generations. We appreciate it because it is so delightfully rural and quiet . . ."

"Dear Chairman Javier," began a missive typed on ivory stationery with an embossed letterhead she couldn't quite make out. "We are aware that there is a town bylaw expressly forbidding helicopter landing anywhere in town except the airport. Please keep it that way."

Next was an email from another neighbor saying almost the same thing. And then another. Then three more. Then a final email: "Mr. Smith is an upstanding gentleman and people should be allowed to transport as they please. I recommend, and request, that you allow him the helipad but restrict usable hours. That should suit everyone. I know my neighbors will give me all kinds of grief for this but it seems fairest."

When the correspondence was complete, Helen announced that it was now time for Mr. Smith to have his say.

A bland fellow in an expensive navy suit, about forty, stood up from the front row. He held a briefcase and was adjusting his maroon tie. His physique screamed College Crew Team, as did his haircut. In Manhattan he would have been just another suit and Joanna would not have registered him in the sidewalk throngs at rush hour. Here, in this rural village in midwinter surrounded by plaid, denim, and camouflage-green flannel, he looked almost provocatively ridiculous. At a guess, Joanna thought he surely used more hair product than the rest of the room combined (including all the women, even the school librarian) and his expensive shoes were hopelessly impractical for January in the country, but sure looked sharp. He did not seem nearly hip enough to have his own helicopter. After a beat, he sat down and decided to talk from his chair.

"I'm here on behalf of Orion Smith," he said.

Ah, that explained it. *A minion*, she could see all the ZBA members thinking to themselves.

"Hello," said Helen gruffly, glancing down at the agenda, the margin of which she tapped absently with a pencil.

The Minion continued, looking grim. "Mr. Smith received a cease and desist order from the West Tisbury zoning inspector in late December, informing him he was not allowed to use his own personal helicopter on his own private property."

"That's right," said Helen, too patiently, looking back up at him. "It's against the bylaws to have a helipad anywhere but at the airport, so he can't land a helicopter on his property." Thumbing through papers in a manila folder in front of her, she went on. "If I recall correctly, Mr. Smith disregarded the cease and desist and brought the helicopter back just a week or so ago, making several trips to bring over multiple parties from the mainland?"

"That's correct. After he filed for an appeal, which is his right to do, he was using it to shuttle guests to a private party at his home, as the ferries had stopped running for the night."

"Is Mr. Smith unable to appear in person?" asked another board member.

"Mr. Smith's tenancy is seasonal and he is currently traveling on business. At his request, I am appearing as his proxy to appeal the decision."

Once Minion Lawyer was finished, Helen called on comments from the crowd. It was a Thursday afternoon in winter, so they were a lackluster group, but a united one.

And they were familiar to Joanna. Even the ones she didn't know, she knew. A particular type often tended toward Island government: hefty men, not fat so much as gristly, radiating a repressed bluster. Each man absolutely definite about his place in his own world, but grudgingly cognizant that the real world was much bigger. As with Hank—an exemplary model—they were boisterous with each other, but with outsiders they tended toward a sheepish belligerence. After decades of painful experience watching their homeland transmogrify into a real estate market, they were wary of being tricked or cheated out of their diminishing resources. Easily a third of the faces in the crowd were that man.

Everyone was against the helipad, even those who lived miles away from Mr. Smith's property. A mousy middle-aged woman in batik rayon could barely bring herself to speak at all, but speak she did, sounding like an NPR announcer. She spoke on behalf of the Wetlands Protection Act, a piece of legislation that *required* only a 200-foot buffer but which *implied* far more, as they all knew perfectly well, but which couldn't *state* more than 200 feet because of lawmakers who were actively determined to poison the planet. Helen very graciously caused her to stop talking. Then there was a brash man in his thirties who started off in a normal voice but— without anyone naysaying him—worked his way into a lather of defensiveness against the big-city rich people who don't give a crap about other people's quality of life. Joanna's money was on his heading straight from here down-Island for a few beers to blow off steam after. An eight-year-old girl, speaking with permission because she was not a registered voter, said she was worried that if she flew her kite on the beach while the helicopter was flying by, it would suck her kite into its rotors and destroy it.

"Hard to top that one," said one of the board members. "I make a motion to close the hearing."

Another seconded it, and all four voted in favor.

Immediately, the same member said, "I make a motion to reject the appeal." This was immediately seconded, and the board unanimously voted to reject.

Helen turned to the Minion Lawyer to make sure he understood that was the end of the matter. "It's in the bylaws," she said, not unkindly. "If Mr. Smith doesn't like the bylaws, he has to take it up with the Planning Board and ask them to change the bylaws. And in the meantime, 'cease and desist' means cease and desist. No more helicopter rides."

"What will happen if he continues to use the helicopter?" asked the Minion.

"I just told you that he can't do that," said Helen. "We're not allowing him to do it."

"What happens if he continues to use it anyhow?"

The four officers all sat up straighter, as if they'd been tugged. They glanced at each other in surprise. "We don't have to deal with scofflaws very often," said Helen. "Generally people are law-abiding."

"Maybe we confiscate the helicopter?" one of the other board members posited, half joking.

"Can we do that?" asked the third. All eyes turned to the administrator who was seated with the largest pile of folders at one end of the table. Other than the Minion Lawyer she was the only person in the room who looked as if she might work in an actual office, and this impression was based mostly on the fact that she had manicured nails. "Rachel?"

"You should ask town counsel," Rachel said. "I think she'll tell you to threaten Mr. Smith with legal action, but I'm not sure."

Said the Minion, "It sounds like there is no answer. Currently, the official position is that nothing will happen if Mr. Smith ignores the cease and desist order and continues to use his personal transportation device as he sees fit."

There was a millisecond of perfect silence in the room. Every set of eyes was staring at the lawyer. Then several grunts burbled up from the audience.

"Are you serious?" demanded Helen, finally.

"How can you enforce a ruling when there are no consequences for disobeying it?" he asked.

"There are consequences," said Helen in a forbearing tone. "We'll find out what the consequences are and communicate them to Mr. Smith."

"Please communicate them to me," he said briskly. He stood again, and held out a card. "Here is the best way to reach me."

After another pause, the officer directly across from him reached out and took the card. She read his name aloud, but nobody took notes. Finally, looking bemused, she offered the card to the clerk, who nodded toward her large pile of files. The officer shrugged and tossed the card onto the pile.

"We'll let you know," said Helen, in a voice of bored dismissal. The suited minion nodded tersely and turned to exit, picking his way past faded Levi's and weathered L.L.Bean. Joanna didn't like him much but she felt bad for him anyhow, because she knew that in most parts of the East Coast he would seem relatively normal.

After another pause, the board members all exchanged glances and rolled their eyes.

"What an asshole," James Sherman muttered under his breath beside Joanna, in a distinctly nonjournalistic tone.

"Any other business?" Helen asked.

As soon as Joanna got home, she turned the oven on again and put what was left of the turkey lasagna in to heat it up. She went into the pantry to check how many Sam Adams were still left (meaning: how many Hank had gotten up to drink while she was at the ZBA meeting, and the answer was miraculously only one) and her eye fell on the spot where the coveted honey jar had been. There was now an empty spot on the dusty shelf, like a missing tooth.

"Henry Holmes," she said in a scolding tone, speaking over the evening news.

"Joanna Howes," he said in exactly the same tone.

"Did you really think I would steal your honey?"

"Oh, so you noticed it was gone?" he said slyly. "That means you had your eye on it, so it's good I did something about it."

"You are amazing," she grumbled. "I can't believe Anderson Cooper puts up with you." She crossed past him into her bedroom to get a sweater.

Sitting on her bedside table was the honey jar.

"Oh!" she said, and back in the living room Hank burst into his Hank Laughter.

"Thank you," she said, coming out of the bedroom and, of course, now feeling bad that she had pressured him to give it up, because that's how these things work.

"Oh, sure," he said. "It's going to taste even sweeter than it would have if I'd just let you have it when you first asked."

That evening, after feeding Hank and double-checking his meds, she exchanged a few "sitting here in limbo" jokes with Brian via text, then wrote up a brief, clear, and objective description of the meeting. She emailed it to Everett along with her notes, feeling as proud and nervous as she had after her first restaurant review.

An hour later, he sent it back to her, not one sentence left un-changed:

> A large crowd was present this week to witness
> the West Tisbury Zoning Board of Appeals re-
> soundingly reject an appeal from Orion Smith of
> New York City, a seasonal resident who sought to
> build a helipad for his personal 5-seater Bell
> 505 Jet Ranger helicopter on his North Road
> property near the much-loved protected wetlands
> of Beechwood Point. Mr. Smith defied a cease and
> desist order earlier in the month by using his
> helicopter on at least two unauthorized trips,
> and has made it clear (through a representative
> who appeared in his stead) that he intends to
> continue to do so. The ZBA is waiting for the
> town counsel to advise on Mr. Smith's actions.
> "We don't have to deal with scofflaws very of-
> ten," said Ms. Javier, by way of explaining why
> counsel was required. This is Mr. Smith's third
> contentious run-in with the ZBA over the past
> 12 years; he had previously sought variances
> for a 5-hole golf course and an oversized out-
> building, neither of which were granted.

"I didn't know any of that," she said to Everett the next morning in his office, trying not to sound defensive. Or pathetic.

"I know," he said kindly. "Sort of ironic, since Hank was chair of the ZBA for at least one of those, and I think they even got into a shouting match in public. Hank is reliable for good copy that way."

The next day, the *Newes* published James Sherman's version: "The West Tisbury Zoning Board of Appeals did not grant an appeal by Mr. Orion Smith, who wishes to build a helipad on the North Road property where three generations of his family have summered."

She blinked at the sentence.

"Susan's gone for another couple weeks," said Everett over her shoulder, seeing what she was reading. "I'm keeping you on the West Tisbury beat. That means selectmen's meeting every Wednesday, and a couple of Planning Board meetings, maybe an assessors' meeting and I think the Conservation Commission meets next week."

"I thought you wanted me to do features," she said, feeling pallid. "Not news."

"When I said no news, I meant no investigative journalism," he said cheerfully. "Covering town politics isn't news, it's just official gossip. You must deal with that all the time in the big city."

II
FEBRUARY

JOANNA NEEDED A ROUTINE TO FEND OFF THE ENCROACH-
ing sense of limbo. Not exactly limbo, though. It was more a dual
desire to evade and yet to claim everything around her all the time,
a hybrid of claustrophobia and covetousness. It was hard to simply
be, when half the time she was anxious to get back to New York
and figure out her future, and the other half wondered what would
make her most homesick for the Vineyard once she got back to New
York. She determined to spend one afternoon per week cooking
easy-to-reheat dishes—stews, casseroles, lasagnas—that she could
feed Hank on short notice. His narcotically enhanced boredom
both fueled and suppressed his appetite in turn, and she required
a quick-fire defense against Hangry Man. This meant he would be
eating the same two or three dishes for lunch and dinner all week,
something he was happy to complain about.

"You don't have to insult my clam chowder [seafood stew, tuna
casserole, turkey lasagna]," she would say, to which he would reply,

the diagonal smirk on his face, "Oh, but I insist! It's no trouble at all." And then he'd bust out with an affectionate chortle.

But most days found him in pain, sometimes too wobbly from the painkillers to get around safely, even for his allotted thirty minutes. Then he would sag against her as she helped him toward the bathroom or his bedroom. *This is our dress rehearsal,* she would think. *Someday we'll be doing this for real.* She'd be filled with tenderness, and she'd see in his eyes that it was mutual.

Then he'd make a fart joke, and things were back to normal.

(He also managed, infuriatingly, to win every game of Scrabble they played, although it was usually because of one extraordinarily lucky play, such as "jinx" on a triple-word score.)

She tried to talk with Brian every evening, but the unspoken question of their future weighed down the silence between their words. Especially when he asked how she would feel if he saw other people, casually, until they finally had The Talk. Both relieved and annoyed, is how she felt. "You should do what works for you," is what she said. She tried to walk with Celia and her dog every other afternoon, weather permitting. "Weather permitting" was a subjective phrase, it turned out. It meant one thing to hardened New Englanders and something else to former New Englanders.

"But kiddo, this is the best time of year for walking the beach!" Celia would insist. "No tourists! No summer people! We get all the sea glass to ourselves!" And so Joanna would bundle herself in Aunt Jen's shapeless down coat—not the one with the duct tape—and join Celia and her yellow Lab, Hops, on Lambert's Cove Beach. Depending upon the mood of the weather gods, the beach was either soft, smooth sand, or else tumbled with stones. The water and wind displaced tons of sand, and then deposited it all hither and yon with a capriciousness even seasoned beach walkers could never predict. The sand was finer here than on the long straight stretch of the south shore, and the water marginally warmer, since it was Vineyard Sound and not the Atlantic Ocean. Not that anyone went into the water this time of year. Not even Hops. It was soothing to walk the mile stretch up to Split Rock and back, listening to Celia's entertaining patter about the personalities she worked with at the bakery, and the unsurprising melodrama of the early morning customers: tradesmen, mostly; caretakers about to make their rounds; ER nurses getting off duty; teachers up early for a morning run before school started. Everyone's life touched everyone else's, usually through some liquid conduit: blood ties, or sex, or drink. This one was the brother of that one's ex. That other one had once been this one's landlord, or perhaps they'd tried to start a business together and wanted to gossip to the bakery girls about why their former partner was the one to blame for the failure. As a written narrative it would have been tedious and predictable, but colored with Celia's buoyant expressions it was good distraction as they pushed against the frosty wind, leaving boot prints in the damp sand.

"Until you're ready to come back to New York and test-drive my new bedroom, I don't see much point in chatting," Brian said pleasantly one day. "I love hearing your voice, but let's not pretend things are normal. I'll spring for your plane fare. Come home as soon as you can, even for an overnight. Until then, have a nice February."

EVENINGS WEREN'T GOOD for Celia. She was a baker, and up hours before dawn. But she braced herself one week, and came to dinner. She brought a nice bottle of red wine, even though she knew Hank, a self-described Cheap Yankee Bastard, only drank beer and rum these days.

So she also brought some beer her boyfriend Ted had just made. "Here y'go," she said, grinning, placing an unmarked brown bottle in front of him. "This is better than cheap, it's free."

Hank, sitting upright at the table, looked tickled by the gift. "And what's this called?" he asked. He pushed the cat off the table and twisted the bottle cap off with callused hands. "Is it another *Game of Thrones* drug like the valerian?" He sniffed it. "Mm, smells hoppy."

"We call it Takemmy Brew," said Celia, watching him take his first slug of it. "Cuz we brewed it right here in Takemmy."

"Isn't that cultural appropriation?" asked Hank, mischievous. "Are you even allowed to *say* 'Takemmy' for 'West Tisbury' if you're not a member of the Wampanoag tribe?"

"Hank, you're absolutely right," said Celia. "That's why white people never call it *Massachusetts*. Instead we say Wicked-Pissah Red Sox Nation of Asshole Drivers. Speaking of the valerian, how'd you like it?"

He swallowed, set the bottle down, grimaced. "Haven't tried it yet," he confessed. "It looked murky."

"That's what happens when you soak fibrous roots in vodka for a month," Joanna said.

His eyes widened. "Vodka? Celia, honey, you didn't tell me it was *vodka*. That changes everything. Dear Celia," he said briskly, as if dictating a letter, "I would like to order a fifth of valerian tincture, please."

"We have to find you something productive to do," Joanna said, trying not to sound exasperated.

"You mean other than drink?" He said it with a defiant but self-conscious grin. "Can't imagine why I'm doing that. There's such an embarrassment of riches to do while I am stuck on my ass on the couch, in the middle of the woods, in the middle of winter. Oh, look," he said, with exaggerated glee, and picked up the remote control. "I can argue with Sanjay Gupta!"

"I think," said Celia, "that it is finally time for you to host a poker game."

Hank burst out laughing. "I'm a dreadful poker player," he confessed proudly. "What I *can* do—you know what I *can* do? I play a *mean* game of Scrabble."

"That's true. Let's invite some people over for Scrabble," Joanna said immediately.

He gave her an incredulous look. "You don't invite people over for Scrabble. You invite people over for *dinner*, and then *after* dinner, you play Scrabble. Maybe. If everyone else has had enough to drink." And then conspiratorially to Celia, "That's the best way to win."

She nodded. "Thank you, Hank," she said. "I will remember that tip and use it to beat you at Scrabble sometime soon. Meanwhile, maybe you need to improve your poker game. Ted can come teach you. Show you a few tricks. He's kind of a shark, but he'll take good care of you."

"Well," said Hank, shooting a glance in Joanna's direction, "I'm glad *somebody* will."

"Hey," Joanna said, more sharply than she should have. "I've been feeding you, doing your laundry, helping you in and out of bed—"

"But you're not entertaining me, Anna," he said. "Right now, more than anything else—even more than valerian tincture—I need some fucking *entertainment*! Gah!" He said this to the ceiling. "There is nothing more boring! Than this! Just *existing*! It's enough to make me get back into *politics*."

"God forbid," laughed Celia.

God forbid, thought Joanna.

Realizing Joanna would never rally as a sportswriter, Everett took her off basketball patrol. Now she wrote about the state Scholastic Awards. This mostly meant taking the press release from the high school and beefing it up with brief personal interviews of all the happy student winners. It was strange, almost eerie, to wander the hallways of her youth and see that some of the teachers were younger than she was.

Martha's Vineyard Regional High School existed in the midst of a few hundred acres that would never be featured on postcards or coffee table books: a flat expanse of fields, scrub oak, and lanky pines, straddling one of the dullest roads on the island, a narrow inland highway from Vineyard Haven to Edgartown (called, imaginatively, the Vineyard Haven–Edgartown Road by most, and the

Edgartown–Vineyard Haven Road by others). Across the street was Community Services, the ice rink, the YMCA, a cement skateboard park. The youth of the island could, and many did, spend most of their waking hours in this self-contained enclave, enjoying each other and their shared activities, but indifferent to all the things that made Martha's Vineyard the Martha's Vineyard of the off-Island imagination. No wonder so many were so ready to fledge to America, where they'd stare dumbly at the off-Islanders who waxed rhapsodic about how lucky they were to have grown up on such a picturesque island. Having become a summer person over the years, she'd wiped all this from her memory, but it crept back in as soon as she'd parked the truck in the high school lot.

Everett also sent her to report on a "merger" between Our Vineyard Bank and ABB, a massive off-Island financial institution. (That would be the Vineyard description of ABB. Most other humans would describe ABB as a massive international financial institution.) She interviewed old friends whose families had had accounts at Our Vineyard Bank for generations. It seemed to her that Everett skewed his editing to highlight the people who were happy about the buyout and underreport the ones who were disgruntled.

"I'm not doing that," he assured her with his terrier zest, when she brought this complaint to him at his unfurnished desk. "I'm not saying we don't have a bias here, but that's not an example of it. *You* don't like the idea of the buyout, but you can't say that in the article. You want to quote people who share your perception but are free to speak it in a way you aren't. My allowing you to write such a piece— *that* would show a bias."

"I'm used to my perception being a valued part of what I write," she said. "That's how I pay my bills."

"Maybe we'll keep you away from business reporting, then," he said. "I hate to think of you starting a local recession accidentally."

That was also Joanna's first week writing up the news briefs. She liked these because her name was not attached to them, so if she got something wrong she didn't have to worry about being scolded at the post office or the grocery store. Writing profiles of litigiously narcissistic celebrities wasn't stressful. Misrepresenting the neighbor's opinion on feral turkeys while misspelling his name—*that* was stressful.

And as for the news on charming, picturesque Martha's Vineyard, that bleak fortnight in February: A public forum was called by state wildlife rangers to discuss the merits of extending the deer-hunting season by an extra two weeks in an attempt to cull the herds, which would hopefully, in turn, rein in Lyme disease. The Vineyard had a Lyme infection rate twelve times the national average. Everyone knew deer ticks relied more on white-footed field mice than on deer, but Bambi always took the rap on this topic, possibly because Bambi was tastier than white-footed field mice.

Also in the news:

The hospital and Community Services were celebrating the one-year anniversary of partnership with Falmouth Halfway House, on the Cape. Everybody always wanted to see addicts getting help—as long as it wasn't in their neighborhood.

A new affordable-housing project was coming up for review at the Martha's Vineyard Commission. Everybody always wanted to see affordable housing get a green light—as long as it wasn't in their neighborhood.

(The exception to this had been Henry Holmes, who'd cannily donated several acres to the town for such a development, with the agreement that he retain timber rights.)

There were also a couple of updates on trials related to domestic violence, and in one case, sexual assault of a minor.

Finally, the Possible Dreams Auction was getting a new home. This annual fund-raiser was an authentic intersection of the Vineyard's wealthy summer population, its famous summer population, and its actual population. The celebrities offered themselves, or perks only they could provide, to the wealthy people. The wealthy people paid extravagant amounts to have cocktails, or a sunset sail, or a walk-on role, or a view from the owner's box, or a serenade, or a painting, or a portrait, or a peanut butter sandwich, with the celebrities. All of the profit went to Community Services, the nonprofit that strove to keep the year-round working-class population from going off the rails.

She dutifully read the competition's news briefs. The *"Newes* in Brief"* covered the Possible Dreams Auction, of course, for who would not enjoy reading about such gracious generosity on the part of our very own celebrities and benefactors?

Oh, God, Joanna thought, cringing. *Sometimes my inner Hank is such an asshole.*

The *Newes* did not mention any of the other things the *Journal* found worth reporting on. On the other hand, it offered updated info on the monthly poetry slam in Oak Bluffs and discussed several well-known historic buildings that would be getting face-lifts before summer. It also had an entertaining little paragraph titled "Stealing Heritage," about nouveau-riche seasonal types pilfering the gray lichen-covered boulders from their neighbors' ancient stone walls to create the illusion that their walls were ancient too. Newly quarried local rocks had a telltale orange hue to them, from so much iron in the soil. A reddish wall meant a newcomer's wall. Nobody wanted to be known as a Johnny-come-lately.

She wished Everett would send *her* to poetry slams.

BY THE FOLLOWING week, Joanna had finally achieved something like a routine. Regular work hours. The regular Hank-chores of shopping, cooking, laundry, driving to PT appointments. Her childhood onus of filling the humidifiers in the rooms too dry from heating and emptying the dehumidifiers in the rooms too damp from lack of heating. Regular Scrabble games with Hank, which he kept winning. Regular Celia-coffees (or in Joanna's case, tea) and Celia-walks on the windy, sometimes rocky North Shore beaches, wrapped in layers of wool and flannel. Regular affectionate-but-insubstantial texts to Brian, who responded with equally affectionate, equally insubstantial texts, and never with phone calls, which was both sad and relieving.

EVERETT TRUSTED HER with news briefs for a second week, and of course, she went to the next ZBA. This time, she felt slightly less like a deer in headlights.

The room had only a handful of people in it this time, mostly the usual suspects in the usual plaid and flannel. The cloudy gray day was darkening, as gray trees and gray-shingled houses began to fade from sight out the window in the gray dusk.

James Sherman was there again, lanky and bespectacled. His surprised pleasure from their previous meeting had shifted, though: now he eyed her almost suspiciously.

"Hey, James," she said, settling into the chair beside him, grateful to feel, if not his peer, at least competent to be there beside him.

"You're still doing this?" he asked, at his leisurely rate of speech. "I thought last time was just a one-off."

That felt a little like a slap. "Well, I'm here for a while," she said, unzipping her heavy coat and shrugging out of it. "Hank is going to need me around for a few more weeks at least, maybe longer. And, you know, it's work, it's income." Seeing his expression unchanged, she added, with false heartiness, "Plus not a bad way to pad a résumé, since every off-Island outlet assumes anything associated with the Vineyard is glam."

"You should be padding your résumé with real journalism. Why don't you come work for the *Newes*? I'm sure Lewis and Laurie would be thrilled to have you there."

"I couldn't do that to Everett," she said. She thought James would understand that, but she'd misjudged, for he made a face as if he smelled something terrible. She scrambled to undo whatever faux pas she'd just made: "I guess my loyalty to Everett doesn't make sense to you since he abandoned the *Newes* for the *Journal*—"

He looked even more disgusted. "Oh, it's not that. I get the whole changing camps thing, not everyone has the right sensibility for the

Newes. I meant what I said before, about the *Journal* being an advertising rag. But it's doing well because people like Everett are in their element there. And, sure, everyone has a right to thrive, and okay, yes, local businesses need more of a friend than maybe the *Newes* is willing to be."

"So . . . ?" she prompted.

"He supported the YMCA."

A pause. Joanna waited for the rest of his explanation.

But that was it, apparently. That was the crime.

"And?" she asked.

He shook his head. "If the whole point of the *Journal* is to be a pro-business paper for the Island, how can they justify supporting a mainland incursion like that?"

"James, it's a nonprofit," she said. "It's independent from any other Y. That's how the YMCA works."

"It's a huge ugly building that takes business away from the local health clubs."

"It *is* a local health club."

He shook his head. "It's as much of a franchise as McDonald's. It's an incursion. I lost all respect for him when he made the editorial choice to be pro-Y."

She hadn't been here for the hoopla around the YMCA getting built, but she recalled there had been hoopla. Not having read anything either paper had published about it, she channeled her inner Hank now, possibly even reciting something he'd said to her in an email from years back:

"Speaking as a kid who grew up here, I gotta say maybe Everett was thinking that if the youth of the Vineyard are bored and drunk and high and heroin looks attractive, but then again so does aikido, and aikido is right across the road from the high school, then who cares if it's a big ugly building? It's keeping them functional."

He gave her a look. "I don't think this is worth getting into a tizzy about. Let's drop it. Anyhow, they're about to start."

Irritably she turned her attention to the agenda. An artist wanted a variance on the setback for his studio. A small affordable housing project sought a comprehensive permit. Joanna's boyfriend from second grade, now shockingly thinning on top, wanted to add a guest cottage; a proposal to expand the bike path up-Island was referred to the Commission. Once the board had addressed all the new business, it was time for old business, and the first of these was correspondence. The Minion Lawyer of Mr. Orion Smith wrote to announce he intended to go to superior court to institute a lawsuit under Chapter 240, section 14A, challenging the legality of the town bylaw forbidding helicopter use. The ZBA and the selectmen would be kept abreast of any legal developments if they did not choose to annul their vote on the helipad.

"He's suing us," said one of the board members, staring truculently at the email.

"He's trying to scare us," corrected Helen, and said very deliberately to James Sherman and Joanna: "This is not a legal document. He is not suing us."

"He's not suing us *yet*," said the first board member.

"We get these kinds of threats all the time, these days," said Helen. "It doesn't mean a thing." But she did not look happy.

". . . AND THEN HE totally froze me out," she said, as Hank howled with approving amusement from his recliner. "When the meeting was over he got up and left without even a nod goodbye. I mean he said goodbye to Helen and the others but walked right past me!"

"You bitch-slapped the *Newes* reporter!" he chortled, saluting her with a beer can. Raising his eyebrows hopefully, he asked, "Did Helen see? Did she hear what you said?"

"I doubt it, Hank. She was trying to start the meeting, she didn't have time for the two reporters sitting in the corner getting hissy with each other."

"I'm proud of you," he said. "Now just write up the ZBA report making it clear Orion Smith is a dick, and you've really earned that honey I gave you."

JOANNA EDITED THE Valentines. Some of them were very Vineyard ("I love cuddling with you when the fish aren't running"). Others were more generic, and led her to feel unpleasantly single. Single-hood was dreaded in winter on the Vineyard. Some excruciatingly unfortunate unions occurred in attempts to lower heating bills. Joanna had cousins enough that she had seen this in action over the years. She would *not* fall into that trap. She hoped.

On the thirteenth of February, as she sat in bed staring out her bedroom window at the hard, cold black of an up-Island winter night, Brian texted her: Will you be my Valentine? And a moment later added: In Manhattan?

She gathered the comforter around her, turned the space heater down so that she could hear better, and called him.

"Are you calling to say yes?" he answered, sounding happy.

"If I was closer I would," she said. "But there's no direct flights in winter, Hank won't let me take the truck off-Island, and the bus takes seven hours if you include the ferry." *No wonder Orion Smith likes his helicopter*, she thought. For a brief, shameful moment she wondered how she could meet Orion Smith, charm him into taking a fatherly interest in her, and then hitch a ride to Manhattan with him, to finally have The Talk with Brian. A moment later, she was very glad this couldn't happen, as she still did not know what she'd actually want to say.

"You can get a lot of reading done in seven hours," Brian was meanwhile suggesting, in his reasonable tone.

"Good point," she said. "And I know you like to read, so why don't *you* come *here*?"

There was a pause long enough to measure in heartbeats.

"Um," he said. "I have no reason to go there. I mean except to see you, of course—but you have lots of reasons to come back here for a few days. This is where you *live*."

It is? she almost asked aloud. Instead, after a steadying breath, she said, "It's a big schlep for just a short visit, this time of year when the weather is so crappy. But I promise I'll get back as soon as I can."

"Here's hoping 'soon' turns out to be one of those words we have the same definition for," he said.

"I understand if you're tired of waiting for me—"

"Joanna, sweetheart, no, you don't get to do that," he said. "I've given you an invitation. Reject it if you want to, but don't try to make it look like I've rescinded it."

She nodded, alone in the chilled bedroom. "All right," she said, enervated. "Thanks for being patient. I'll be back in town for sure by mid-March at the latest."

"And then we can finally have The Talk," he said, a shade too eagerly.

THAT WAS THE closest thing she had to nightlife. There really was no place to casually wander to up-Island. So much of the Vineyard was shuttered in February. There were only two places on the hundred square miles of island to buy a bag of potato chips after 9 P.M. And when she wanted something more than potato chips, well . . . Celia had an early night and everyone else her age had kids. She had never been one for bars. Sporadically—for amusement only—she would cruise local online dating sites. There were very few available men on the Vineyard, and most of them had photos of dogs, pickups, or fish in place of their profile photo. She did catch herself wondering about the availability of decent-looking men under forty whose path she crossed—in the feed store getting grain for the chickens; the propane-delivery man at the *Journal*; motorists waiting to be served at the gas station across the street from the paper, when she went there for cheap coffee. After a few days of idle contemplation, Brian in comparison seemed exactly right for her. But every time she'd pick up the

phone to call him and tell him so, some part of her did not want
to admit it.

The following week, Joanna did a feature on a new hardware store
opening up-Island. She also covered the West Tisbury selectmen's
meeting, at which they decided to call a public forum to discuss the
increasingly unfriendly situation with Mr. Orion Smith, infamous
helicopter owner, who had used his helicopter at least once again.
And there were news briefs, including a court date for the domestic violence case she'd mentioned, without going into details, the
week before. It was Everett's position as editor to keep the "ugly bits
of life," as he called them, on readers' radars. In his childhood—
which was also Hank's childhood—nobody ever talked about anything tawdry or unpleasant, and so wives and children suffered in
silence, for the sake of appearances, while their parents or husbands
behaved atrociously and everyone just looked the other way. Everett
had survived such an upbringing and now was adamant about never
looking the other way, something Joanna had her own reasons to
appreciate. Names were kept out of the paper, and sensationalistic
details omitted, but every issue of the *Journal* had at least one article
intended to rob readers of complacency. This week it was the domestic violence case.

But the big news, that final week of February, was Hank's health.

Joanna had thought she'd soon be New York–bound. That she'd
be returning to finally have The Talk with Brian. His texts (they

had stopped speaking on the phone, again) made it clear he was very aware of her anticipated return date.

Hank had started physical therapy, but he hadn't weaned off the prescription pain meds, and couldn't put any weight at all on the broken foot, not even to test how much weight he could put on the broken foot. So it was no surprise to learn that he wasn't healing right.

Joanna took him in for the X-ray that they thought would be the precursor to his getting the boot removed. But the same doctor who had spoken to her back in January called them both in to the overbright lab room to stare at the icy, backlit negative of Hank's leg.

"You're not laying down enough calcium here," she said, pointing with a pencil eraser at what was obviously the fracture. "Which means the bone is not rebuilding."

"What does *that* mean?" Hank demanded, as if she were accusing him of something.

She sat up straighter in her cushioned swivel chair. "Just that it's going to take a little longer," she said, briskly comforting. "Just means we keep on keeping on, maybe even dial it back a little, okay? No weight-bearing at all, use the crutches one hundred percent of the time, and keep it elevated. Come back in two weeks for another X-ray."

"Oh, great," Hank muttered.

"And I'll renew the scrip for the pain meds," she added.

"Oh, great," Joanna muttered.

BACK HOME, SHE emailed Everett, Celia, Helen Javier and her husband, Paul, and a few others with an update. Then she fed the cats, slipped a couple pieces of eggplant parmigiana in the oven to reheat, went into her room, and called Brian to tell him her return would be delayed.

It went to voice mail. She considered just asking him to call her, but then it felt less exhausting to simply leave a message now. So she did. Three hours later, he sent a text saying, OK. Sorry to hear it.

SHE COULD HAVE gone to New York for a check-in, a weekend, a few days. Objectively she certainly could have done that. But Island Psychology seized up her brain, perhaps because it was always in control of Hank's and she was trying to calibrate to him. According to Island Psychology, off-Island was very far away. It could have been Boston or Taiwan, there was just a few hours in the difference. The obstacle—also the buffer, also the safety net—was Vineyard Sound. This band of water, traversable in fifteen minutes if you happened to own a motorboat, made a trip to New York feel five times more time-consuming and exhausting than it really was, especially now that she was so out of the habit of making the trip. Hank claimed he didn't care if she went, but he said it with enough petulance in his tone that she knew he'd consider her going back to New York even for a weekend tantamount to abandoning him permanently. Could she have simply bought a bus ticket? Objectively speaking, yes, of course. But it was out of the question. Especially given her increasing discomfort and confusion about The Talk With Brian that awaited her.

So a friend in New York vetted a subletter for her, but they needed a place for a year. She went with it. This took some pressure off financially. But it added a different class of pressure because now she would have nowhere to live in New York when she finally returned—unless she moved in with Brian. She could barely remember what Brian looked like. Sometimes she thought she was inventing him.

She was still stressed about money, and the only time the Vineyard was as quiet as February was March. At least April had Annual Town Meetings to get upset about, and by May everyone was bracing themselves for summer.

On the plus side, March was three days longer than February. But that wasn't enough to amend her take-home pay.

So she called Mr. C.

SHE STILL THOUGHT of Paolo Croce as Mr. C even though she'd graduated from his Advanced Algebra years ago and had the right to address him as a grown-up. Her class had called him Mr. C; the name stuck and now some parents weren't even clear what his whole name was. In addition to teaching math at the high school, he'd also moonlighted doing payroll for the *Newes*.

He'd been a fan of her writing on the school newspaper, and introduced her to the *Newes'* editor-back-then, who had offered her the cushy internship of restaurant reviewing. Mr. C had retired from teaching by now, but last she'd heard he was still doing the *Newes* books.

The historic district in Edgartown was a close-nested neighborhood, with brick sidewalks and the morning aroma of baked bread wafting down narrow streets. The houses were old, in a tidy, grandmotherly way. Unlike the other towns, the empty streets did not feel abandoned in February, but simply quaint and quiet. In Oak Bluffs it was easy to imagine horse-drawn vehicles on main streets, and in Vineyard Haven one could imagine Model Ts. Edgartown evoked chiefly the foot traffic of past centuries.

The *Newes* offices were housed in a building nearly as stately as the paper's masthead. Growing up, Joanna had known these as Whaling Captains' houses, but when she went off to college and took an elective in architectural history, she realized most were Greek Revival and had been built by plenty of people, all over America, with no relationship to whaling. Broad whitewashed clapboard, dark louvered shutters framing the windows. Regal, but understated. A stoic Yankee retort to the southern plantation manor. The Whaling Captains' houses mostly clustered here, at the eastern end of the Island. The grandest ones looked out over Edgartown Harbor toward the islet of Chappaquiddick. Edgartown, the first place white settlers had put down roots, had grown to be one of the great whaling ports of the Eastern Seaboard. Its sense of maritime exceptionalism never deserted it; a hundred years after whaling died out, it still boasted the "yachtingest of all yacht clubs" in New England.

The *Newes* building lived on a neat little one-way Edgartown street, where all the yards had thigh-high whitewashed fences with bare-branched bushes, over which roses and hydrangeas would later gush in time for the Fourth of July parade. Unlike most of its neighbors, the *Newes* building had given up its white clapboard sheath. Now it boasted simple cedar shingles, long aged to a velvety gray. Inside was an eccentrically intoxicating blend of architectural reserve and knuckle-down work environment. The receptionist, in her restricted little booth that had once been the coat closet, smiled politely, not remembering Joanna from fifteen or eighteen years ago, and asked what she was there for.

"I'm here to see Paolo Croce," she said. The receptionist nodded, informed her desk console—freakishly out of place in a nineteenth-century house—and then smiled politely up at her. "He's down the hall to the right," she said. "Do you know it?"

"I can get myself there, thanks," Joanna said, and passed by. The bare floorboards—wide, painted a steely blue-gray that matched the sky on a sulky winter day—croaked in tired protest under her step. The ceiling was lower than modern buildings, and as she traveled deeper back into the house, it gradually inched even lower. She passed by two narrow thumb-latch doors, then turned right through another thumb-latch door that stood ajar, to find a slender, dark-eyed man hunched behind a desk overflowing with files. Mr. C smiled when he saw her and sat up, more resembling the lithe figure she remembered from her youth. "Joey!" he said, and got up from his creaky wooden chair.

Until the name came out of his mouth, she'd nearly forgotten about her high school nickname. And until the name came out of his mouth, she'd also forgotten that she wrote those restaurant reviews under that name. Anna Howes had never had a byline in the *Newes*. Due to an ephemeral obsession with her Azorean middle name, she had insisted on publishing as Joey Dias that long-ago summer.

"How are you, Joey?" Mr. C asked, patting her on the back. "What are you doing back on the rock?" His voice was wispier than it had been when he was teaching. His pomaded hair was wispier too. With his Boston accent he could have passed as a genteel barber for the mafia.

"My uncle had a spill," she said. "Helping him to get back on his feet."

"Oh . . . I think I heard about that."

Of course he'd heard about it, his wife worked at the hospital.

"It could have been worse," she said.

He nodded sagely. "Glad it wasn't. So how long you here for?"

She shrugged. "I dunno, maybe another month, month and a half? Depends on Hank's health. Are they looking for freelancers here?"

"You want to write for the *Newes*? Man, Joey, they'd be lucky to have you, go talk to Lewis . . . Oh, do you know Lewis? I don't think he was here yet when you were here."

"Pamela was the editor," she said.

"Yeah, Lewis is great, he came a couple years ago," said Mr. C. "Want me to introduce you?"

"I'd really appreciate that, but there's just one thing . . ." She hesitated. "Have you heard about how you can't write for both papers?"

He smirked. "Yeah, the *Journal* apparently has some kind of policy about that."

"The *Journal*, are you sure?" she asked. "The *Journal* thinks the *Newes* is the one with the policy."

He jutted his lower lip out thoughtfully, shook his head. "I've never heard that. I mean it doesn't really affect me down here, but everyone here thinks it's the *Journal*. Why? Oh!" He gave her a con-spiring look. "You're writing for the *Journal*? Everett hired you?"

"Just as a freelancer. Y'know, for this short time I'm here."

"Yeah, that guy loved you," said Mr. C with a chuckle. "We used to debate which of us would adopt you. Nothing against Jen and Hank, but we never felt like they were worthy of you."

"That's sweet, but I don't need to be adopted anymore. What I need is more work."

"I'll get you upstairs with Lewis. Let me see if he's free now. It's Friday but I think the edit meeting just ended, so he might still be around." He punched something into his phone. An indicator light went red, then green, and a soft baritone voice said, "Lewis Worthington."

"Hi, Lewis, it's Paolo, downstairs. There's a young woman here, an Islander—" And he quickly explained who she was. He didn't use her name, whether by design or accident she couldn't tell. Lewis was willing to see her, so Mr. C brought her up the steep old stairs that had once led to the servants' quarters, and into the room that she remembered from years earlier as the editor's office. It was a converted bedroom—not the master bedroom, which was reserved for the publisher—and overlooked the narrow, quiet street outside. The walls were lined with bookcases, with *Banks' History of Martha's Vineyard* being given pride of place, close at hand to the desk. The shelves not filled with distinguished-looking hardcovers had duck decoys nestled on them. Resting on the mantel above the decommissioned fireplace was a framed collection of Wampanoag arrowheads.

Lewis himself was precisely what Joanna would have expected for a *Newes* editor: oxford shirt (over a turtleneck, as it was winter), expensive wire spectacles, well-behaved yellow Lab lying on the braided rug.

"Lewis, this is Joey," said Mr. C, before she could introduce herself. Joey. Not Joanna.

Lewis stood. He was very tall, with the slight apologetic stoop that some tall people have. He reached across his broad oak desk to shake her hand. His hand, she saw, had the mild calluses and short nails of a day sailor's. The dog, happy to have visitors, rose and dawdled across the rug to press its damp nose into her other hand.

"Hi, pooch," she said.

"That's Nevin," said Lewis.

"Hi, Nevin." Then, because she couldn't help herself: "I'm a Nevin, on my mom's side. Who's he named for?"

"The former owners of our house were Nevins," said Lewis.

"I thought you were a Dias on your mom's side," said Mr. C.

"I am," she said. "But on my mother's *mother's* side, I'm a Nevin."

Both men chuckled, exchanging the look that wash-ashores gave the native-born when they grew precious about family connections. She ignored this. "That house on Pease's Point way? The little Cape? That was my great-uncle's."

"Yes, that's the one," said Lewis, looking pleased. "Okay, so you're a real Islander." A glance to Mr. C. "And she used to write for us?"

"She worked under Everett when he was here," Mr. C said unhelpfully.

"High school, summers," she said. "It's been a while."

"What have you been doing since then?"

"Oh, um, writing. Under various names," she said awkwardly, trying to think if she had ever published anything else under the name Joey Dias. Nope.

"Newspapers? Magazines?"

"Both," she said, trying not to sound jittery. If he asked for links to her work, he'd see she was actually Anna Howes. Anna Howes worked for the enemy paper.

"She wrote that article about Nina Brown," said Mr. C proudly. "You know, that one somebody had hanging by the coffee station for—"

"Oh, boy, I do remember that," Lewis said, and smiled with respect. "The rock-star's-favorite-cereal thing, right? Everyone was so proud that a former intern had hit the big time, even though you wrote it under some other name, didn't you? For some reason?"

She made a dismissive gesture. "Yeah, I got a lot of work out of that piece. Grateful for it."

"Okay, well, that sounds good to me," said Lewis. "You're in."

Good Lord, she thought, *that was easy*. Small-town newspapers! Where else would a bookkeeper's recommendation score you a position as a reporter? "We're understaffed. Let me look at some of what you wrote for us, and we'll take it from there. Did you go to J-school?"

"No. I took some journalism classes, but I was an English major, and I'd be much more comfortable doing features," she said. "Or, y'know, reports. I have too much respect for investigative journalists to try to pass myself off as one."

"Can you cover town government?" he asked, and turned his attention through his reading glasses to something on his computer screen. "Have you ever reported on, say, a committee meeting?"

"Yes, actually, I have." *Thank you, Everett.*

"That's great, we're short next week because James Sherman just became a grandfather for the first time so he's in Connecticut for a while—"

"She can absolutely cover James's beat," said Mr. C heartily.

She knew there was a problem with that. She just couldn't rearrange the pieces in her mind to figure out what it was.

"Okay, introduce her to Laurie and see if she's still in the system." He gave her a patrician smile. "Thanks for stepping in. Glad we're the ones to get you, instead of Everett and his salacious little coupon-delivery system of a paper." He said this in such a gracious tone she almost didn't register the meaning. "Looking forward to working with you."

"Thanks," she said, a little wide-eyed. "Mmm, how will I get my assignments?"

"I'll call you directly, or else Laurie will handle it. Do you know her?" She shook her head. Her brain was trying to identify what the problem was with her taking over James Sherman's beat.

"She's sorta new," said Mr. C to her. And then, almost apologetically, to Lewis: "By Joey's standards, I mean." He winked at her. "I'll introduce you. Thanks, Lewis."

"Thank you," said Lewis. To Joanna: "And thank *you*."

They let themselves out. Mr. C walked her toward the back of the building, down a narrow corridor with more thumb-latch doors along the length of it, and occasional small skylights to redeem the corridor from total darkness.

The *Newes* offices were spread between the antique house and its barn, connected by a breezeway with a little break room. The barn having been in disrepair, its innards had been torn apart decades ago leaving a capacious cavity—newsroom above, printing press below.

In the open newsroom, full of cubicles and whimsical found objects hanging from the walls, Mr. C directed her to an attractive blond woman in her forties named Laurie. As Joanna dutifully stared around the room, distracted by all the changes wrought over the last twenty years (spiffier computers, ergonomic chairs, a paint job), he explained—in a rapid, casual tone—who she was and what Lewis wanted of her. Laurie shook Joanna's hand, welcomed her aboard, and got her contact information.

"So you'll be covering James Sherman's beat this coming week," Laurie said. "Can you turn things around quickly? There's a big ZBA meeting in West Tisbury on Tuesday and we need a write-up by Wednesday, early afternoon, so we can revise it if we need to. It's the helicopter thing."

"No problem," Joanna said, finally grasping what the problem was. When filling in for Susan Grant on the *Journal*'s beat of the ZBA, she had sat with James. Now Joanna would *be* James, but the *Journal*'s usual reporter—Susan Grant—was back, so she would recognize Joanna (they'd never met, but Helen always greeted the reporters by name), and the jig would be up. Susan would out her as a two-timing journalist.

"No problem," she said again, mechanically, now that she realized it was a problem.

Mr. C took her back down to his office. When they were alone, he grinned, winked, and chucked her on the shoulder.

"You told them I was Joey Dias, not Anna Howes. I thought it didn't matter to the *Newes*."

"It doesn't. But since you're already Joey Dias here, why do something that will get you in trouble with the *Journal*? Don't you need both gigs? You're on the books each place with two different names. Just simplify it and keep it that way. I want to help you out, Joey. I know you're not in an easy situation."

"Thank you, Mr. C," she said.

"Hey, you're a good kid," he said. "One of my favorite students. Too bad you didn't stick with math."

"I hated math."

"I know!" he said. "Broke my heart. So tell you what: go forth and prosper, and don't hate math quite so much."

It's a bad sign when you ask for something and then cringe upon getting it. When the only thing that is going to save your butt is something that could actually just get your butt in deeper trouble.

Joanna asked Everett if she could cover the ZBA meeting on the grounds that she had covered the last two ZBA meetings. Everett was pleased. He was pleased for two reasons: Susan Grant, whose beat it was, was off-Island again, researching the regional heroin crisis; she had a reservation to come back on the 3:45 ferry, but there was a winter gale expected that would keep the boats from running, so she'd already asked to have somebody on backup. More than that, though, Everett liked the notion that Joanna was invested enough in something that she wanted to make it hers.

She almost told him the truth: if she was covering it for the *Newes*, she had to also cover it for the *Journal*, so that the regular *Journal* reporter couldn't see she was working for the *Newes*. Perhaps she could have sat in the back of the audience and just not spoken to anyone, but most meetings had sparse attendance and everyone seemed to know her.

But now she had a new challenge: although only a single human being, she had to appear as two different individuals, because both papers would be sending a reporter. And those reporters would be nearly the only people in attendance, so neither would be getting lost in the crowd.

So she called Celia, of course.

Celia was both mortified and amused. "You want me to impersonate you while I'm with you?" she echoed, with an uncertain laugh.

"Sort of. Not really. I mean you don't have to *impersonate* me exactly. I just need to be with somebody who kind of looks like me from the back. If either of my editors ever looked at the video for some reason, I can't be the only reporter in the room—there has to be *somebody* else, but the somebody else has to be nondescript so that they don't stand out—"

"I've been called a lot of things, kiddo, but never nondescript."

"—and the best way for them to not stand out is to look kind of like me. So you know, wear a hat, wear loose clothes, we can dress similarly. Okay?"

"And this will accomplish what, exactly?"

"It lets me cover the meeting for both papers without drawing attention to the fact that both papers have hired the same person. There's no reason for anyone to know that."

"So which paper are you fleecing?" Celia asked, getting invested now.

"Neither! I get paid by the piece, not by the time it takes me to write it. I'm going to write a different article for each paper, so they will each get what they're paying for—but it's just simpler not to try to explain it to my bosses."

"Yeah, those damn bosses," Celia said. "Always keeping people from gaming the system."

"I will pay you for your time."

"You don't have to pay me if I do it. But I'm not sure I want to do it."

"Please. You're the perfect person—you're about my height, you don't live in West Tisbury, and you're the only person I can be totally honest with about this."

"Well, when you put it like *that*," Celia said, and sighed heavily. "I guess I can't turn you down."

"Thank you! The meeting starts at five. Come over an hour before and we can figure out what to wear together."

Celia laughed. "The last time either of us said that, we were in high school," she said. "So let's do it like we did it in high school. All you have are some city clothes you threw in a bag a month ago in the middle of the night, I have my entire wardrobe. You come over here. Also I don't know that I'd fit in your stuff. You have that tight little city-gym-club butt."

"Do I?" Joanna said incredulously.

"Come over at four," said Celia. "And if the meeting goes late, I'll have to leave because I'm up at three thirty in the morning."

Celia and her boyfriend Ted rented a house in Tisbury (which is a different town from West Tisbury, but the same town as Vineyard Haven ... never mind why. Really. You'll never get that quarter-hour of your life back.). Like so very many houses on the island, this one was built quickly from prefab plans in the 1980s or early '90s, without the soul of earlier houses or the style of later ones. Whoever built it and sold it made a buck; whoever flipped it made more; whoever owned it now and rented it out was also doing just fine. Celia and Ted were waiting on a lottery to buy an affordable building lot near the Tisbury School. Meanwhile, they were growing some of their own food, and other things, in an extra bedroom that they'd converted to a greenhouse, and brewing some of their own beer in the garage, which was otherwise filled with the discarded playground toys of the landlord's now-grown children. Ted worked maintenance for the hospital and moonlighted as a private chef in summer. His clients found him exquisitely quaint and prided themselves on the street cred they got for inviting him to an occasional cocktail party. All the pants he owned were Levi's and most of them had indelible tomato sauce stains on them. This may have been part of the reason people wanted him at their parties. Authentic culture!

But Ted wasn't home. So once Joanna had hazarded the sleety winds of February and warmed up in the kitchen, the two women stood in front of Celia's open winter closet in their underwear, shivering and giggling, sampling dresses and skirts and leggings and yoga pants and sweaters until they came up with two costumes that didn't look deliberately twinnish, and yet were almost indistinguishable at a passing glance. Wrapped in inelegant but warm padded winter raincoats, they carpooled into West Tisbury, past the shuttered farmstands and empty fairgrounds, to the Town Hall, running in through the worsening wind just in time for the ZBA meeting to start.

And just in time for Joanna to realize the flaw in her plan: Helen Javier.

As they entered the nearly empty room, pulling their hoods back, red-cheeked from the cold rain, Helen pleasantly called out, "Hello there, Celia!" to someone she had known casually for thirty years. "What gives us the pleasure?"

Celia looked at Helen as if she'd been caught stealing something. She glanced at the MOCC camera operator; he was futzing with something, and the camera wasn't on yet.

"She's keeping me company," Joanna said, somehow sounding offhand. She tried to think through the ramifications of this: Helen, as the chair, surely read both papers' write-ups of ZBA meetings regularly. Not only would she notice that Celia Hendricks hadn't written either of the ones about to appear, but she might also notice that both of them were written by people with names that belonged, at different times over the years, to Joanna D. Howes.

For the MV Journal, by Anna Howes:

The West Tisbury ZBA voted this week to
grant a comprehensive permit for an affordable housing project, described as
"desperately needed" by the Selectmen,
off State Road near Ghost Island Farm. The
project, called Onkokemmy Fields, has been
held up for the past two years due to spirited disagreements about the architectural
style of the solar-powered residences. "We
are all very grateful that the board has
chosen to prioritize the urgent need for
year-round housing over aesthetic issues,"
said Roger Patz, the developer. Abutters
to the property had argued against it,
which ZBA Chair Helen Javier described at
the meeting as "ironic" since several of
them are part owners of the solar power
company that would be supplying solar for
the project. "Are you so allergic to being
in proximity to people from a different
socioeconomic class that you will argue
against your own business interests?" she
asked.

In other news, the ZBA will hold a public
forum March 1 at 7:30 p.m. at the West Tisbury Public Library. The forum is to discuss the unfolding situation with seasonal
resident Orion Smith, who has threatened to
sue the town for the right to land and operate a private helicopter on his North Road

property. Mr. Smith could not be reached for
comment.

THE GODS OF typography were kind to Joanna that week: somehow, despite two editors and a proofreader looking it over, the
Newes accidentally used the name "James Sherman" as the writer
of the ZBA report. So most of the Island thought he wrote the
following:

> In West Tisbury last week, the Zoning Board of
> Appeals moved swiftly through item after item
> on the docket. Chief among these was a compre-
> hensive permit for the affordable housing project
> Onkokemmy Fields, named after a small fresh-
> water pond to the north of the development.
> Onkokemmy Fields will offer solar-powered, year-
> round rental housing to five local families in a
> townhouse.

THE MOCC TAPES of various meetings were sometimes viewed
after the fact by an overextended reporter who hadn't been able to
get to a meeting in person. So even Helen Javier might be excused
for thinking James Sherman had written this, despite his absence at
the meeting.

But of course there was one person who would know James Sherman hadn't written it: James Sherman.

And as soon as he brought this error to the attention of Lewis Worthington, Joanna knew, they would have a talk that went something like this.

JAMES S: Hey, who actually wrote that piece?

LEWIS W: Joey Dias.

JS: Joey . . . Hang on, that's the name Joanna Howes wrote under when she was an intern here . . . and Joanna Howes is actually writing for the *Journal* under the name Anna Howes, and she defended that no-good hypocrite Everett. She is definitely not somebody you want writing for our hallowed gazette, and furthermore, to pay her back for her scheming duplicity, you should rat her out to the *Journal* as well, and let Everett know of her perfidy! With no means of income available to her, she will slither back, starving, to the off-Island world that is all she now deserves!

And so, when her phone rang on Friday evening and she saw it was an Edgartown number, she braced herself. She did some dexterous calculations—Mr. C would have been proud of her, no doubt—and determined that she could afford to stay on the island without an income until Hank was better, provided she was prepared to then immediately move in with Brian once she went home to New

York. It was not even a matter of whether or not she wanted to, as the choice was about to be taken away from her due to finances.

And in that moment, she realized she did not want to move in with Brian, at least not now. He was a good man and deserved honesty from her, which meant she would have to tell him the truth, which would leave her with nowhere at all to go. Without the social safety net of a place like the Vineyard, she would end up sleeping somewhere in Central Park and living off whatever pigeons she was able to catch and kill, like Hemingway in the Jardin du Luxembourg.

With all of that clear, she answered the phone.

"Hello, is this Joey?" said Lewis, gentlemanly and a little tired.

"It is," she said, not letting on that she knew who it was, in order to postpone the inevitable another seven seconds.

"Joey, it's Lewis Worthington. I'm sorry to be calling you on a Friday night but I got an urgent call from James Sherman."

Of course you did, she thought.

"No problem," she said as casually as she could. "What is it?"

"Well, first of all I want to thank you for covering for James on such short notice, you did a great job, really—"

"Thank you," she said, willing to accept a head pat before her head rolled.

"Here's the thing—"

Oh, God. He was hesitating. Just say it, she thought, just get it over with.

"Well, his daughter just had a baby and he's in Minnesota with her right now, but the baby was a preemie, and things seem a little hectic out there, and I'm not sure when he'll be back."

"Oh!" she said, with inappropriate relief.

"Yes, exactly. He's very preoccupied, it's his first grandchild, and since there really isn't anything much going on with West Tisbury these days, I'd love to be able to give him a long leash in terms of family time off."

She was going to point out that West Tisbury was probably about to be sued, but reconsidered and said nothing. Apparently that wasn't news the *Newes* found interesting.

"So, my question is, would you be able to fill in for him on the West Tisbury beat until he gets back?"

"Oh," she said, unraveling her calculations about being homeless in Central Park. "Um. If you think I'm up to it. Sure."

"That's great, thanks so much, Joey. I'm sure Laurie can find somebody to fill in any knowledge gaps you might have since you've been away for so long—"

"I've got people I can talk to," she said.

"And I haven't forgotten that your strength is writing profiles and features," he said. "I'm looking for some good matches for you."

"Looking forward to that as well," she said. "So, this public forum on March first at the West Tisbury library, about the helipad lawsuit—do you want me to cover that?"

"Oh . . ." He clearly hadn't considered this. "No. It's not actually news, it's just a town huddle over a topic that isn't even very interesting. It won't impact anything. So, no, don't bother. Next selectmen's meeting, though, you should go to that. I'll have Laurie send you the schedule."

"Thanks, Lewis," she said. "I appreciate your reaching out to me. I don't take it for granted."

She would never take anyone's trust in her for granted ever again. Because she no longer deserved it.

III
MARCH

THE COMMUNITY ROOM OF THE WEST TISBURY FREE PUBLIC
Library was crammed full of her childhood—nearly every face familiar, more lined than she remembered it. Winter skin was ren-
dered paler by the pseudosummer of full-spectrum fluorescents
above. More than half of the hundred-odd chairs were filled, and
more folks were wandering in from the darkened main hall of the
library, blinking in the brightness and then seeking friends to sit
with. Suddenly, she felt awkward, not sure where to set up. She crept
along the left-hand wall toward the front, beginning a circumambulation of the room.

Distracted by all the familiar faces, she almost walked into a tall,
broad-shouldered woman with a thick gray ponytail and bright gray
eyes. Joanna knew her but blanked on her name. She'd been the
high school gym teacher, and Joanna had always been terrified of
her. Worse, she was talking to Jenny, now known as the manager
of a popular Oak Bluffs hotel, but to Joanna she would always be

the fourth-grade class bully. There were hardly two women on the Island she was more intimidated by, and here they were standing together. She decided to pass by as invisibly as possible.

"Hey, *Joey*!" they both said robustly, almost at the same moment, and she overcame her ingrained impulse to scamper away. She waved, trying to look purposeful as she pivoted slightly to cross past them and continue her circuit around the room. They didn't really want to talk to her anyhow, she was sure, but she felt their cool glances on the back of her head.

She sauntered a few more rows closer to the front, and a kindlier face presented itself: this was Dr. Tavers, her family optician. He was sitting in the third row, on the end, his wife beside him. "Hello, Joanna," he said, in the soft, reassuring tones of his profession.

"Hello, Dr. Tavers!" she said, glad to see him although suddenly mildly awkward about now having an off-Island eye doctor.

"You home for Jen's fund-raiser?" he asked. This was an annual event held in honor of her aunt Jen, to raise scholarship money for high school seniors.

"That's in May," she said. "I'm home to see Hank."

"Oh, of course you are! Sorry. Give him my best."

"Will do." She resumed circulating. At the front of the room, where the miked podium waited, she crossed quickly to the other side without looking around, to avoid being greeted by vaguely familiar faces she couldn't put names to.

Nobody was greeting her as if she were a reporter, even though they had probably seen her byline in the paper over the past six weeks. Maybe they didn't want to embarrass her by commenting on her new status as professional gossip. This thought made her so self-conscious she felt something like stage fright. She decided to eschew the chairs and settle someplace unobtrusive, to make it easy for people to pretend they didn't know she was a reporter.

There was a long folding table at the back of the room, just to the side of the entrance. It was used for serving refreshments at more amicable library functions, like readings or memorials.

There were few people by this table. Only one was familiar, a fisherman Hank used to scallop with, with wiry hair that stood up all over the place as if caught in a perpetual nor'easter. He didn't notice her now, any more than he'd ever noticed her in childhood, so that was safe. All the rest were strangers. There were a man and a woman about her age, both nondescript, and one bright-eyed octogenarian with the broad, humped back of a stonemason, dressed in musky work clothes but hair neatly combed. Nobody else. Nobody to distract her from her duties. She leaned back against the table, staring out over the sea of (mostly graying) heads. Leaning, without actually sitting, felt safe. It was noncommittal. If anyone she knew approached to chat with her, she could sidle away without seeming to avoid them. So here, among strangers, she could put on her reporter hat and focus.

"Nothing like direct democracy in action," said a man's voice, close by.

"Absolutely," she said with gusto. It was the man about her age. His skin was pleasantly cappuccino-colored for a local in March—he might have been a Brazilian with accentless English, but something about him seemed very yacht club, so probably he was just a banker with a snowbird tan. He wore faded jeans, a heavy corduroy jacket over a down vest, and a Red Sox cap but his carriage, the closeness of his shave, the boring neatness of his coiffure, were too suburban for the clothes.

"It's my first Town Meeting," he said quietly, looking reverent. "It's fascinating."

"Ah. You a wash-ashore?"

"I'm from America. See, I know the lingo." He grinned at her. "And you?"

"Family's been here since 1692," she recited. "Or maybe 1705. Depends on which great-aunt you ask."

He chuckled. "You Islanders, man," he said, affably. "You're more obsessed with lineage than the British royals."

"Our land's more fashionable than theirs," she said. "We cost prohibitively more per square foot."

"Is that why you're anti-immigrant?"

She blinked. "What?"

"You're xenophobes. You don't want outsiders coming in." He had a friendly smile that took the sting out—it was just a description, one he found mildly entertaining. "In fact, you're anti-immigrant and *foolish*, because *most* immigrants to the Vineyard bring cash *into* the economy instead of taking money out of it."

She blinked again. What Vineyard did he live on? "No, a lot of people send money back to Brazil or Estonia or the Czech Republic. We're okay with that because they work very hard for it and they're more reliable than a lot of the college kids."

He shook his head. "I mean the immigrants who come here to

settle down and make a long-term home for themselves. The wash-ashores."

She smiled dismissively. "That's a misuse of the word *immigrant*. You're a *transplant*. From one part of America to another."

"This place really could be its own little country, and anyone moving here to make a life for themselves better be on board with that, because things get done differently here. Isn't that why you all call the mainland America? As if you *weren't* America?"

She nodded. "Okay, fair point."

"Sounds like immigration. But it's immigration that adds money to the economy. People who come here because they want to *live* here tend to have cash to sink into a nice piece of property, and they pay people to build their house and maintain their yard and teach them yoga and feed their kids." He gestured around the room. "*And* subsidize their public buildings. I've seen photos of the old library. It was two little rooms on Music Street, for, like, a century. A few decades later and you've got the Club Med of bibliothèques. Wouldn't have happened without immigrants like me." He shrugged, and gave her an almost sycophantic smile.

She liked his eyes. She had a thing for dark eyes. Too bad he was talking nonsense.

Beyond him, eclipsed by his coat collar, she saw a crutch and the sleeve of a familiar plaid shirt in the doorway. Helen or her husband, Paul, must have picked Hank up. She'd assumed he wasn't well enough to come. Now she felt both guilty and excluded that she was not the one he'd asked for a ride.

Paul Javier passed by Hank. His curly black hair was grayer and thinner than the last time Joanna had seen him but otherwise he was unchanged—gentle, slightly goofy Paul, the hapless Peter Pan to Helen's Wendy. He headed quickly toward an aisle chair down front and draped his wool coat on it to save it, then gestured for Hank to notice. Hank himself was making a slow progression. People greeted him boisterously, a few with surprise but most with affectionate hard-ass Yankee ribbing. She heard them tell each other to get out of the way for the invalid, for the crazy guy, for the acrobat, and Hank took it all in with his slanted smile and occasional back talk. Nobody noticed Joanna and she decided to stay engaged with her new friend. After all, he wanted to debate.

And he was nice to look at. Nobody had been nice to look at for ages.

"You so-called immigrants make it too expensive for most Island families to continue to live here. You've priced me out of the market in my own hometown. I grew up on seven acres that my uncle bought in his twenties on a fisherman's income, from a retiring farmer. If I tried to buy the smallest possible buildable lot from him, for a hundred times what he paid for the whole thing, I'd be ripping him off, that's how insane real estate has become. I don't think most immigrants have *that* kind of impact on a local population."

"Actually, most American communities do well economically when they welcome immigrants."

"Let's check with the Wampanoag tribe. I'm not sure they'll be on board with that."

"I'll rephrase it," he said. "The United States historically does well to welcome immigrants."

"But you've already made the convincing point that we're not like the rest of the United States," she said triumphantly. "Whatever truisms you want to push about America are meaningless here."

He shrugged. "You look like somebody who appreciates a good library," he said. "You're welcome." And then he gave her a killer smile.

"I need a moment to process this conversation," she said.

"Take your time," he said, expansively. After a weighted pause: "I'm enjoying this. It's not your usual nice-to-meet-you banter, is it?"

"Actually," she said, with a nod toward the other side of the room where the mic awaited, "if you consider the setting, it kind of is." She looked down toward her backpack, unzipped it, and began to pull out her laptop. "Excuse me, but I need to find a place to set up shop."

The laptop surprised him. "You're taking notes?"

"I'm covering the meeting for the *Journal*."

"Oh, that's the reactionary one that hates immigrants," he said.

"That is a ridiculous statement," she said. "We have two Brazilian columnists who write in Portuguese."

"Well, your readers hate immigrants," he said. "I've seen the online comments about Brazilians—not to mention the online comments about the wash-ashores. If you're not a seventh-generation plumber, you're not welcome here."

"That's not true," she retorted. "My cousin's a seventh-generation plumber and he offers below-market rental housing to a bunch of Brazilians." The rental part was true, but she doubted indoor plumbing existed seven generations ago.

"Really? Good for him!" Despite the suburban blandness, his expression was incredibly agreeable when smiling. It was the kind of smile most men lost forever when they hit adolescence.

"Yes," she said, trying not to enjoy his face quite so much. "He does it on principle, because he believes everyone who works for a living should have a place to live." And she couldn't help but add, "It's a sort of passive-aggressive protest against people whose McMansions are driving the price of housing up."

"Oh, so he likes only *certain* immigrants," the fellow said, as if *he'd* scored a point. "The sort that match his idea of what the Vineyard should be. While disapproving of the ones that don't match his idea of what it should be. Totally unlike what happens to immigrants in mainland America. Right."

She saw the town moderator moving up toward the podium. She had to focus.

"That's an interesting but specious comment," she said. "Your parallel won't hold up to scrutiny. I could tear it apart in fifteen seconds but I have to don my reporter's hat now."

She focused on her laptop but she could feel him giving her the once-over. "I'd love to hear you tear my parallel apart. How about a coffee sometime?" She darted a look at him to see the mischievous gleam in his eye.

Her mouth dropped open. She closed it quickly. A date? With a nice smile? Who lived here in *March*? Was she allowed to date? Brian had told her he wanted to be free to see other people, although she was pretty sure he wouldn't do so.

She shrugged. "Okay, sure," she said with forced nonchalance, and studied his reaction from the corner of her eye.

He looked surprised. "You don't think I'm being inappropriate?" he asked.

"It's a little forward," she said. "But I don't get hit on very often and at least you're asking to hear my expert opinion instead of telling me I have nice eyes."

"You do have nice eyes," he said.

She felt herself blush, although she was not the blushing type. There was a silent moment as she tried to contain the blush, but this only made her blush more. Finally she answered, "Thanks."

He bit his lower lip. "Oh crap. Did I just ruin the vibe here?"

"No, you just changed it a little," she said, knowing she absolutely had to retreat from this conversation and put her reporter's hat back on.

"Enough to make it a drink instead of coffee?"

Butterflies. Instant case of butterflies. Wow, that was fast. "Let's start with coffee," she said, as calmly as she could.

"Of course. And seriously, if you think I'm inappropriate, I get it."

"I don't think you're inappropriate," she said, and smiled despite herself.

"You prefer text or email?" he said, and almost before she realized what she was doing, she had recited her cell number to him.

But at this moment—*thank God*, she thought—Peter Cooke, the town moderator, who looked like a bearded hippie-farmer version of Richard Burton, called the meeting to order.

"If everyone could just turn your attention up here," said Peter Cooke, "we can get started." A pause as the buzz settled. "As all of you know, this is an informal forum. It's not a selectmen's meeting or a ZBA meeting or a special town meeting. We're not here to make any decisions or to look at any language, but we want to get the sense from the town about some possibilities. Including, at the request of the selectmen, the possibility of raising and appropriating an extra one hundred thousand dollars as a war chest in case of unexpected legal action. Or not. We're looking at all possibilities, and we're looking for your ideas."

"Okay, so should I text or call?" her new friend whispered. He used the excuse of whispering to lean toward her, and she felt—or imagined she felt—his breath faintly against her neck.

"Um. Text," she whispered back. Then, pointing at her computer. "I have to work now—"

"Right, sorry," he said, quickly righting himself.

"The warrant has closed for the Annual Town Meeting," Peter Cooke was continuing, "but the selectmen are interested in hearing people's thoughts on this. Tonight is mostly in the interest of maintaining transparency. Okay? So let's get started with a presentation of the situation from ZBA chair Helen Javier."

Joanna flexed her fingers, launched her phone's voice recorder, and began to type. She was an Olympic-level typist; she could type faster than most people talked, as long as she didn't get distracted by cute men trying to chat her up about local socioeconomic tensions and the like. She pushed him from her mind and focused on the voices flowing into her ears, and the words flowing out of her fingertips.

The evening was for temperature-taking. Yankee townships were famously parsimonious and nobody wanted to feel bullied into spending money that wouldn't result in some obvious town improvements. So while it was a given that the selectmen would release legal funds, they wanted to be politically sensitive about how much money could be in play. Especially since two of them were up for reelection.

First the gathering heard from the town counsel, a sharp-voiced blond woman Joanna didn't recognize, dressed more formally than anyone else in the room, but still a slacker compared to the Minion Lawyer. She advised them on all the legal ramifications of the situation and also cited three similar helipad cases from Edgartown over the past thirty years, all of which the plaintiffs had lost. She also pointed out that it would be unprecedented for the selectmen to decide *against* using the legal fund. Then the head of the Conservation Commission reminded everyone about the Wetlands Protection Act, which applied even to private property. He shared his concern about the effects of noise pollution on the local wildlife, not to mention peril to birds who might get caught in the wind disturbance. Amy Walsh (Joanna's WASPy former kindergarten teacher) took the podium, representing a group that Joanna's fingers typed accurately without her brain quite registering, lamenting that the spiritual soul of the town was being wounded by these gross incursions of conspicuous consumption. Joanna agreed with her, but the argument sounded reverse-snobby. As her future coffee date had pointed out, the residents only wanted *their* kind of transplants. People who helicoptered were not their kind of transplants. The chairman of the Board of Selectmen also spoke, asking for a straw-poll show of hands about adding a line item to the annual budget for legal spending. There was grumbling, and only four hands went up.

In between each of the speakers, hippie Richard Burton stepped in toward the podium and spoke gently into the mic, introducing each speaker almost apologetically. Could she describe his tone as "apologetic" in her write-up? Probably not. Everett wouldn't like it and anyhow, Peter Cooke would look at her sadly the next time she crossed paths with him at the post office.

"The next speaker was not originally slated to speak," he said. "We're grateful that Mr. Orion Smith was able to come here on short notice and contribute his thoughts on this matter." There was a rustle of surprise . . . The malefactor himself? Joanna was the happiest person in the room: that would make *fantastic* copy.

"Thank you, Mr. Moderator," said a voice, and *oh no oh no oh crap she knew that voice*. She looked up, her stomach sinking. Yes, it was him. The fellow who had just asked to take her for a drink.

Clarification: Who had asked to take her for a drink as soon as he realized she wrote for the *Journal*.

She had just been played.

He had such nice eyes.

"Let me start out by stating," said Mr. Orion Smith, "that even though we're here because of a conflict, I'm really glad that we *are*

here. I mean here in this room, talking about this in a civilized fo-rum. I'm honored to be part of a great New England tradition, and happy that everyone has the opportunity to practice direct democ-racy, and to be an activist in your immediate life. That's pretty un-usual and I hope that none of you take it for granted. Just wanted to say that. So. With that understanding, let me explain a few things about why the issue of the helicopter is headed for court. I mean 'why' in the big-picture sense." He paused briefly, as if for a response, but appeared not to hear the grumbling and muttering that filled the pause. He continued: "I hope you can set aside your preconcep-tions for a moment and really hear what it is I'm saying. First of all, everyone here knows how bad the traffic is in summer." Again muttering, which was again disregarded. "Whether it's getting on and off the Cape, or ferry traffic, or getting through Five Corners or the Triangle, it's a nightmare. I'm just one person, with one set of guests, but that's one set of guests who won't be adding to your traffic headaches. I know abutters have been saying it's about noise pollution—which I don't think is fair, by the way, and we'll get back to that—but the noise really doesn't last very long. Even if you're home when the copter is landing or taking off, the period of noise pollution is very short compared to the period that you're likely to be stuck in traffic."

Joanna grappled with the illogical algebra of his reasoning, as an attendee closer to the podium went on the offensive:

"You're saying you want to use your helicopter as a *favor* to *us*?" Hank demanded with a snarky laugh, and there was a collective guffaw of hostile amusement. "Wow. That sticks in my craw."

Orion Smith smiled at him, as if he had expected the jibe and was glad everyone was playing along. "It's my old friend Mr. Holmes, Mr. Henry Holmes. May I call you Henry?"

"You may call me Mr. Holmes," said Hank, as if Orion Smith should have known this. More laughter from the peanut gallery.

"Mr. Holmes," said Orion Smith, "I'm not saying I make the difference between a traffic jam and no traffic jam, but I am saying that anybody in a position to *not* add to the traffic problem should do so to the degree that they logistically can. So there's that. More than that, though, moving beyond the traffic and on to a more abstract and general note, we are a nation of people free to make their own lifestyle choices."

"That's true," said Hank heartily, as if holding court. "And our lifestyle choice here in West Tisbury is to eschew unexpected helicopters buzzing over our houses and violating our sense of privacy."

Orion Smith gave him a pedantic smile. "I was talking about a given individual's choices," he said. "A lot of people are against my helipad, claiming it's about noise pollution or an environmental issue, but in fact they just don't like that an individual who lives among them has a different set of values. Vineyarders seem to take this kind of thing very personally. I wish to do something out of the conventional way of doing things. That's true for a lot of you too! People here tend to believe that everyone can do their own thing in this town, to each his own and all that. But in fact, if people make choices that you all aren't comfortable with, they pay for it in some way. You make sure of it. *If* the ZBA had allowed me to fly the helicopter in and out, *then* I could have demonstrated all the collateral benefits to the town itself. But they didn't, and that leaves me with no option but legal recourse. I respect my neighbors' privacy and their lifestyle choices, and it saddens me that they will not return the courtesy."

"Oh, c'mon, that's a load of crap," said Hank. "If you respected our privacy you wouldn't be trying to fly unencumbered over our private property."

"I don't moonlight for the DEA, Mr. Holmes," said Orion Smith. "My helicopter isn't black. And I'm not a drone. I'm not interested in invading anyone's property, I just want to get from Point A to Point B—"

"Which takes you over Point C! My house! Or Point D! Their house!"

"There would be one established FAA-approved flight path—"

"Great, so one set of families gets the privilege of being in your flight path every time." Hank pulled himself up straighter in his chair and looked around the room, grinning viciously. "Any volunteers? No? C'mon, Mr. Smith might give you a free ride! You can spy on all your neighbors and see who's growing the best weed!"

"Hank," said hippie Richard Burton, stepping toward the mic.

"It's fine," said Orion Smith, dismissing this with a flick of the wrist. "We've done this before." People laughed at that—so, a reference to the previous tussle Everett had mentioned.

Orion Smith went on, but Joanna had to fixate on typing more than listening, because she was afraid her head would explode. Hank was surely looking for more opportunities to heckle but Joanna didn't hear his voice again. Despite the snubs coming out of

Orion Smith's mouth, he spoke in a friendly, can't-we-all-get-along-here voice, as if he were mediating a conflict instead of creating one.

When he finished speaking, he walked away from the podium politely, declining to answer questions. He walked calmly down the center aisle toward the back of the room, ignoring catcalls and irritated questions from the audience (some of whom were eyeing Hank hoping for an encore from him), and then kept walking, right through the door into the main hall, and then out of the building itself. As with the Minion Lawyer's exit at the ZBA meeting, incredulous, inarticulate noises and expressions were exchanged among the tribe. Peter Cooke asked for more comments. Finally Hank used a colorful epithet that caused embarrassed laughter to ripple across the room. Someone else asked for a new straw poll, a show of hands in favor of a war chest being raised to keep that bastard from crossing anyone's land ever again. Every hand in the room shot up. That was that. Peter Cooke gently reminded everyone that was just a straw poll, not a legally binding resolution, but the selectmen could be seen exchanging whispered words, with something approaching excitement.

Meeting over, townspeople filed out, muttering to each other. Joanna shut down her laptop, shoved it into her backpack, and moved against the human current toward the front of the room, where Hank was clumsily getting up with his crutches. The temperature in the room was dropping quickly with the abrupt loss of body heat. Outside, headlight beams swung across the room through the windows, and gravel rattled, as cars and trucks began to pull out of the parking lot.

"Want me to take you home?" she asked, offering Hank a hand.

"Nah, Paul's car is easier to get into than the truck," said Hank. "Anyhow, I might go over to their place for a nightcap."

"That's a great idea," she said. "We just don't have enough alcohol at home to mix with your pain meds."

"Sagacious posterior," he said, affectionately. "You should've gone to the package store and restocked."

"Too late now."

He gave her a private, knowing look, then rolled his eyes. "What a spoiled little jackass. Probably never had to work a day in his life."

"He doesn't like traffic," said Paul Javier, affably.

"He doesn't like . . . *I* don't like traffic," said Hank. "That doesn't mean I feel entitled to use a *helicopter*."

"You don't *go* anywhere," Paul pointed out.

Hank's diagonal grin. "Well, there's that," he said, but already the helium was leaking out of his buoyancy and he looked a little fatigued. Sagging onto his crutches, he pivoted toward her. "See you back at the house," he said. Yes, definitely fatigued. That happened fast.

"I'll set your meds out for you," she said. "Have fun." She pecked him on the cheek, which embarrassed him. She pushed past him in the emptying room, to check some legal details with the town counsel.

By the time she exited into the raw night, Paul and Hank were gone and the lot was deserted. Or seemed to be.

Wherever he had been lingering to avoid the crowd, suddenly he was at her elbow, between her and the truck.

"So when are we having coffee?" he asked, with that same disarming grin. His breath misted in the streetlamp light and gave him a gossamer nimbus.

She stopped. She was too abashed to look directly at him. "You have committed a lie by omission," she said to the gravel of the parking lot.

"You've done worse," he said blithely. "You've committed crappy journalism. You didn't even ask me who I was."

"You invited me to coffee without getting my name."

"Of course I did, that was strategic," he chuckled. "If I asked your name, you'd have asked me mine. But now that the cat's out of the bag"—he held out his gloved hand toward her—"hello, I'm Orion Smith. When can I take you to coffee?"

"You can't. Obviously. I can't accept any gift from you since I am a journalist and you are a subject of my journalism."

"I flirted with you before knowing you were a journalist," he argued. "I would genuinely like to chat with you over coffee."

She was mildly appalled with herself for wanting that as well. "I'll pay for my own coffee, then," she said. "If I pay for my own, it's not a gift and you can't be seen as trying to buy my favor."

He laughed. "Oh, is that how it works."

"Yes, and it's not something to laugh about. Tomorrow. Hubert's Bakery. Ten thirty."

Then she rushed home to google him.

THERE WERE 384 references to the Vineyard's Orion Smith on the entire internet. Most of them gave no real information at all.

He settled across the wooden table from her as the morning sunlight glanced off the pale blue walls. "So," he said, fresh latte in hand. Joanna had plain coffee, black. She preferred tea at home, but a properly brewed tea while out in the world was impossible to find. "This is the famous Hubert's I've heard about."

"Not quite," she said. "This is a satellite of the one you've heard about. The original Hubert's was up-Island, not too far from your place, actually. The family that owned it had an internal feud and ended up selling the property. It was bought by someone like you, who tore it down—"

"Anyone who would tear down a landmark business is not like me," he said, with pleasant firmness.

"—and built a fortress in its place. Now it's nearly a plantation. The landscaping alone takes a crew of ten."

"I wager they put more people to work than the bakery did," he said peaceably, stirring raw sugar into his latte. He tapped the balsa wood stirrer on the rim of the compostable cup, then set it on the table. "That's good for the local economy, right?"

"They're employing people but they're not offering a service," she said. "In a locale that needs services. The bakery was built decades before there were any zoning laws. It was grandfathered in—the way zoning works now, nobody else can start an eatery in that part of the town. That was it. It was the only place to get lunch in the whole area."

"Must have been a throng around midday then," he said. "Traffic congestion must have been terrible. Did that contribute to the Island Way of Life?"

"Concerns about traffic congestion seem to be a cornerstone of your life here," she said. "Which I approve of, if that matters. Anyhow, yes, there was traffic, but there was also *communing*. People from many different backgrounds came together, ate together, sat together at the outside tables, and now that's all gone, now it's just rich people inside the house, their workers outside it, and everybody else can just go stuff it."

He winked at her. "I know the Brightons, who bought the property. They seem supernice. Anyhow, now that you've made your point about the horrible greedy wash-ashores destroying your childhood paradise, tell me about yourself. You're an attractive woman in the prime of life, I'm sure you're well-educated and capable, what are you doing living in this Podunk community in winter?"

"I'm looking after a sick relative," she said. "I'll be heading back to New York soon."

His brows raised approvingly. "New York. *My* hometown."

"New York? You were wearing a Red Sox cap last night," she said, eyes narrowed.

"When in Rome," he said. "Where'd you go to school? Or more important, since you're such a sleuth, where'd you go to journalism school?"

"I went to Boston University. And I majored in English, which explains my dazzling and intrepid journalism skills. English. You know, the degree for people who don't know what to major in."

"I majored in English too," he said. "Because I wanted to major in English. That's the whole point of a college education: you read, and then you think and talk about what you've read."

"Spoken like somebody with a lifetime of privilege," she said.

"Excuse me, but didn't we just establish that you're an English major too? Anyhow, college isn't a trade school. If you want a vocational education, go get it. Nobody's forcing anyone to study liberal arts."

"There's privilege talking again."

"You assume a lot about me. You don't actually know how I wound up with a helicopter."

"Good point," she said, and reached for the backpack. "Tell me."

"Don't take out the laptop, this is off the record," he said, suddenly firm. "This is a get-acquainted chat."

"I want to *interview* you," she said. "That's the whole point of not letting you pay for my coffee."

He shrugged. "If I say something you think is really germane or vital for you to do your job, jot down a note on your phone or something, but this is not a formal interview. If it were, I wouldn't be meeting you in a public place, I'd want you to come to my office."

She lowered the backpack, determined to get herself invited to his office. "Okay," she said, "I'm listening."

"My grandmother was a German Jew. She was on the kindertransport as a young child and her family was all killed in the camps. She married my Anglo-Indian grandfather, named her son—my dad—Christian and didn't get him circumcised, and lived in terror of being found out as a Jewess for most of her life." He was matter-of-fact, as one is when rattling off an overly familiar anecdote. Not rushed, but not impressed with his own story. "Christian married Marie, my mother, who was raised in a brutal Irish Catholic orphanage. My grandfather imported Indian goods to the UK and America, a very small enterprise, he had no business sense. My father expanded that to a shipping company, which wasn't doing so hot until he made me partner. I'd gone to B-school on a scholarship and had a knack for it. The business took off under my direction. The helicopter was originally bought as a way to monitor a facility in Singapore."

"That's fascinating," she said.

"Yes. It's also completely fictional," he said in a mordant tone. Then he winked. "Well, not completely. The bit about my grandmother is true, but she didn't marry an Indian, she married a WASP from old money."

"That's more believable, I guess," she admitted, deflating a bit.

"Also fictional," he said. "Or maybe not. Do your research. If you're interested. Verify. Identity is such a fluid concept in the twenty-first century, don't you think?"

For a moment she thought he was somehow calling her out for being both Anna and Joey. "Yes," she said uncomfortably. "Yes." Then, not wanting to linger on that, she asked, in a conspiratorial tone, "Have you actually filed the lawsuit?"

He smiled, as if pleased she wanted the scoop, and leaned in closer to her across the table. Joanna leaned in too. He smelled good—autumn leaves and wood smoke, a hint of cardamom. She hadn't noticed that in the library. He glanced around the empty bakery. "Off the record?"

"Yes."

"Off the record, I don't talk about it." He laughed. If there had been a hint of malice in the laugh, she would have dismissed him as an ass, but this just made him cuter.

"As I understand it," she pressed, "you're continuing to use the helicopter. Why not just keep that up? Let the town fine you or sue you if they're serious about wanting you to stop. Or go to the Planning Board and ask them to change the bylaw."

"That would take forever and I don't want the whole thing hanging over my head. Plus it will be an ongoing drain on my time and resources if they sue me. If I go on the offensive, I have some sense of agency about things. I call the shots."

"Ah."

"That's off the record. Also, of course, I'd be happy if the selectmen decide not to fund the town's defense, and then the town would crumble and I'd get what I'm looking for without actually going to court."

"You do know that never happens, right?" she said. "That was part of the point of last night's forum. The selectmen *always* agree to fund a defense. Their vote on it next week is just a formality."

"Of course I know that," he said, patiently. "I'm assuming it. The meeting last night, the upcoming selectmen's meeting, those are just the necessary opening acts to my lawsuit. That's not well said so it's also off the record."

"This is going to be a crummy interview if it's all off the record," she said with a pout.

"You wanted an interview. I wanted a coffee date. I win!" He gave her a delighted grin. "Thanks for playing." Another wink. "I'll let you win next time, how's that?"

"I didn't agree to a next time," she said.

"You don't want a next time?"

"I didn't say that."

"Of course you didn't. Because you know there's going to be a next time. Because you want there to be a next time, and something about you makes me want to give you what you want."

That was startlingly sexy to hear. (Even though Brian had used the same rationale without effect.)

"It's presumptuous of you to say you know what I want," she said, trying to bristle.

"Am I wrong?"

"... No."

"So it's presumptuous of me to speak the truth accurately?"

She knew there was an articulate rejoinder to that, but she couldn't remember what the words were for it. She was aware of the terrified thrill of feeling transparent while depending on opacity.

"I'll see you the next time we have coffee," she said, then rose, grabbed her laptop bag, and rushed out the door of the bakery.

"Fantastic," he called out. "I'll text you tomorrow."

She was getting good at writing news briefs. She liked them because they were short, pithy, and anonymous.

Community Services to expand addiction-counseling services

Chilmark man charged in DUI moped incident

All elementary schools to begin composting in response to success at MVRHS

Correction: Last week's *Journal* incorrectly identified Samuel Black's oxen as Laurel and Hardy. Their correct names are Lowell and Hoody.

Her phone rang Monday morning, and this time she recognized the number: Lewis Worthington. Her immediate visceral reaction was certainty that he had finally realized who she was. With elegant adroitness her mind raced the steps from his revelation to her doom. She'd be shunned by both papers, and without income or a New York home, she'd be condemned to remain Hank's helpmate until she could get back into the celebrity-interview game, but she couldn't get back in the game as long as she was his helpmate, so that probably meant she'd end up homeless in Central Park soon.

She held her breath as she answered.

"Hello, Joey," he said. There was muted hubbub in the background, meaning he was in the newsroom. "I've found a great project for you, if you're up for it."

"Always up for work," she said, relieved. "What do you have in mind?"

"We want to revive a regular feature that was popular back in the forties, called 'On the Same Page.' There would be a feature article, usually a profile on a valued member of the community, and then—on the same page—a short excerpt from the paper from decades or even a century earlier that paralleled it somehow, that showed a continuity of sensibility. Proof that the ethos of the island hadn't changed much. Or maybe better to say, the more things change, the more they stay the same."

"That sounds interesting," she said carefully. "Do you think that's still true, though? The Vineyard's changed far more in the past century than it changed between the 1840s and the 1940s."

"Oh, I agree, that's why it's even more important to emphasize what *hasn't* changed. Anyhow, you don't have to deal with the archival part, you'd just do the interviews and profiles. Sounds right up your alley, no?"

"Yeah, sounds interesting," she said, as her inner Hank groused *Oh my God, how typically precious, it's like a picture postcard in essay form.*

"Good. Glad you like it. Since you've already agreed to take on the West Tisbury beat, I'd like you to do a profile of Helen Javier, the ZBA chair. She's stepping down because she and her husband, Paul—hang on a moment, Joey." Muffled noise in the background, like one of the grown-ups in a *Peanuts* cartoon. "What? No, not after the way . . . sorry, Joey, hang on just a sec . . . No, that's not acceptable." He sounded like a stern but kindly father. "I think that would put us on their level and we're better than that. Let's just sit tight and wait to see what happens. All right, I'm back, Joey."

"No worries."

"Sorry, the *Journal* did something in poor taste and I just needed to make sure we didn't accidentally follow suit."

Her stomach tightened. "Oh, really? What?"

"It has to do with that affordable housing project—you mentioned it in your ZBA report, the solar-powered one."

"Oh, right."

"The *Journal* emphasized some class tension going on around it, and in fact, it turns out that a part owner of a solar-panel company that would profit from the development is a leading voice against the development, because it abuts his property. So that seems maybe worth investigating, but it was incredibly irresponsible of the *Journal* to include it in such a throwaway manner. They're continually taking cheap shots, like the way they track that domestic abuse case when it hasn't even gone to trial yet."

"Oh," said Joanna, who had written that bit. Which part of Central Park was the safest squat for homeless women? she wondered. Sheep Meadow? Strawberry Fields?

"Anyhow," he continued. "About Helen Javier—she's stepping down and will be leaving the island for a while, and I think it's a great time to do a piece on her. We might pair it with a piece about the first female elected official in Vineyard politics, which was somebody on the Tisbury School Committee in 1905. But for some reason, Helen suggested putting it on the same page with a piece about a woman named Nancy Luce"—and when Joanna chortled, he asked, "What? I don't know a Nancy Luce."

"How can you not know about Nancy Luce? She's the chicken lady of West Tisbury," said Joanna, unable to contain her laughter. "Back in the 1800s. She was a social misfit. Her only friends were all her chickens and when they died she made gravestones for them, and she wanted to be buried with them. She wasn't, she's buried in the cemetery, but her gravesite is strewn with chicken figurines, plastic, ceramic, what have you."

A pause. Then, from Lewis: "That is possibly the most bizarre story I have heard since I moved to the Vineyard. Why on earth would Helen Javier think it would make a good parallel to her own life?"

Still chuckling, Joanna said, "Well, the figurines are sort of an homage to how dedicated she was to caretaking a population that nobody else could see the value of, or had really small brains, or something, so my guess is she's making a little tongue-in-cheek comment about West Tisbury property owners."

"Huh," said Lewis, sounding unconvinced. "Y'know, that's pretty impressive, how you know the backstory to something that randomly weird."

"It's not, really. It's like knowing Bartholomew Gosnold discovered the Vineyard in 1602 and named it after his baby daughter, or that Thomas Mayhew established the first English settlement here, or the fact that the Vineyard is the only community in the New World where there was never armed conflict between the native population and white settlers."

"Joey, my goodness, you're an historian."

"Nah," she said. "I'm an Islander."

Joanna had known Helen most of her life, largely in the context of civic life because, like Hank, Helen had been involved in West Tisbury politics longer than Joanna had been alive. Joanna wasn't even sure what Helen did for a living, and she'd come to Hank and Jen's at least once a month for drinks and town gossip the whole time Joanna had lived with them.

This was the kind of assignment she'd have gotten regularly (with a much higher fee, of course) in New York: celebrating the private side of an august human being. But this august human being knew her. When Joey Dias from the *Newes* showed up to interview Helen, Helen would recognize Anna Howes of the *Journal*.

Helen was an upstanding, honorable, transparently by-the-book model citizen—that's why Joey Dias was interviewing her. She did not suffer deceivers gladly. When Joanna was six, she had snuck into Helen's strawberry patch and eaten all the berries, then lied about it in an inept attempt to avoid responsibility. Helen had scolded her—not so much for eating the berries as for lying about it. Helen disapproved of liars and she would disapprove of what Joanna was doing now.

From the kitchen-door window, Helen gave Joanna a puzzled smile as she crossed the dirt driveway to the door. "Good morning, Anna," she said, opening the door briefly to let her in, then pulling it quickly closed against the cold.

"Morning, Helen." Joanna took in a deep breath of the warm, cedar-scented air. She'd always loved this house.

Helen continued to look quizzically at her as Joanna pulled off her gloves and unzipped her jacket. "Are you interviewing me for the *Newes*? You're covering the ZBA meetings for the, mm, *Journal*." She spoke tentatively, as if afraid of being indelicate. "I wasn't listening too closely to all of Lewis Worthington's details, but if he'd said it was Anna Howes, I'd have remembered that. So I'm sure he didn't describe you as Anna Howes."

Joanna gave her an ironic grimace. "Yeah. I wondered if you'd pick up on that."

Helen considered her a moment. "Joey Dias," she said, suddenly. "That was the name Lewis mentioned. So let's see. You wanted us all to call you Joey when you were about sixteen. For about a year."

Joanna nodded. Helen continued to consider her.

"And . . . oh, of course, Dias was your mom's maiden name."

Joanna suddenly noticed how lovely the knots were in the boards of Helen's kitchen floor.

"I can explain," she said.

"What's there to explain?" said Helen. "You're writing for both papers under different names. Everyone knows neither paper will work with the other's freelancers, so you must be doing it on the sly. You're playing the periodical field?"

Joanna bit her lower lip and nodded.

Helen tilted her head slightly. "I always thought the edict against freelancing for both papers was ridiculous, but you're being dishonest to Everett—and to Lewis. That's not cool, Anna." Her tone resembled how she'd spoken to the Minion Lawyer. Anna felt about the size of a crocus bud. She couldn't speak. "What has triggered this journalistic infidelity?"

Joanna had rehearsed several fantastical excuses to justify herself but now she just said, "Money."

Helen stared at her, sternly, for what felt like a very long time. Long enough for Joanna to meet her eyes, look away again, meet her eyes again, and again look away.

"Okay," Helen finally said, in a long-suffering but decisive tone. "I guess I can respect that. Especially since you're only here to take care of Hank."

"Thank you, Helen," she said. She realized she'd been holding her breath, and sighed.

Helen chuckled grudgingly. "Sorry you're in a tight spot, but my inner bad girl is cheering for you."

Joanna almost gawked. "I didn't know you *had* an inner bad girl."

Helen gave her a look. "Any woman who's ever gotten anywhere by being good has an inner bad girl, Joanna."

Helen Javier stepping down after nearly
four decades on the West Tisbury ZBA
Helped to manage the town's accelerated growth
By Joey Dias

In a cozy home of unpainted wooden walls practically covered with philodendron vines, Helen Javier
huddles before a woodstove, sipping tea. She and her
husband, Paul, built this house in the late 1960s—Paul,
a jack-of-all-trades, dug the well, put in the plumbing
and the electricity (with some professional friends
stopping by now and again to make sure he would
not electrocute himself in the shower). The tea is
an herbal concoction, of plants grown in her garden this past summer; she drinks it from a mug she
made herself back when the Artisans' Guild was still
around. The shawl she's tucked herself into, at least
forty years old, comes from the wool of local sheep—
not from any farm you'd have heard of, just from a
neighbor who kept sheep because sheep were a cheap
way to keep the lawn mowed ("not as good as the
goats," she editorializes. "Plus you can milk goats.").
It was cleaned, carded, dyed, spun, and knitted by
a neighbor, who had taken on such distaff projects
before the Fiber Arts group was a twinkle in its
founders' eyes.

It is a scene for a winter idyll and Ms. Javier has

earned this moment of rest. After 45 years in the trenches of town growth, she has retired to a home that, ironically, she could not build today even if she had the stamina.

Ms. Javier was an original board member of the ZBA. She was 29 when she first volunteered for the position. Nobody had any idea back then what they were getting into. "I think my generation is the one who raised the roof here," she says. "We dove into the scene, so to speak—we were the young Turks when there weren't that many old Turks, and there weren't a lot of young Turks after us, to push us out. So there's an entire generation of us who have pretty much defined town governance. We're the first wave of Baby Boomers," she continues, with a knowing smile aimed at the Millennial who is interviewing her. "We came of age knowing we could change the world. Not merely believing we could, as you all do now—which is admirable of you, by the way. But we had *evidence*. The youth quake of our era was the first of its kind in America, maybe on the planet. I'm proud to have been a part of it, even in this little corner of the world."

Ms. Javier is a wash-ashore, although she's been around long enough that not a lot of folks remember that. She married a "summer kid" whose family name—Pease—suggests an old Island heritage. Their children are Islanders in the strictest sense: they were born here. But their offspring have flown the coop for Manhattan, Denver, and Geneva, returning only for the summers with their own children. The family has cycled through what it means to be a Vineyarder.

Through it all, though, Ms. Javier continued in her position on the ZBA. In those early days, the assessors went around from house to house with index cards, taking notes of what a parcel of land had cost. The police station was in the police chief's living room. The town hall was a 2-room shack by the Mill Pond, and the elementary school consisted of 3 rooms. The ZBA never had to adjudicate built-in swimming pools, cell phone towers were unimaginable, and there was no call for affordable housing in West Tisbury—indeed, West Tisbury was the town nobody wanted to live in, because there was no "there" there.

When she's not overseeing the careful evolution of her adoptive hometown, Ms. Javier is a science teacher at the Oak Bluffs School, where she now educates the children of some of her former students. With a degree in marine biology, she initially sought a job at the Woods Hole Oceanographic Institute on the mainland, but when the teaching position opened up, she applied and upon getting it, went for a low-residency MA in education at Boston University. "Believe it or not, I made that choice because I like disputes," she said. "You get to be disputable as a teacher—your job is not to dictate information to your students, but to teach them to think analytically—and that means you have to engage them interactively, so that they listen and reply. No twelve-year-old kid is going to just inhale the material you give them. They're going to argue, or ignore you, or do things designed to keep themselves from having to really learn. I love taking that on. If I'd been working straight up as a marine biologist, my quarrelsome tendencies would probably have manifested themselves in some unfortunate ways. I'd have ended up arguing with a seal, or being insubordinate to my boss, or exasperating my peers. Put me in a room with twenty truculent junior high kids and I'm in my element."

Ms. Javier has a warmth that makes anyone feel right at home almost at once. A self-described Earth Mother, she grows most of her food in the summer, canning a good deal to go into the winter, and most of her wardrobe is from the "free store" at the West Tisbury dump, embellished with some interesting flourish she creates herself. "I think the term now is upcycling," she says, with a gentle laugh. "Back when I started doing it, there was no word for it. It was just a thing I did."

That attitude pervades her entire worldview—45 years of service is just a thing she did; helping to start the Food Pantry is just a thing she did; being part of the initial urge that got the Emvee Players, the non-profit theater company, started was also just a thing she did. In a spirited but understated Yankee manner, she's always just doing things.

The timing of her departure is, she insists, coincidental. She retired from teaching this past semester, and she and Paul are taking a year to circumnavigate the planet by train and by freight boat. They have been planning this trip for nearly two years. However, foresight is never 20/20, and she could not have predicted the perfect storm of events that would decimate the ranks of the Zoning Board of Appeals. She didn't know that she would be leaving behind her a gaping hole in the already-undermanned ZBA, at a moment when they are most in need of leadership, girding their loins as they are for a lawsuit to be slapped on the town by Orion Smith. Mr. Smith, a seasonal resident, wishes to build a helipad on his property off North Road. With the confrontation pending, Ms. Javier's resignation seems almost like a retreat from battle before it has begun.

"That's got nothing to do with it," she says with her gentle laugh. "Although I don't envy whoever steps in . . ."

Joanna went out early Friday, to the bakery where Celia worked. She bought a copy of the *Newes*, a cup of the Colombian roast Hank liked (but was too cheap to buy for home use), and a bear claw. By the time she got back to the house, balancing these offerings between her mittened hands, Hank had gotten himself up and dressed enough to be presentable. He was in the recliner, seeking the TV remote.

"Here you are," she said sweetly, and placed on his side table the coffee, the pastry, and that which would make him spit both of them out: the *Newes* with Joey Dias's coverage of Helen.

She busied herself with invented chores, watching him from the corner of her eye. She wiped the counter, and then the stove, and began to rearrange things in the refrigerator, which was a precarious undertaking. While squatting down by the crisper, she heard the rustle of the *Newes'* oversize pages. She pushed the crisper closed and focused on stabilizing the various casserole dishes in the main part of the fridge.

"What the hell?" Hank exclaimed suddenly. "*Anna*."

"Yeah?" she said with false offhandedness, standing and closing the fridge. "Okay, I think that's a little more ordered—"

"Anna, this is your interview with Helen."

"Oh. Yeah. What'd you think?"

"I haven't read it yet. It's—you wrote it—this is the *Newes*. You're calling yourself Joey Dias."

"Yeah, remember I wrote as Joey Dias in high school? That's just the byline I use there."

"Anna," he said, in a voice tenor with incredulity. "What are you doing writing for the *Newes*?"

"I need more money than Everett can off—"

"Does he know?"

She hesitated, which gave him his answer.

"Anna! How can you do that? That's illegal."

She chuckled nervously. "It's not *illegal*."

"It's gotta be *unethical* at least."

"What's unethical about it?"

"Well . . ." He looked befuddled that he'd be expected to have an answer. "Nobody who writes for one paper gets to write for the other. That's just not *done*. You gotta tell Everett what you're doing. You could get in big trouble."

"With *whom*?" she asked archly. "With Everett?"

"Well, *yes*," he said.

"I'll get in trouble for telling him? Or for not telling him?"

"For not telling him—"

"If I tell him, and he fires me, I'm fucked, especially if he tells Lewis Worthington, who then also fires me. If he doesn't fire me, but orders me to stop writing for Lewis, then I'm still kinda fucked because I only have one source of income. If I tell him and he doesn't care, then why should I have told him in the first place?" She hated how reactionary she got when there was tension between them. She also hated how easily she started dropping F-bombs around Hank, but it was the language she grew up with and merely walking into this house lowered her verbal finesse.

He took a moment to consider her argument, then rolled his eyes and sighed miserably. "Oh, Christ," he muttered. He stared out the window a moment, his gaze fuzzy, then looked back at her and suddenly grinned with a helpless shrug. He opened his mouth to speak, instead released a pained, voiced sigh, and shook his head. "I dunno. Jeez, Anna, it's dangerous."

"It's two country newspapers. I'm not going to get shot as a dissident."

He giggled a nervous basso giggle. "I don't know what to say," he said gruffly. "I think you're being very stupid."

"If that's the worst you've got, I can live with it."

"Christ," he muttered, then settled back into the recliner and opened the paper back to the interview with Helen.

"But Hank," she said. His eyes glanced up at her, dolefully. "You can't tell Everett. Or anyone. You can't tell anyone. Except Helen knows, of course."

"What did Helen say?"

"She said her inner bad girl is rooting for me." She grinned tentatively.

That worked. Hank started to chuckle again, the anxiety gone. "Well, all right then," he said. "But jeez, Anna, why don't you just go get one of your big-ticket interviews off-Island somewhere?"

She bit the inside of her cheek to stop herself from saying she was stuck on the Vineyard taking care of him. "I'll work on it," she said gruffly. "I've got a sandwich in there for your lunch, and some cheese and crackers for a snack later, okay?"

"Yes, *Mom*," he said, in an ironic tone, and then muttered, "*Christ.*" He continued muttering to himself as she made a sandwich for herself, brushed her hair, organized her backpack, and put her boots on. The muttering never stopped, and sounded increasingly irritable. Why was he more stressed about her dual identity than she was herself?

"Are you okay?" she asked.

"Of course I'm not okay!" he said, with a sudden vehemence that startled the cats. "I've got a goddamn broken leg!"

It was the first time he had acknowledged that.

THURSDAY MORNING WAS usually the *Journal*'s staff meeting, but the ferries were canceled due to high winds, and Everett was trapped off-Island, so the meeting was pushed to Friday. As a freelancer, Joanna wasn't required to go—in fact, if Everett knew she was freelancing for the *Newes,* he would not have allowed her there. But she was desperate to impose structure on her life to keep from losing her mind while trapped on a rocky little island all winter. So come Friday, she wrapped herself up in layers of Jen's most gale-proof sweaters and coats, and went.

As usual, both Island papers were lying on the table. Even in the era of online news, there was a constant game of one-upmanship, since the *Journal* (published Thursdays) could get the week's news out in print sooner, but the *Newes*' print edition (on Friday) could be more up-to-the-minute. Her *Newes* interview with Helen had come out that morning, and she was afraid to look at it sitting here in the *Journal* office, lest she somehow draw attention to the fact that she had written it. Everett was the only one to whom this would be obvious, but surely it would be obvious to him as soon as he recognized the pseudonym. She had only a few hours before she'd be called to the carpet.

The paper was functioning on a skeleton crew: two front-of-house staff juggling clerical, ad sales, classifieds, and reception; two young bearded guys handling IT and production; and an entire editorial and reporting staff of six: Everett, Joanna, two women younger than her (smart, cutting their teeth before moving on to greener pastures, and unintentionally intimidating), and two middle-aged men (smart, clearly with impressive résumés and nothing left to prove, rewarding themselves after decades of off-Island journalism with a plum job here). They were covering an area one hundred miles square with seven different governmental bodies—the six towns plus the county. They had all bonded in the trenches. Joanna felt like a fraud.

Everett praised the team for the issue that had just come out and congratulated them on their sweep at the New England Press Awards, a thing Joanna had never heard of, further confirming her fraudulence. "I'm not impressed by awards, but it's a nice excuse to get off-Island in winter," Everett said. "Now . . . what's on for next week? Will the DACA story be ready?"

"We have to pull it," said Rosie, one of the young women. She had pale, luminous skin and everything else about her was black: hair, clothes, boots, eyeliner, and an arm tattoo Joanna could only grasp a glimpse of under her long-sleeved T-shirt, and which seemed to be written in runes. In response to Joanna's puzzled look, she explained brusquely, "There's a Brazilian student at the high school who's probably going to be valedictorian, got into Harvard early admission and he's planning to study genetics. But he's a Dreamer—he and his parents are undocumented—and they're afraid to draw attention to themselves or he might get deported."

"Oh crap," Joanna said.

Rosie nodded unhappily, then began to turn her attention back to Everett. A distant throbbing hum seemed to move through the room, and she paused.

"That's the helicopter," Joanna said. "Too bad we didn't have enough warning, we could have gotten a photo."

Rosie looked at her. She was not rude, but the look made it clear which of them was actually a journalist. Spoiler: not Anna Howes. Anna Howes was the one who interviewed celebrities.

"So I'm going to wrap up the story about the halfway house tomorrow. Also we're still working on a piece about the Food Pantry. We found half a dozen families willing to let us interview them if we don't use their names, but nobody wants their picture in the paper."

"Snap some volunteers," said Everett.

"That's what we thought," she said. "And let's see . . . Oak Bluffs is considering plans to upgrade Ocean Park and reroute the ferry traffic, I'll cover that."

"Okay, thanks, Rosie," said Everett, and turned toward Sarah, the second young reporter. There was a melodic *bing* from right behind Joanna. Her phone.

Need some more coffee? read the text.

Thank God she had not programmed Orion Smith's name in. It was just an off-Island number, which would mean nothing to Sarah or Everett, on either side of her.

"Excuse me," she said, and typed in, If I buy my own again.

It was normal to have phones on during edit meetings, in case a story broke, but if she gave it too much attention she would be expected to share the breaking news with the rest of the table. She set the phone beside her laptop and looked with forced interest toward Sarah, the smallest, youngest, and perkiest person at the table.

"So, Edgartown and Chilmark both have coastal erosion issues," she said, with an earnest intensity that made her sound like she was describing a fabulous movie she'd just seen. "There's a house at risk of sinking into the Gut on Chappaquiddick and we're negotiating with the owners and the town to cover it on a week-by-week basis, what they decide to do about it, who they're working with, what island contractors and experts are doing and who they have to bring in from the mainland, the environmental impact, and so on. In Chilmark the erosion threatens the boat basin. I'm going to get more information at the selectmen's meeting next Tuesday."

Everett nodded as Joanna's phone tinged again:

Not buying. Brewing. Come scope out the helipad. House will offend you nicely too. 5:30-ish. Catch the sunset.

And then an address, off North Road.

"Also," Sarah was continuing, "I'm meeting with the chair of the Possible Dreams Auction to discuss a series that we could publish over the summer. I need to crunch some numbers, but the idea is to track how the amount of money from each Dream can be used in Community Services. So, you know, let's say somebody bids six thousand bucks to go fishing with Keith Richards, what does that translate to in terms of their budget? Is it a year's worth of mental health counseling for four people, does it cover the expense of one safe house for victims of domestic violence, does it go toward addiction recovery that sends people off-Island, does it all get eaten up in admin and office expenses, and so on."

"Nice," said Everett, looking like a pleased godfather.

"I'm not sure yet if it should start right after Memorial Day or wait until the Fourth of July."

"Let's see how big it is, and go from there," said Everett. "Anna, do you have any outstanding stories? I mean besides the helipad, but there's nothing new with that this week, and I've mostly got you on news briefs otherwise, right?"

She stared at him. Surely there was a productive way to take advantage of the insider status Orion was offering. She could pitch a feature article about him to Everett. Or if the place was really gorgeous, acquire a photographer and do a feature for *Architectural Digest* or *American Home* or *Oh, jeez, Joanna, shut up, stop hustling.*

"That's about it," she said. "So I'm free for other assignments."

"Christopher?" Everett asked one of the older male reporters, and she felt all the eyes in the room shift to her left. She reached for her phone.

I'm not going up in the helicopter, she typed.

>Did I invite you?

Bet you were going to.<

>Now you'll never know. See you at 5:30.

SHE WAS DISTRACTED all day. She left the office after the edit meeting and went home, and managed to write up a more detailed report on the forum than the graphs she'd already given Everett. But somehow that took five hours without being worth five hours of her time. She tried to convince herself she didn't need lipstick but in the end she put on some tinted lip balm.

When she walked out of her bedroom, she found Hank in the living room standing upright, leaning on his metal crutches.

"Not putting any weight on it, are you?" she asked.

He startled slightly, and jerked his head around to stare at her. "What are you doing there?" he said sharply. "I didn't know you were home. I have such a goddamned headache, and your surprising me like that makes it worse."

"I've been in my room all day," she said. "Writing."

"You need to *tell* me when you're doing something like that."

She shrugged. "I got nothing to hide, Hank," she said. That

wasn't true. She was hiding the reason for wearing tinted lip balm. Not that Hank would notice this detail. He looked pallid and tired.

"I won't need supper until late tonight," he said. "Helen's coming over and we're going for a little spin."

"That's nice," she said. "Where to?"

He shrugged. "Oh, just around," he said, shifting his weight uncomfortably on his crutches. "Gotta get out of here now and then or I'll really go nuts."

"I can take you out sometime, you know," she said, reflexively conscience-stricken.

"I'm going out with *Helen*," he said, sharply, still staring down at his boot. "If I wanted to go with *you*, I'd have *asked* you."

"Whatever works for you," she said, pacifying. "I think you're handling this whole thing really well."

"Nice that it *looks* like that," he muttered. She walked past him toward the door, reaching for her coat on the wall hook. "And where are *you* going?"

"I'm going to tail you and Helen," she said immediately, "make sure you don't start makin' out with her or I'll have to rat you out to her hubby."

He grinned, and then chuckled, and then laughed, and she was off the hook.

At 4:45, she drove to her favorite bakery and bought coffee. She also bought a chocolate chip biscotti—baked by Celia at dawn— and shoved the wax-paper bag in the smallest pocket of her backpack. In case Orion had bought something, she didn't want to be tempted to eat it. Like Persephone in Hades, one bite of food from the man she was resisting might somehow bind her to him for eternity.

North Road was exquisitely peaceful, brushing along the northwest line of the Island. Even in winter, its leafless canopy and lichen-dappled stone walls welled with Old New England rustic charm. This time of year, there were almost no other cars, and certainly no fool day-trippers on mopeds wandering all over the road with illegal pillion passengers. In the summer these up-Island roads were so lusciously green it was impossible to remember or believe they ever looked otherwise—now, in winter, it was equally hard to believe they had ever been or could ever be anything but this dull gray.

Open fields lay fallow or were grazed by livestock. There were few homes off this part of North Road, and especially few to the north side and Vineyard Sound. They were generally owned by people who were wealthy but not interested in showing it. These were Islanders' preferred sort of wealthy people. Some lived there year-round, put their kids through the school system, ran for office. The sandy soil grew more clay-heavy farther up-Island, so these homes were uniformly accessed by potholed dirt driveways, often very long. Most folks here drove SUVs or pickups. Because they actually needed to.

Orion Smith lived at the end of such a road. Here the Island was hilly, and there were shallow pockets of mud, and corners that would become blind turns when the scrub finally leafed out in late May. This dirt road was so long that Joanna knew, even before she arrived, that it would have a view of Vineyard Sound and the Elizabeth Islands, even the mainland. As kids, Celia and she had trespassed in this area on their bikes before they understood the concept "trespassing." A stone wall to one side of the road was splattered with sage-green lichen, and to either side of the drive were a mix of tall scrubby oaks and scraggly pines, with an occasional beech stretching its branches out like a dancer, last fall's pale copper leaves still fluttering.

He had said in a text that it was about half a mile in. There were turns and twists but she finally veered to the left and the woods opened out to a broad field. Settled in the field was a large house whose backdrop was a bluff overlooking Vineyard Sound.

The house was a colonial-era manse of sorts. She knew there were a few of these in this part of the Island, since back in the day people in such remote settings tended to live in clumps with extended family and servants. This one had all the original lines but had been given such a thorough overhaul that it could almost pass as new. She was expecting something grander, gaudier, more custom-made. Something that would "offend her nicely," as promised.

On the other hand, the landscaping struck her as a bit over-the-top, even in winter. It was a prissy English cottage look, writ too large for a real English cottage. It didn't seem like a bachelor's aesthetic . . . was he married? Google had said nothing about a wife.

She parked in the clay-top parking area a hundred feet from the side of the house and walked toward it, appreciating it. The view from the upstairs windows must be amazing. The front door faced south, toward her, the English cottage busyness spilling out like an apron. To the left was a little stone terrace and to the right a screened-in porch, both designed to blend with the original aesthetic.

Orion, in a hunter-green cashmere sweater, had opened the front door and was waiting for her. He raised a hand in welcome, and gestured her inside before disappearing in himself.

"I'm in the kitchen," he called out cheerily as she crossed the threshold. "Feel free to look around! Take your coat off and stay awhile."

Joanna had never been a house craver, but this was a house worth craving. Stepping inside through the front door—ancient oaken slats nailed together by ancient crossbeams with ancient nails—she was in a tiny vestibule. It smelled of Antique Home: as if mothballs were tucked away in every corner and decades of steam heat had left an invisible haze of ozone in the air. A winding staircase directly before her led upstairs, and to either side were thumb-latch doors, both ajar. She knew the basic layout of these old houses well enough to guess what to expect through both doors: each led to a public space, perhaps a living room and a study; at their far ends, they would both open into the great room with its large fireplace, which centuries ago had been the kitchen; beyond that would likely be an extension added later with a modern kitchen. Upstairs, of course, would be a warren of bedrooms.

But she had never seen any house this old so well maintained. She couldn't tell how he had insulated it effectively, but it seemed to have both the original internal plaster walls, adulterated with Victorian wallpaper, as well as the original exterior ones. So he must have blown some kind of space-age insulation into the narrow plaster-and-lathed space between them, to keep out the wet New England chill.

Joanna walked into the right-hand room, sparsely furnished with colonial farmhouse furniture lit by a patinated Tiffany torchiere. The grandfatherly smell of old wood overpowered the mothball-and-ozone. She crossed through to the great room—even more sparsely furnished, just a wrought-iron daybed near the hearth and another torchiere. She went through to the kitchen.

The kitchen was in sharp distinction to everything else, modern and high-tech. It smelled like fresh gingerbread. *Damn you, Smith*, she thought, as she set down her backpack on a high stool, and opened the smaller pocket.

"Hello," he said. "A little sweet is about to come out of the oven, want some?"

"Nice try," Joanna said. She brandished her cookie bag with insolence. "Brought my own."

"Is it still warm? You can use the microwave to heat it up."

She hesitated, trying to determine if this was a violation of ethics.

"You're being ridiculous," he said, intuiting her thoughts.

"A journalist I know accepted a bluefish from a fisherman he was writing about during the Derby. The journalist brought it as smoked bluefish pâté to a potluck dinner at someone's house that both the fisherman and the editor were also at, and long story short, the editor learned the provenance of the fish and the journalist got a tongue-lashing the next day in the office for accepting a favor from someone he was writing about."

"I won't tell anyone," he said confidingly.

"I'm just going to dunk it into my coffee anyhow," she said, and pulled out the thermos.

He seemed tickled by her having brought her own snacks. "As you like. I can at least offer you a real mug for your coffee. Help yourself." He nodded toward the smaller of two walk-in pantries. It was painted grayish-blue inside, very old-school even though lit by modern pin lights, which glanced off rows of dinnerware that looked like it might have come with the original house. There was an NPR mug in the midst of all the teacups, and Joanna plucked it off the rack, along with a small plate for her biscotti. She came back out and sat at the granite counter. The small rows of recessed lights made the kitchen look like it belonged in an ad for interior decorating. They made the owner look pretty good too.

"All right then," she said, pouring her coffee into the mug and setting her cookie on the plate . . . and then she watched him pull the gingerbread out of the oven. That bastard had timed his baking (his *baking*?) to torment her when she arrived.

"Take your coat off," he said with a cordial smile, setting the gingerbread directly in front of her on a trivet.

"Do you do a lot of baking?"

"Only when I'm trying to impress girls."

"How often is that?"

"More often since I got divorced. So, a few years now." He turned back to the stove, made sure the oven was off.

Good, there was an ex-wife. Google hadn't mentioned her, but there were other search engines specializing in such things.

"Too bad you won't have any," he continued. "Hard to impress you if you won't even try it."

"Another time," she said.

He grinned. "Just got here and already committing to another date? That's great!" He smoothly pulled off the oven mitt, dropping it into a linen-lined wooden basket with other mitts. He did it with the casual grace that comes of performing a familiar ritual: he genuinely did bake.

Noticing where her eyes had gone: "My grandmother wanted a granddaughter. The least I could do is let her teach me to cook."

"That's sweet," she said.

He nodded, dwelling on some pleasing remembrance. "It *was* sweet. We had our seasonal projects—Thanksgiving, Easter, Fourth of July. I especially miss her on the Fourth." He looked almost choked up. "The Fourth of July was a special day in my family." He seemed about to say more, but then stopped himself. "Maybe someday I'll tell you about the Fourth of July."

"Was your family from Edgartown?" Joanna asked with dry humor. Different towns claimed different annual rites—West Tisbury had the Fair, Oak Bluffs had Illumination Night, Aquinnah had the Wampanoag Cranberry Day, but Edgartown owned the Fourth of July.

She could imagine his family—evenly tanned father in the preppy uniform of green and pink Izod clothing, mother in khaki slacks with an athletic haircut that could withstand the breeze of a morning sail, sitting on the porch of a Whaling Captain's house (the grandmother with perfectly coiffed, very white hair, and thick pink lipstick that stained her teeth), watching the parade pass directly in front of their house while sipping grasshoppers or Pimm's.

Her question seemed to startle him. Rather than acknowledging her astute assumptions, instead he asked, "Do you cook?"

"Enough to survive," she said.

He grabbed a tailored wool jacket from a peg and slid one arm into it with the same smoothness he'd discarded the mitt. "Since you won't take your coat off, why don't I give you a quick tour while the gingerbread is cooling," he said, pulling the jacket the rest of the way on. "If your coffee gets cold we'll just reheat it." And before she could disagree, he was nodding toward the kitchen door.

This opened directly onto a broad expanse of scruffy grass and scraggly bushes—unreconstructed Vineyard Meadow. About two hundred feet distant, a bluff dropped away to the steel-blue water of Vineyard Sound. The chain of the Elizabeth Islands—Nashawena, Gosnold, Naushon—rested on the horizon, rocky and bare. The sky above them was a watery lavender, accented with orange cirrus clouds. The contrast made the world look enormous.

Just to either side of the door was a kitchen garden, now dormant, with herbs within reach of the threshold and raised beds radiating out in a fan pattern.

"My chef's passion project," he said, a statement that sharply reminded her this man was not one of her people. "I have a brown thumb."

"That's an impressive garden up front," she said. "Even in winter."

He nodded, disinterested. "My ex designed that, and I have the landscapers come in to keep it shaped. It's based on a Renaissance garden or something. Down there"—he gestured toward a very large wooden building she hadn't seen from the drive—"that's the barn. This used to be a working farm like everything else around here, but now that's my home theater and there's a couple of pools, inside and outside. And a sauna and hot tub and all that. Want to see it?"

"Oh, why not, sure," she said, making certain not to sound impressed. What was wrong with her that she had not yet amassed the dough to buy a house, let alone smarten one up as he had done? To which of her many bad choices should she attribute that failing? "Actually, can I see the helipad?" she asked. "That's really why I'm here."

He shrugged. "Not much to see, but sure." He led her around the side of the house—an outdoor shower with elaborate stonework built against the western wall, behind the screened porch—and then pointed down a slope that spilled away from the extensive front yard. "There it is," he said.

She looked. There it sat, a huge mechanical dragonfly resting in a field where Celia and Joanna used to play Little House on the Prairie nearly a quarter-century ago. It was almost precisely where they had, absurdly, tried to build a log cabin one spring, out of foraged oak branches.

"There are no markings," she said.

"Not yet," he agreed. "That's not where it will stay, I want to clear a section of trees and move it about five hundred yards that way"—he gestured into the woods from which Joanna had once foraged the failed logs—"so it's not an eyesore. But for now when I use it, I just land it right there. It's convenient." He nudged her shoulder with his—she felt a pleasant shock from the intimacy of it—and began walking toward the front door.

"It must be awfully loud," she said, following him.

"It's not like I'd ever use it to run errands," he said. "I just want to get to and from Manhattan. And sure, once last summer, I chartered a pilot to bring guests because their timing didn't match mine. But even then, I avoid the traffic, and—you'd think this would matter to people—I don't *add to* the traffic, even at the airport—"

"Yes, I remember that polemic from the meeting."

"I come in by copter and then I barely ever leave this place. Can you blame me? In the summer I have a housekeeper and chef, but they time their errands so they're in town when everyone else is at the beach." He shrugged. "So, you know, it's ultimately a boon. Without the copter I'd be one more rich asshole adding to the traffic. I use it maybe twice a week in summer and it's only in earshot briefly, usually when most of the chartered jets are making a ruckus anyhow. It seems like a no-brainer to me. I don't see why the ZBA was so stubborn about it. It couldn't be any worse if Henry Holmes was still on the board. C'mon, let's go back in before your coffee gets cold."

For a moment she couldn't breathe. "Henry Holmes?"

"Sure, you know him, he's an old-timer," he said easily, as he unlatched the front door. "The jerk with the broken leg heckling me at the meeting. He gave me such grief about a storage shed—seriously, a storage shed!—that I wanted down by the boat launch, when he was on the ZBA, but apparently he's got his nose in all kinds of town business. You know him? You must know him."

She nodded, averting her gaze as she crossed past him into the house. "Yep, I know Henry Holmes."

"He has a *huge* chip on his shoulder toward anyone with money."

With a terse laugh, she said, "It's not that exactly. But he is known as the town contrarian." She felt some depraved pride about that.

"I totally get that," he said, closing the door behind himself and gesturing her through the Colonial-Furniture-room back toward the kitchen. "If he handled his own prejudices with some kind of *integrity*, I could respect that. But he's one of those windbags who just, I don't know, his moral compass lacks a true north. He seems to be defined by what makes him personally comfortable or uncomfortable."

Now she felt herself bristle. "Is that so strange? How do you set *your* moral compass?"

"I think my values are pretty consistent," he said. "But for instance, here's a story about Henry Holmes I heard at a cocktail party. He's always going on about how the government should have no right to limit people's freedoms, right? He's famous for that. Early on—I have heard—everyone loved how he chaired the Zoning Board because he didn't even *believe* in zoning. He believed everyone should have the right to do whatever they wanted on their own property."

"Yes," she said, remembering those days, which lapsed as she was weaning off training wheels, and the annual average building-permit rate quadrupled over a decade.

"So," Orion continued, as they settled back into the kitchen. He slipped his wool coat off and laid it on a stool. "Will you please take your jacket off? You make me feel like a terrible host."

"Can't have that," she said quickly, and disrobed.

He had reached for a knife to cut the gingerbread. "Here's the man who doesn't believe in zoning because he feels everyone has a right to do whatever they want with their own resources. Got that? Except he thinks that private schools should be abolished because they give rich kids an unfair advantage." She laughed a little, pained: oh, yes, she remembered that diatribe. "He wants the government to ban private organizations. So depending on his whim, he's either a libertarian or a fascist. He takes a position on things depending on his mood, or something-or-other, and then he tries to impose it on everyone else."

She focused on her coffee mug, on the letter P in NPR, and said nothing because she couldn't think of a way to respond without exposing herself. Ironic how those qualities in Hank that exasperated her also made her feel defensive of him.

To distract him, and herself, she looked out the window. "Y'know, I used to traipse around out here," she said. "As a kid. My best friend and I would ride our bikes to the beach with picnic lunches in the spring, then walk down the beach a ways and sneak up the cliffs. We pretended we were Wampanoags and had the whole Island to ourselves."

"Isn't that cultural appropriation?"

"Is that worse than geographical appropriation?"

"Wow, it's already time to have an argument about the concept of private property? This is only our second coffee date." He strolled into the pantry.

She smiled, abashed. "I admit the ship has sailed on the issue of private property. However—"

"There is always a *however,* and it's always about the good old days," he said, like an understanding parent. "Go on."

"We had permission to trespass. Sometimes it was tacit permission, but it was a time when that just happened a lot. People weren't as fierce about guarding their property lines as they are now."

He came out of the pantry with a small dessert plate. "You were a kid. How rough is anyone going to be with a little girl?" He considered the loaf of gingerbread, curlicues of steam still hovering over it as he assessed which piece to take. "If you were a grown-up caught trespassing, you'd have paid hell for it."

"I don't think so. It was the same for fishermen and hunters. It's the law of the land that fishermen can go anywhere below the high-water mark, but that's becoming acrimonious in a way it just didn't used to be. More and more, the people with summer homes want to be here because the Island is trendy and pretty, not because they have any real understanding of what the Island *is.* They have no deep ties to the community, and they're really disinclined to form any—I mean they become buddies with each other and say things like, *Oh, yes, I really feel like I'm part of the community*, but they just mean the community of well-heeled summer people. They just mean their own enclave." She could feel herself physically heating up. This was the part of her that Hank had molded and fed, and she did not want it to get the better of her at this moment, but she felt its anger, and she couldn't shut it down. "I mean, sure, they might invite a real working Islander to their cocktail party because it gives them street cred, and they'll give generously to all the fund-raisers, which is great, but they don't actually want to *know* the natives. They don't want to really face, with any kind of intimacy, the people who have no stable housing or are struggling to make their mortgage or who dive into depression every winter when there's no employment. They want to appreciate them without embracing them. They will open their pocketbooks, but not their gates. So the whole issue of access comes down to money—nothing but money."

He looked up from his gingerbread contemplation with that diffident smile. "That's the main reason people like to have money, Anna."

The intimacy of his using her name gave her another shock.

"Well," she said peevishly, "that mentality is why you'll never be loved here."

He laughed. As always, without malice. "You're a snob. You know that, right? You're all reverse snobs. I'm bad because I'm not poor. You're good because you're not rich, even though you covet what I have." He picked up a serving spatula and reached for his chosen piece of gingerbread, right in the middle of the loaf.

"We don't covet your *money*," she shot back. "We covet your access to things that feel like part of the common good but which we no longer have access to. Even if we don't legally have a right to those things—I'm not knocking private property, for Pete's sake—it *feels* like we are being deprived. By you."

He was so incredulous he almost dropped the spatula. "I'm not responsible for what you *feel*—"

"I know that," she said impatiently, "but we're going to *treat you* like you are, whether you deserve it or not, unless you offset that somehow. That's just how things work here."

"Offset it?" he said, bemused.

"You know, do something generous for the community."

"I'm very generous. You won't discover that if you try to google me, which I assume you've finally done. I keep my donations anonymous, but you would give me lots of brownie points if you saw the figures." He picked up the spatula again.

"Are you generous *here*?" she asked, waving her biscotti toward the window. "Are you acting *locally*?"

He made an exasperated sound. "Oh, I get it, it's like an inverse of NIMBY, it counts *only* if it's in my backyard." He put the spatula back down again and faced her across the granite counter. "What would that be, there's a lot of *i* words in that—" counting them on his fingers: "if, it's, in . . . so that would make it . . . *oiiimby*. On Martha's Vineyard, philanthropy counts *oiiimby*! Sounds like a war cry." He picked up the spatula again, now with resolve, and finally got the gingerbread onto the plate.

"I'm just telling you what would make it easier for you here. You can judge it all you like, it doesn't change how people are."

He gave her a conciliatory smile. "What if I opened the property up to the local kids once a year? Let them come in droves to study the flora and fauna, have an all-day field trip with a naturalist, that sort of thing."

"That'd be good," she said. "Of course, they're already doing that right next door at the Beechwood Point preserve, but sure, people would feel more generous toward you in turn. Not that it would impact the decision the Zoning Board made, but you know, it couldn't hurt. Anything involving kids is good."

"Okay, and what if I *didn't* do that," he continued in the same friendly tone, moving toward her and settling onto a stool. "But instead opened it up to *really* needy kids who have *no* access to nature. Like brought in a bunch of them from Detroit."

"Easy to do on your helicopter," she said.

"I know, right?" He laughed. "Actually, the helicopter only holds five and its range isn't that long—it's just a little Jet Ranger. Anyhow. Tell me." He leaned closer to her, and again she smelled a hint of cardamom. Or maybe that was from the gingerbread. "If I made sure everyone here knew that I was doing this wonderful thing, even if it didn't help the locals . . . how would that fly, so to speak?"

She thought for a moment. "I guess you're right, we're hypocrites, we'd like you more if you let the local kids onto your property as part of your generosity."

He nodded a little, understandingly, as if he knew she'd say this. "And why is that?" he prompted.

"Because we feel the need to take care of our own. Put our oxygen masks on first. 'Course, you probably don't have oxygen masks in your helicopter."

"Cute," he said.

"But yes," she went on. "We're an island. There are finite resources here, you can't simply go a little further afield to forage, there is an innate awareness of limitation, especially since the poverty rate is over ten percent, and the cost of living here is twice what it is in the rest of Massachusetts while the average year-round income is half. That sense of lack, it percolates down into how we see things unconsciously. Especially when there's suddenly a gazillion people here in the summer, wanting, wanting, *wanting*."

"And giving, giving, giving," Orion returned. "Maybe your problem is with the whole notion of give-and-take. Everyone's all about Yankee self-sufficiency here, or kid themselves into believing they are, anyhow. You don't get to live that way in a resort community. Especially one that, as you just said, has limited resources. You need tourists as badly as Venice does."

"I've been to Venice," she said. "Venice gets to regulate what outsiders do to Venice. We don't have that kind of control. Even if you think the ZBA is fascist, we're libertarians compared to Venice. We feel very vulnerable to the whims of off-Islanders. That's why new things scare us. We are suspicious of change."

"So my real crime here isn't that I'm rich, or that I'm damaging the environment, or that I'm cheating anyone of anything. It's just that I'm doing things differently."

"In part, I guess," she said quietly. "I mean, maybe."

"Now we're getting somewhere," he said. He took a triumphant bite of gingerbread. "Will you please have a piece of this."

It smelled better than the best gingerbread of her childhood. "No, thanks," she said. "I'll just dunk my cookie in my coffee, I'm happy as a clam."

He gave her a penetrating look. After a pause, he asked, rhetorically, "How do we know clams are happy? I get *happy as a lark*, because they sing, and *happy as a pig in shit*, because pigs make those contented little snorty sounds. But clams—"

"Happy as a clam at high tide," she said. "That's the whole phrase.

Clams are safe at high tide. Nobody can get at 'em. They are impervious." She raised the coffee mug. "Cheers."

He mirrored her with a gesture, as he'd nothing of his own to toast with. "If you feel better depriving yourself, that's fine. It's a great recipe."

It smelled like it. "Enter it in the Fair," she suggested. "Once you win a blue ribbon at the Fair, people might respect you more. Plus there's a five-dollar prize, that could help you with a retainer for your trial lawyer. The Fair's not until August, though. I'm guessing you want to get all this thrashed out well before then."

He winked at her. "Not sure if you're trying to talk me into suing faster, or not suing at all."

"I'm freelance, I get paid per piece. There will be more to write about if you actually go ahead and sue."

He laughed. "I like you for thinking that way," he said in a bright voice. Then, lowering his tone to something more intimate and knowing, he amended, "But what I like even more is, I'm pretty sure you don't mean that. I think you love this place a lot—all of it, even the hotheads like Henry Holmes—and you want peace to reign supreme. Right?"

She went red when he said Hank's name, and trying to camouflage the cause of the blush, made sure to look sheepish. "You got my number."

"Yes I do, which means I can call you for another date. Should we schedule it now, get that out of the way?" He twisted like a cat and leaned in her direction, until his ear was resting on the counter and he was grinning up at her. It was an unselfconscious, goofy thing to do, and she giggled uncontrollably in response. "You have a great laugh," he said. "Come on, admit it, you like me."

She recovered from the giggles. "Can I just ask—are you *living* here now? In *March*? You're here a lot for a summer person."

"I'm here when I can be," he said, and straightened up. "I've gone round-trip to New York since I last saw you, but I'm hoping to roost for a bit here now. Probably be a few weeks before I head off again."

"Why?" she asked. "What do you *do*?"

He winked at her and took another bite of gingerbread. "That's for me to know and you to find out. If you're a good journalist. Which so far you don't seem to be. No offense. I mean, they're giving you diddly-squat to do, I've been following your byline in the paper."

"To be fair to them, there is diddly-squat going on."

He shook his head. "The *Newes* has some great feature writing. Do you read it? You should probably read the competition."

"Of course I read it. It paints a very different picture of the Island."

"Obviously," he said. He took a bite of gingerbread. "They're much nicer to people like me, for starters. It's as if they have some awareness that we add something of value to the economy. Like, I dunno, *money*. Also—the writing itself, some of it's great, like the piece they just did about an outgoing member of my personal nemesis, the ZBA. This person has made my life difficult, and if I'd read about her in the *Journal* she'd probably just strike me as an irritant, but I read about her in the *Newes* and suddenly I appreciate her as a human being. I'd enjoy getting to know her. I value a newspaper that allows for that kind of reporting. Plus they have poems sprinkled through the paper, and little artistic images, and aphorisms. They really capture the nuances and ethos of what makes this place so special—no offense, but the *Journal* presents the Vineyard as if it were just any small town. The *Newes* really luxuriates in teeny little specific . . . *Vineyardishnesses*. Is it okay to make up a word when I'm talking to a writer?"

"Eh . . . yes," she said. A pleasant shiver sped across her shoulder blades. He liked her piece about Helen. He had no idea it was her, and yet he liked her writing and it had, however humbly, done some good. That felt nice. But the brush with her double identity did not. "Made-up words are great as long as they have lots of syllables that don't really add to the meaning."

"I see. So short meaningful words are not okay? I can't use, let's see, *stroot*, or *chish*, or, mm, *bleg*?"

"Those kind of phrases sound like they belong in the word market in *The Phantom Tollbooth*," she said. "Around here we only accept fabricated words if the meaning is self-evident. *Vineyardishnesses* passes muster. *Stroot* does not."

He grimaced. "The meaning of *stroot* is perfectly obvious to anyone listening to the sound of the word. *Stroot*."

"Ummm . . . no."

"It's the opposite of a lie," he protested. "Obviously. You know, as in, I think that's a lie—no, it's *stroot*."

"That is so dopey," she said, but she laughed.

"Well, what do *you* think it means?"

"It's the texture on your fingertips when they're red from handling raw beets."

He snapped his fingers. "Oh, that's right, I got mixed up. See, it is *totally* obvious what *stroot* means, it's a perfect fake word."

"Unlike *bleg*."

"Oh, *chish*," he said dismissively, grinning.

She'd hoped to beat Hank home, get dinner on before he got back so that if he asked where she'd gone out to, she could deflect him by asking how he wanted his potatoes. Come sunset, Hank could be distracted pretty easily by food. Then she would try to dive a little deeper on the internet in search of information about Orion Smith.

But when she got in, Hank was already settled in his reclining chair with his leg propped up, a Sam Adams on the table beside him to the right, a pile of manila folders congested with papers on the table to the left. He had one such folder open on his lap, lounging against his belly. He had loosened the walking boot, and his foot and ankle were swollen. The TV was on, muted. It was showing the last ZBA meeting Joanna had attended, and the back of her and Celia's heads were clearly visible. She found the remote and clicked off the screen. Hank didn't notice.

"Hey," she said, lowering her backpack onto a kitchen chair.

"Hey," he said, without looking up from reading.

"Want some dinner?" She pulled off her outer sweater and hung it on a peg by the door.

A pause.

"Sure," he said, absentmindedly, and kept reading.

A pause.

"What do you feel like?"

"Whatever. What we got?" He did not look up.

"There's the last of the bay scallops from Joseph and there's about one meal's worth of kale still in the freezer downstairs. Marie and Bill brought over a chicken pot pie. Nice that people are still bringing food."

"After all these weeks? That's a comment on what they assume about your cooking," he said dryly, finally glancing up. And he grinned to soften the insult.

"Thanks," she said. "Anyhow, what's your preference?"

"I do like Marie's chicken pie," he said.

"Okay, I'll heat it up," she said, and moved to turn the oven on. "Feel like a game of Scrabble?"

"Maybe later," he said, rustling the document he was reading. "Busy now."

"What you reading? Is that something for Jen's fund-raiser?"

"Oh," he said, vaguely. "No. Some stuff Helen loaned me. I need stronger reading glasses. Will you check my foot? My ankle is throbbing."

She went to it. It looked painfully swollen, but there was no discoloration or anything else she'd been told to look for. "It doesn't look great. Aren't we due for a follow-up X-ray this week?"

"*We* are not. *I* am. Paul can take me. Or Helen."

"Well, suit yourself, but I've got it in my calendar already. So is that pleasure reading?" She went back to the oven, opened the creaky oven door, and slid the chicken pie onto the top rack.

"Of course not pleasure reading," he said. "Do I look like someone who would read regulatory documents for pleasure? When I am in a state of discomfort?"

"If it was about your hometown? Maybe."

"*Maybe*," he echoed sardonically under his breath. "No, this is ZBA stuff."

She froze very briefly, before closing the oven and straightening up. "Why are you reading ZBA stuff?" she asked.

"Well, you know Helen retired—"

This could not be happening. "Of course I know Helen retired, I *wrote* about it," she said. To her bemusement, Hank had expressed no curiosity about her continuing double identity. That said, he hadn't been curious about much at all lately. Joanna was worried there was a correlation between his general indifference and his health. "And I'm the one covering the ZBA, remember?" There was more fierceness in her tone than she intended, but it didn't matter. He was insulated in a cocoon of beer, pain, and self-absorption.

"Well," he said, as if spelling this out for a cheeky toddler, "her retirement created a big problem. They don't have a quorum for the ZBA, so they asked if I would step in until the selectmen could find—"

"Hank, I'm under your roof and I'm covering the story. That's a conflict of interest."

"Don't be ridiculous," he said, emerging slightly from the cocoon. "It's not like there's a trial or anything."

"There's *going* to be a trial!" she said, stepping out of the kitchen area toward his recliner.

"No there isn't. That asshole Smith is going to back off, he just doesn't know it yet." He had briefly sat up, but now slouched back into the chair as if exhausted. "Or maybe he does. Which kind of makes him more of an asshole. He backed off five years ago when he wanted to build a fucking *boatyard* within shouting distance of Beechtree, on that stretch where the erosion is terrible. What an idiot. People get their Ivy League educations and they don't even understand *erosion*. Christ. He backed off then. He'll back off now."

"Whatever he does, I'm writing about it, and you're my immediate family so you shouldn't be gratuitously inserting yourself into the picture."

"It's not gratuitous. The selectmen came to me and *begged* me to take over."

It was worse than she'd thought. "Take over? You're the *chair*? You went from being uninvolved to the most involved, just—when? This *afternoon*?" She was looming over him and forced herself to take a step back. He barely noticed.

"I went in to talk to them yesterday, but we all had a chat today and agreed I'd lead it. I've done it before, when there was legal action pending. I know the ropes, it just made sense to make me chair." Finally registering her consternation, he added quickly, "It's not like we're going to actually *do* anything. It's out of our hands now, it's with the selectmen and the legal team. But it makes the town look incompetent if the board in question isn't even operational because it lacks a quorum. They just need a front man who doesn't give a rat's ass if abominable things are quoted about him in the paper by rich presumptuous jerks. And that," he said, grim and conclusive, "describes *me*."

"When was I going to be informed of this?"

"Don't get bent out of shape, Anna. They'll do it formally tomorrow at the selectmen's meeting."

"While I'm there taking notes? And they all know me?"

"So tell the paper to send someone else."

"It's my beat. And I need it."

"What is it, fifty bucks? And it's temporary. My work for the town eclipses that."

"How come *you* get to decide that, without even checking in with me?" She could hear her voice rising to an adolescent pitch.

"What was there to check in about?" he retorted. "What was I supposed to do, say, 'Thanks but I can't do it because Anna writes for the papers'? I bet every writer on both papers has these kinds of conflicts come up all the time." He made a grand, dismissive gesture. "Just get yourself moved to another beat. Everett likes you, he'll find you work."

She rubbed a hand over her forehead. "I wish you had at least talked to me about this before it happened."

"Well, now I've talked to you about it *after* it happened," he said. "If you want corroboration, go to the Town Hall at four thirty tomorrow afternoon, second floor."

In her irritation, she forgot to research Orion Smith.

It was snowing the next day. Just as they all got used to it being a snowless winter, and the equinox was days away, it snowed. Or nearly snowed. It was more like being peppered with slush by an unfriendly weather sprite.

The *Journal*'s parking lot was too small even for the staff, so she'd taken to parking across the road, in front of a T-shirt boutique that was closed for the winter. She parked with the truck facing out, in case this turned into real snow and stuck, and then she trudged across the street as angry cold kisses of precipitation stung her cheeks. In the overheated *Journal* office, she shrugged out of her wet coat, settled into one of the free chairs around the news table, and got her marching orders from Everett: this week, as well as continuing to cover the West Tisbury beat, she'd be writing a couple of movie reviews, and a feature about the owner of an up-Island hardware store.

"Can I talk to you for a moment in private?" she asked after the meeting. He gave her a puzzled look, then gestured toward the steps. They went upstairs, where Sarah and Rosie had already commandeered the best seats at the conference table. Everett led her into his office, which always felt to her like being below deck in a wooden boat. The soft wood absorbed sound, and it was exquisitely quiet up here.

"What's up?" he asked, closing the door behind him. It was the first time she'd ever seen the door closed. He settled into his chair.

"Hank is replacing Helen Javier as chair of the ZBA board," she said. "Effective this afternoon."

"Ah," he said.

Then he looked pensive for a moment.

Then he laughed. It was a resigned laugh.

"Well . . ." And not actually having anything productive to say, he settled for, "Yeah. That happens." He shrugged, and added rhetorically, "What can we do?"

"We can take Hank's caretaker off the ZBA story, for starters," she said.

He held his hands up. "Anna," he said. "You know how few people I have here. If there were no helipad story, I wouldn't bother covering West Tisbury *at all* until I got my staff back. Everyone's already going full-tilt, and I can't just swap you out with someone. Everyone else is in the middle of complex stories on issues that'll be coming up at all the Annual Town Meetings, and there is no time for you to get up to speed. There's nothing I can do."

"When board members have family connections to an issue, they don't vote on the issue—"

"You're not voting, you're reporting. Voting *creates* policy. You're just *describing* policy. We can add a disclosure statement that you're connected to a board member, we've certainly had to do that before. But in this case that makes it more of a big deal than it is."

The chords of Django Reinhardt's *Belleville* burst forth from her back pocket.

"Go ahead and take it," said Everett, looking relieved, and made a dismissing gesture. "Really, Anna, this is fine. It's not ideal, but it's okay."

"Hello," she said. She gave Everett an unhappy look and exited his office, into the open area with the conference table.

"Hello, Joey? This is Lewis," said the patrician voice of Everett's rival.

"Oh, hello!" she said, too briskly. Sarah and Rosie both looked up from their laptops. She wished there were an empty room that she could meander into. Taking a call into the bathroom would be weird.

"I just wanted to tell you what a positive response we've been getting from your Helen Javier piece," he said. "I don't know if you check the website for comments, but about twenty-five readers have written nice things about it—that's a big number. Usually we only get a lot of comments when they're negative."

"Thanks," she said, adapting a casual tone to avoid continued interest from Sarah and Rosie.

"And we're getting positive snail mail about it as well."

"That's so nice to hear, thank you."

"I like your tone, it really fits the Vineyard in winter, and so I'd like to keep up this 'On the Same Page' project, if you're good with that?"

"Absolutely," she said.

"Great, well, you can come in to talk it over in more detail, but one idea we had was to interview some Island fishermen in the off-season."

"Okay," she said, carefully. She wanted to answer him without saying anything specific that the reporters here would note. "You know they work in winter too, right? It's not like March is off-season for *them*."

"No, of course," he said, with a reserved chuckle. "I actually do know that, but some of our seasonal subscribers don't. That's why I think it would be affecting. We would set it off against a piece from

1943 about the *Alice Wentworth,* the final sail out of Vineyard Haven harbor, marking the end of coastal schooners under sail."

"Sounds great," she said, bemused by the notion that all seagoing vessels belonged on the same page. "Also there's a selectmen's meeting tonight."

"I appreciate your being on top of the schedule, Joey, but don't worry about it. I called about the agenda and the only thing they're voting on is Henry Holmes being made the new chair of the ZBA. That fellow is a chronic activist board member; he's constantly trying to get his name in the paper to get column inches for his causes. He can pull strings at the *Journal* but I don't have the time for that kind of thing. So it's not worth it."

"Okay," she said lamely, then arranged to come in to see him the next morning. She couldn't stop glancing at the young women out of the corner of her eye. They took no notice of her, but the knot in her stomach at the fear that they might was itself almost too unpleasant to withstand. She would not be able to keep this up for long.

She left the office just after four, to head to the West Tisbury Town Hall. It was below freezing but the precipitating slop had not coalesced into snow, so now she was stomping through nearly three inches of the coldest slush in North America. It was almost translucent. The road had been sanded, but she was glad to have four-wheel drive getting out of the parking lot. Heading up the hill to go up-Island was like driving through a black-and-white photo. She remembered this from childhood: the end of winter into early spring was the dreariest interval of the Island year. Even those who liked quiet and solitude were climbing the walls by now. If they had actual snow, if they had the drama of it, that might have helped a little, but no, despite the bitterest of winds, most of the time they just endured grungy skies and halfhearted frozen drizzle that couldn't commit to a texture once it landed. Sunset was later now that they'd sprung forward an hour, but it was already gloomily dark from the slush-clouds.

She drove the desolate roads past little vestiges of civilization—Cronig's supermarket was still open, and SBS, from whence came the chicken feed and the cat food and the nesting straw and, most likely, her dead aunt's insulated rain boots that she now wore almost daily. Once upon a time, she recalled, she had dressed well enough, her emphasis on harmonious palettes and tailored curves and tasteful makeup. Since returning home, she had slipped by degrees into wearing the same three pairs of Levi's over high-tech long underwear, and a rotation of four sweaters, three of which almost went with the burgundy cap she had taken to wearing even indoors. She had no idea where her mascara was and had never once considered wearing blush. She realized, reflecting, that it took genuine effort to break out of this monotony, and she had only done it for Orion. "I guess he's good for something," she muttered to herself.

She passed the farm stand and fairgrounds, the empty fields and the graveyard with Nancy Luce's hen-festooned gravestone. Past Alley's General Store ("Dealers in Almost Everything"). Past the neat white Congregational church, because rural New England.

She pulled into the Town Hall parking lot facing the Grange Hall. This was rarely opened this time of year, but in summer bustled with the Farmers Market and various artisanal fairs, adored by those with disposable cash, cursed by its neighbors who could never exit their driveways due to the traffic backup. This was a peaceful little village that people flocked to see in such numbers that it was no longer peaceful. She remembered on summer visits, timing her yoga classes to avoid Antiques Fair traffic. Come to think of it, she could do with a yoga class or two as soon as possible, and those at least seemed to be in supply even in the dark of winter. She'd have to crunch the numbers and see if she could spring for one. Amazing how her mind wandered on these empty, familiar roads.

Inside the Town Hall, she settled grimly into her chair. There was nobody else present but the camera operator and Helen's husband, Paul.

And Hank. *Let's not forget Hank*, she hummed sardonically to herself. Paul Javier had driven him here. He entered moments after she did, and he was breathing as if everything took effort. Paul moved a chair into the aisle to make it easier for him to sit.

The agenda was, of course, short.

Chairman Bernie Burt picked up the gavel lying on the table, rapped it twice, and said, "I call an abbreviated meeting of the West Tisbury Selectmen to order on the evening of March 11. We have one item of business, and we're putting off minutes and the like, and going right to the issue of filling the ZBA vacancy." This was stated as if for the camera, as there was nobody else here but Joanna. And Paul Javier. And Hank. With his sheepish grin aimed just above her head.

"Would you like to make a motion?" the chairman asked fellow selectman Mel Sanders.

"I would like to make a motion that we elect Henry Holmes to the Zoning Board of Appeals," said Mel.

"I'll second that motion," said the third selectman, whom Joanna didn't know.

"Any discussion?" asked Chairman Burt.

No answer.

"Okay, then, all in favor," he said. They all raised their hands and said, "Aye," in slightly tired voices.

"All opposed?" No answer.

"Okay, that passes," he said laconically. "Welcome back to the ZBA, Hank."

"Thanks," said Hank.

"Do we have any correspondence to review?"

"No correspondence," said Rachel, the administrator, who was perkily taking minutes.

"Do we have public comments or questions?" Chairman Burt asked this, without irony, to the rows of empty chairs. "Any press comments or questions?"

She kept her mouth shut. It was fine that Hank was the chairman of the board that she was reporting on. Of course it was. Totally fucking fine.

"I make a motion that we adjourn," said Chairman Burt.

"Seconded," said Mel.

The chairman struck his gavel again. "Meeting adjourned at . . ." a glance to the wall clock behind Joanna's head. "Four thirty-four. Everyone go home before we succumb to bombogenesis." Score one for the locals, thought Joanna: their weather vocabulary rivaled the National Weather Service's.

She glanced back at Hank. He appeared jaundiced compared to Paul's ruddy complexion. Except the apples of his cheeks, which were redder than Paul's. "Do you have a fever?" she asked, like a scold.

"Sure," he said, mellow. "I'm in a delirium of joy that I get to be chairman of the ZBA again and do battle with Orion fucking Smith."

ONCE HE WAS back home, swaddled, fed, and medicated, she took his temperature, but it was only 99. She gave him aspirin and made a note to call his doctor in the morning. He was due for his follow-up X-ray anyhow.

And she tried, again, to find more information about Orion. The databases and search engines she had learned to rely on coughed up almost nothing. His name was attached to residences in upstate New York, suburban Connecticut, and Manhattan. He had owned, and then not owned, a couple dozen companies, or possibly pieces of commercial real estate. It was all generic and unhelpful.

Which made him more intriguing.

Dinner? Finally?

She stared at the text and glanced guiltily around the beige waiting room. The table lamp beside her sported paintings of ducklings, and these were the only nonbeige things in the room besides a raft of watercolors of the painted Victorian houses of Cottage City. Otherwise, all beige. Linoleum, walls, padded chairs, laminate tables—as many variations of beige as the island in winter had of gray.

She glanced again at the text. She should have already recused herself from the helipad story. She was falling sweet for the plaintiff and living with the defendant. Neither aware the other one meant a thing to her.

Maybe they canceled each other out. She didn't want either one of them hurt even though both of them drove her a bit nuts. The scales still hung evenly. With that as a justification for continuing—at least temporarily—she texted back, Can't accept a meal. Will bring my own. Date?<

>Yes, so glad you concur that it's a date! How about tomorrow night? 7?

Have to cover the improv comedy show, it's a fund-raiser for Affordable Housing<

>Next night?

The three-day Film Festival had started but she'd already done most of the research. Anna Howes would be writing up the documentaries, and Joey Dias would focus more on the dramatic films. Anna Howes needed to review the locally produced doc about the locally produced housing crisis, but the Festival staff had already sent her a link to watch it online, so she couldn't believably use that as an excuse to back out of a dinner date. Anyhow, she didn't really want to back out. She just *wanted* to want to, which was not at all the same thing.

There was a County Commission meeting the night Orion was asking about; that meant if Hank was well enough, he would get a ride there from some fellow civics junkie, and would be preoccupied. He hadn't been on the Commission for years but he was constitutionally incapable of keeping his nose out of everything. He'd be exhausted by the outing, and therefore asleep by the time she got back.

Even as she was thinking this duplicitous thought, the inner beige door opened, revealing a darker beige within. Hank hobbled out with his aluminum crutches. She rose to her feet, instinctively hiding the phone behind her back. Hank didn't notice.

"I'm fine," he said in a surly voice, before she could ask. He spoke as if he were addressing someone in the next room. "I told you I was fine. The X-ray is fine and I'm fine and I'm supposed to call in if I start to feel worse but I'm not going to feel worse. What a waste of a morning. Let's go." He hobbled past her, without waiting.

Sounds good, she typed to Orion, then shoved the phone into her back pocket and followed Hank.

"Wait for me," she said. "After I dropped you off I could only find parking in the dirt lot. That's too far for you to walk on crutches with everything frozen." He made an indistinct noise and kept walking. As she hurried down the hallway after him, wishing she could be elsewhere, she wondered what she would make for the supper. It had to travel well, but mostly she wanted to impress

Orion. Puerile, but still true. Sea scallops? Expensive. Cod? Cod fell apart too easily, hard to make an attractive dish. Maybe mussels. Sloppy to carry, or had to be cooked there. Oysters. Yes, oysters!

It was unsavory, how satisfying she found it to contemplate dinner with Orion nearly under Hank's nose. The irony was not deliberate, but it certainly was tantalizing.

And if Orion also got oysters? And made some incredibly sophisticated dish? She had to one-up him somehow.

Actually, that would be easy.

The dirt road to Orion's was treacherous from the slush and the peanut-buttery mud lurking beneath it. But it was worth the odyssey: Orion made Oysters Rockefeller. The aroma of the bacon made her mouth water before she was entirely inside his house. She gave him a small smile and planted her canvas grocery bag on the granite counter.

"Welcome," he said. "Sure I can't tempt you?"

"You're already tempting me, I'm just not succumbing," she said.

"It's all geographically correct," he boasted, gesturing to the exquisitely assembled meal, resting in a Williams Sonoma dish designed exclusively for baking oysters. She recalled Hank once fashioning something similar out of a bunch of wired-together glass butter trays. Or something. "The oysters are from the Edgartown Great Pond, the bacon's from Tisbury, and all the veggies are defrosted from my chef's kitchen garden harvest."

"Smells lovely," she admitted.

"Oysters were harvested this afternoon," he added.

"So were these," she said, shrugging out of her coat. "I went at low tide."

He paused a tick, and then returned to fussing over his dish.

"Nicely done," he said.

"Thanks," she said, offhandedly. She reached into her back pocket for the shucking knife, waving it in his direction. "You don't mind, do you? I can open them over the sink."

He smirked. "Okay, you win," he said. "The laurel wreath for Authentically Local goes to Anna Howes."

Her leather shucking gloves were on the top of the heap; she put them on, then grabbed an oyster. She cupped the rounded side in her palm and pushed the tip of the knife into the hinge, running it up and around the edge of the shell and forcing it open. Oysters don't pry open easily.

"You do that like a pro," he said, in an almost reverential voice. "I'm a gentleman and intend to remain one but I have to tell you— it's kinda sexy."

She laughed and held up one gloved hand. "Sexy as Shackleton," she said.

"Seeing somebody do something with dexterity—" he pressed.

"Oh, well, if you think *this* is sexy, you should get a load of my uncle," she said, before realizing how foolhardy it was to mention that uncle. So she just kept talking. "You'd hardly be able to contain yourself."

"You know what I mean," he said.

"Where should I put the shells?" she asked.

He shrugged.

"I'll take them home, then," she said. "Chickens can have them."

Since she was eating her oysters raw, they were able to sit down together at the dining table a few minutes later, with their respective *Crassostrea virginica* dinners. She eyed his, envying that it was a warm dish. He eyed hers as she squeezed a bit of lemon on each one. She pretended he wasn't watching, and brought the first oyster to her lips, sucking it into her mouth and swallowing it nearly whole. He watched her without even raising his fork.

"No wonder they're considered an aphrodisiac," Orion said, sounding almost pained. His face was pinker than she'd ever seen it. "I could watch that all evening."

Her stomach flip-flopped. "Ha! Can't be that much of an aphrodisiac if you're happy just to *watch*."

He grinned, laughed a little. "I'm not sure if you're combative, or just competitive. You never just accept anything I say, you *always* have a retort. Do you realize you do that?"

"We both do that. It's not just me."

"You're almost the only person who does it with me, though."

"Well, that's a remarkable coincidence," she said, "because you're almost the only person who does it with me too." *Along with Henry Holmes*, she did not add.

"So . . ." he considered. "It's kind of special, then, our little banter. Right?"

She shrugged. "Kind of." She picked up another oyster and brought it to her mouth with a flourish. "Hey. Watch this. This'll be more special than banter."

"You little siren," he said, shaking his head. "I'm determined to keep this aboveboard, and shall therefore avert my gaze." He turned his face away but then immediately turned it back. "Eventually, I mean."

"It's fun to watch, isn't it?" she said slyly.

"I have no idea what you're talking about, ma'am. So. Ahem. To keep this budding friendship on its current platonic flight path, and since you're the expert and I've never thought about it, tell me: how does one get an oyster?"

"They're so easy," she said. "They don't burrow or anything, they find a rock or a shell right on the floor of the pond and grow in clumps. All you need are waders and a basket, really—maybe a rake, but if you go at low tide you can just reach down and grab 'em off the bottom. It's ironic they're considered such a delicacy; clams are harder to harvest. Maybe it's like lobsters—they got overfished at one point and were basically extinct up here, so suddenly that made them a commodity. And they're a little harder to shuck than, say, scallops. But otherwise they practically grow in your lap."

"That's not fair, you can't do that. This evening is supposed to be chitchat and repartee. You can't talk about oysters and your lap in the same sentence. Not unless you intend to seduce me."

"I can't seduce you. I'm still trying to research you," she said quickly. It was pleasing to have his attention, though. She began to stack the slick oyster shells unsteadily, one atop the next on the plate.

"Those two objectives need not be unrelated—seduction and research."

"I'm really not an expert on seduction," she said in mock apology. "And I'm only getting to know you because I want to write about you for the paper."

He laughed. "I don't believe that for a moment!" he said. "You want a piece of me. All the locals do."

She had not seen that coming. "*Wow*, that's arrogant," she said, and paused from her shell stacking. "Or condescending. Which?"

"Neither," he said. "I just mean it's a cause-and-effect thing. I have money, I have resources, and people hope I'll do something with it to their benefit. My background made it impossible not to be aware of that. It very nearly defined my grandparents' relationship to everything."

"Oh, you poor child," she said. "How tediously first-world that must have been for you."

"I'm not judging anyone for it, it's only human—"

"That's very big of you—"

"—and so *I* would like to not be judged, in turn!" he said, so sharply it shocked her. "The having of money does not make me evil, it does not make me selfish, it does not make me indifferent to other people's needs. Don't treat me that way. That's for the fucking Henry Holmeses of the world to do!"

The buoyant music of Django Reinhardt erupted from her back pocket. Hurriedly she wiped her oyster-dampened fingers on her napkin, then pulled out the phone and saw the call was from Hank.

"Sorry," she said, flustered. "Excuse me." She pivoted away from Orion on the stool, as if he would be able to recognize Hank's voice if she were facing him. Then she answered and said, "You okay?" in lieu of greeting.

A brief pause. "Probably," he said grudgingly, which meant he probably wasn't.

"I'll be right there," she said. "Don't move." She hung up and looked dolefully at Orion. "I'm sorry, this is a family emergency."

He nodded gruffly. "Hope it's nothing serious. Go on. Sorry about the rant." A small grin. "Need a helicopter ride to the hospital?"

"Ha," she said, getting up and reaching for her coat.

"He had a fever," said the ER doctor, who looked younger than Joanna, which did not reassure her. "But it's going down now. And he was dehydrated, so we've given him fluids, and started him on intravenous antibiotics."

"Intravenous?" She might have winced. "That sounds serious."

He waved his hand reassuringly. And it might have reassured her if he hadn't been younger than she. "It's just to get his blood levels up—a sort of launch event for his immune system. We worked up the fever, did a blood culture—"

"It's his *leg*," she said, wondering if he were too young to have studied anatomy. "It's his *ankle*."

A nod. "Of course it is, but we wanted to be sure there was nothing else going on. He needs to follow up immediately with his orthopedic doctor. We'll keep him for another hour or so for observation and then if things continue to improve, we'll send him home with a scrip for oral antibiotics. He really needs to stay quiet with his leg elevated until he can be seen. Whatever he's doing, he's doing too much of it."

She nodded, feeling hapless. He patted her arm, reassuringly, and left.

She looked at the clock on the ER wall. 2:30 A.M. Too late to call Brian. But she could text.

> Have to stay longer because Hank has gotten worse

Ten minutes later, a response.

> Sorry to hear it, LMK what happens.

And ten minutes after that:

> Really hope things are okay. Thinking of you and your
> family. Give me an update when you can ...

That was from Orion.

The next morning, while still curled up under the musty woolen blankets of her childhood bedroom with a cat purring at her feet, she left an urgent message for the orthopedic doctor asking for an appointment. She left Hank's landline as the callback number, since he had recently accused her of trying to take all control away from him. So she made a mental note to check the answering machine hourly. Then she pried herself out of bed, wrapped herself in a flannel bathrobe from tenth grade she'd found in her closet, and hurriedly made a fire in the woodstove to take the stale damp out of the air. When it was warm enough to remove layers without her teeth chattering, she got dressed. She put on her good boots, the suede ones she'd worn home from the city, now ringed white from salt. Arranged her hair more carefully than usual. Put on blush and eyeliner. She looked almost like her New York self as she strode into Everett's monastic office twenty minutes later, triumphant from having traversed ice patches in the parking lot without slipping in her city boots.

"Armed for battle," he said, eyeing the war paint. "I assume you have something to say that I won't want to hear. Let me guess. You're going back to America."

"No," she said, although that now seemed like an attractive option. "I need to speak to you off the record about a potential conflict of interest."

He sighed patiently. "Anna, I already said we'll make it work. We have to make certain allowances for how tight the gene pool is here. And you're only reporting facts, you're not doing features or—"

"Not Hank," she said. "The other guy."

"What other guy?"

She grimaced, blinking stupidly. She couldn't get it out.

The penny dropped. "Smith?" Everett blinked stupidly too. "What's the connection with Smith?"

"He thinks I'm cute."

Avuncular delight. "Fantastic! Use it."

"I might be starting to think he's sort of cute too."

He looked amazed. "I did not see that one coming. Doesn't seem your type."

"He's not, but he's working on it."

He rubbed the back of his neck, stared at his bare desk a moment, and then looked up at her. "Moment of truth, Anna," he said. "Can you separate your work from your personal life?"

She took a breath. Moment of truth. Yes. "I believe I can," she said. "Just like you said about Hank—I'm reporting facts, I'm not doing feature articles or editorializing. There's no reason for my personal opinion of him to appear in my reporting. But I wanted to mention it now, in case the objective bit doesn't pan out."

He stared at her for a long, level moment, his ginger-toned terrier eyebrows puckering. "I'm trusting you," he finally said. "I'm trusting you because you told me."

"Thank you, I don't take that lightly," she said. "And if I start to feel that the situation is getting in the way of my doing my job with integrity, I will let you know right away."

"All right," he said after a moment. He gave her a mischievous grin. "Never took you for a gold-digger."

"Everett," she said affectionately, "fuck off."

Dear Brian

I think

Dear Brian

I wish

Dear Brian

You are

"HEY," BRIAN SAID, when she called him that afternoon, huddled in her heaviest coat outside the *Journal* office. "I was just thinking of calling you."

"We need some clarity on what our status really is until we get to have The Talk," she said, trying not to rush, and realizing she was perhaps being rude by not having said hello first.

"Right," he said. "You found someone."

"No!" she said, too quickly. She squinted into the sun, and pushed back against the old gray shingles. She took in a deep breath scented with creosote and seawater, and was comforted by it as others might be comforted by their mother's perfume. The frozen slush from earlier in the week had sand and clay so mushed into it that the ground looked like gritty caramel taffy. "I just want to know what's appropriate if I *do* find someone."

"On the Vineyard in March? From what you've said about that place in March, I think the most appropriate thing might be genetic testing."

She said nothing. He chuckled gently.

"Okay," he said. "I get it. It's not a guy. It's a place. You want to have a monogamous live-in relationship with a place, despite all the stuff you hate about it."

She stared out over the quiet harbor. Hmm. "I didn't realize that's what I was asking for."

"I did. I want a monogamous live-in relationship with Manhattan, so I get it."

". . . Thanks," she said. The harbor was suddenly mesmerizing, perhaps because she didn't want to focus on the phone call. A handful of the larger sailboats were at their moorings, but most of the inner harbor was empty, snug behind the long protecting rock jetty. In the summer, every mooring had a boat, and there were ad hoc moorings in the outer harbor too—out beyond the jetty, but still sheltered between the two chops. It was the marine equivalent of a ghost town now.

"I think you're making a bad choice, but I respect your right to make it," Brian was saying. "When you realize the folly of your ways, Manhattan will be big enough to take you back. I'll probably start dating again, though."

"Heard that before," she said, trying to make a joke of it. This time, probably, he really would.

HANK'S FEVER WENT down. A little. Not enough for her to relax about it, and his ankle was still inflamed. He contended he was fine and let her know "casually" after the fact that he had informed the doctor of this when the doctor returned her call on the landline. He would not be calling the doctor again. Because he was fine. The proof was that he could still beat her at Scrabble. He had come apart the other night and called her during a weak moment, but he would not make *that* mistake again, not now that he saw how susceptible *she* was to overreacting.

Orion texted to see how things were.

I'm going to be busy with family things for a few days, she said.

Keep in touch when you can, he texted back. Hope it's all okay.

From Brian, she heard nothing further.

Celia and Joanna walked Celia's dog on raw, unsheltered North Shore beaches. Long barrows of eelgrass flanked the shore like soggy black fettuccine and the shifting tides had exposed ten thousand rocks on a beach that had been smoothly sand just two months earlier. "How metaphorical," she said to Celia. "You can never tell when things will suddenly get rocky."

Celia stared at her a moment, then burst out laughing. "That's what you have to show for your English degree?"

They also saw a few movies. Made gleeful idiots of themselves bowling in Oak Bluffs. She took her first yoga class in three years, in a cedar-lined up-Island studio in the woods. Joey Dias began a series called "Librarians of Martha's Vineyard" for the *Newes,* which was on the same page as a story about the first microfilm reader coming to the Edgartown Library in the early 1960s. For the *Journal,* Anna Howes wrote up a piece about the annual Martha's Vineyard Chili Fest and the money it raised for the Red Stocking Fund. The Chili Fest had been around about as long as she had been alive, but it was immeasurably bigger than in her childhood and almost convinced her the Vineyard had off-season nightlife. Hank continued to pretend he was fine, despite his demeanor seeping into even his most public moments.

Moments she was now paid to describe to *Journal* readers.

West Tisbury Will Let the River Run, by Anna Howes

After nearly 100 years of sitting silent, the Look Farm will once again operate a grist mill, thanks to a variance granted by the West Tisbury Zoning Board of Appeals. The variance will allow light industrial use in the residential/agricultural zone. The proposal allowed the addition of a culvert to a stretch of Beechtree Brook within the farm bounds, to power a small hydroelectric mill. The hotly contested issue was passed three votes to one, with newly appointed Board Chairman Henry Holmes dissenting.

"Despite Chairman Holmes' obstructionist inclinations, this is a win for the traditional character of the town," said BOS chairman Bernie Burt, who attended the meeting as an audience member. "The farm has been in the family for generations, and for more than a century, a small mill was operational on this site. We have that in the historical record." The mill fell into disuse in the 1920s, when the original culvert carrying water from the stream was broken during a botched Prohibition raid on a nearby still. The culvert fell into disrepair and was destroyed by Hurricane Carol in 1954.

"The stream has a stronger current than it did a century ago," says jubilant property owner Lucy Look-Dawson. "There's higher water volume—that means we can divert some of the flow but keep most of the stream undisturbed. This is the best possible outcome. We're thrilled." The Conservation Commission and DEP had previously reviewed the project, issuing an Order of Conditions. Both groups will continue to monitor the situation as the culvert is being rebuilt, to ensure that no damage will be done to the surrounding area, and to ensure that the plan is built to approved specs.

Lone dissenting officer Henry Holmes argued: "Moving water around constitutes trespassing. . . . If other properties have water rights to that stream, then diverting the water is actually theft."

To which Ms. Look-Dawson replied, placing a two-inch pile of correspondence on the table before Mr. Holmes, "All of the abutters are in support of this. We want to power the mill mostly so that school kids can come and see how to grind flour. We're working with the Heritage Grain Project and Whole Loaf Bakehouse to develop a grain-to-table project that will make sure the local kids understand how bread is made, and encourage their families to buy from local farmers."

While the other three members of the ZBA commended the project, Mr. Holmes continued to balk, saying, "The culvert is within the setback zone, where construction isn't allowed."

"It isn't *construction*," commented Mr. Burt. "It's a *pipe* . . ."

Nice article, said Orion's text. You get brownie points for mentioning Henry Holmes' obstreperousness.

"Did you really need to include the quote about water theft? Jesus," complained Hank, dozy on pain meds and beer.

PS: Stop trying to get yourself kicked off the ZBA beat, said Everett in an email.

HANK SHOUTED WITH pain in the middle of the night. The orthopedic doctor had warned Joanna to be vigilant—especially after Hank had canceled his follow-up appointment—and Celia had swapped vehicles with her in anticipation of things getting worse. They were worse.

Somehow, between his crutches and the hay cart, Joanna got Hank safely over the icy ground and shoehorned him into the Forester. His ankle was so swollen it pushed over the edge of the boot like a cupcake top, and each breath sounded like he was about to break into Gregorian chant. His breath had the sickly-sweet stench of rotting meat. When she put her hand to his brow, he was very hot and her palm came away damp. The route to the hospital had never seemed so long, even breaking the speed limit the whole way on the dark empty roads.

She had to wait an agonizing hour in the empty ER waiting room before anybody would tell her anything. At 3 A.M., a soft-spoken Jamaican nurse called her into the hallway to explain that Hank had osteomyelitis. Infection of the bone.

"I didn't know bone could get infected," she said weakly.

"They are going to have to drain the wound," he said. "And that means opening it up and possibly removing all the metal that is in there, because the metal causes a reaction—you know, there is a foreign body in the wound and the body doesn't like that."

"So . . . so what does that mean?" she asked.

"He's back on intravenous antibiotics right now, and we need to keep him here for a day or two to monitor him, make sure the antibiotics are working and that he doesn't get sepsis." She just stared. "As soon as it's drained and the swelling has gone down, sometime tomorrow, the orthopedist can immobilize the injury with external fixation. Like a cast, or a surgical sleeve," he added, seeing her confusion. "And then you may take him home."

"And then what?"

"Then it's just as if you're resetting his recovery back to day one. But hopefully it will all go smoothly now." And he smiled reassuringly.

Reassuring smiles were a dime a dozen in that ER.

IV
APRIL

JOANNA SPENT THAT DAY AND THE NEXT TRYING TO DIS-tract herself. First with a thorough cleaning and airing of Hank's bedroom and his corner of the bathroom, which the cats protested raucously. Then by contemplating the immense project of tidying up all the junk in the yard, but it was too muddy. March on the Vineyard equaled mud, and it was only the first of April. Instead of tackling the yard, she baked piles of food to get them through the next few weeks—casseroles, lasagna, chowder.

Hank came home after forty-eight hours in the ICU. His swollen, angry shin and ankle were now exposed and haloed by a sinister-looking bit of metal scaffolding, a sort of open-air Death Star/Erector Set mash-up. It took up more room than the boot had, making locomotion even clunkier and more cumbersome. He was furious at fate, and trying not to act furious at Joanna. Or at the patient home health aides who once again paraded through. She trimmed her schedule to be at home more often, as when she'd first arrived.

Orion texted her in the middle of that Thursday morning edit meeting at the *Journal* while Everett was crowing about the pinkletinks.

Each spring, the two papers competed, compulsively, to report the first pinkletinks. This year, a plumber had heard the shrill chorus of spring peepers—as pinkletinks were called off-Island—on his way out of a client's house off Lambert's Cove Road. Being nonpartisan, he had informed both of the papers, and both had immediately posted it online. But the *Journal* came out the day before the *Newes*, so the *Journal* got to herald the good news in print: It's spring! You read it here first! Everett, with close-lipped grin and terrier eyebrows raised high, was triumphant.

> Hope things are better with the family emergency . . .
> and if so . . . dinner? Tonight?

Her happily partnered friends in New York always warned her that saying yes to a spontaneous dinner was a terrible idea. But she wasn't in New York, and she was not enthusiastic about sharing reheated casserole with Hank while he sniped yet again about that asshole Orion Smith and then insisted upon using a Sam Adams lager to fortify the effect of his pain meds. She texted back under the table.

> Will meet you but will bring my own food again.

Almost immediately, Django Reinhardt's music began to play between her hands. All eyes at the table jerked in her direction. Reddening, she slid the ringer volume to mute and stared very deliberately in Everett's direction to demonstrate that she was not distracted. ". . . because when the shadbush blooms, that means the shad are running," he was explaining.

"Actually I don't think that's true anymore, because of climate change," said petite Sarah.

"I saw some in bloom," said Rosie, the Goth reporter with runic tattoos. "So I guess we could get a shot of that." She did not sound enthusiastic. Joanna could almost hear her thoughts: *This isn't our thing. This is the* Newes' *thing. Are we so pathetically short on real reporters that we have to write about flowering shrubs instead of issues?*

Under the table, Joanna felt the phone shudder slightly between her hands: a voice mail message. After a brief discussion about how heroically the herring were running, the edit meeting ended and she was able to huddle in a corner and check the message.

"I know you don't want to accept a gift from me, but I would love to cook you my grandmother's favorite recipe. Baked scallops with mushroom and cheese. Doesn't that sound delicious?"

She pulled her coat on and stepped outside into the sunshine, shielding herself from the harbor breeze behind the scraggly yellow of a forsythia bush. "Baked scallops with mushrooms is my favorite food group," she said into the phone, as soon as he answered.

"So come eat them," he cajoled.

She considered this as she watched a trio of seagulls circle, arguing, over Beach Road. "How about I pay you for the value of my share of the dinner. That way it's like we're going Dutch."

"All right." He chuckled. "I'll even give you a bill. It can be a business expense."

That evening she heated up a slab of tuna casserole for Hank, played a game of Scrabble with him while he ate it, and helped him to get into bed. He did not ask where she was off to. He was too dampened. It was early, but he was supposed to be horizontal most of the time anyhow. The narcotic painkillers meant he'd lost the Scrabble game, but also that he did not mind much.

She arrived at Orion's to a kitchen so full of tantalizing scents she felt she could almost recline against the aroma. "Four more minutes till it's out of the oven," he said, pacing slowly before the stove. "Exactly long enough to mix you a Manhattan." He headed toward the smaller pantry.

"Just a glass of wine," she said. "Add it to my tab."

"Yes, so about that tab," he said, rerouting toward a small refrigerator that sat on the counter beside the regular icebox. "What were you planning to pay?" He opened the door of the smaller icebox and pulled out a bottle of white wine.

She improvised. "A dinner like that would run about thirty bucks at a respectable restaurant. With the wine, let's call it forty."

"We don't eat at the same restaurants," he said. "I was thinking something closer to a hundred, and that's just for what's on the menu." He opened a drawer near the stove, which moved silently on its expensive runners, and retrieved a bottle opener. "When you consider the added artisanal value of an heirloom recipe . . . I think we're talking more like two hundred."

"Well, nice seeing you," she said, reaching for her coat.

He grabbed her arm with his free hand. "Wait, now," he said, soothingly. "You don't have to pay in currency."

"We agreed—"

"Oh, you have to pay," he said, with a sly smile. "But not in cash."

For one dizzy moment she thought he was pulling a *Fifty Shades of Grey*. And she felt something inside her clench as she admitted to herself that yes, she would allow that.

"You are transparent, Anna," he said, releasing her. He turned his attention to opening the wine bottle. "I don't mean anything indecent. I mean you can pay me back some other way. I would consider it fair payment for you to tell me some stories."

". . . what?" she said. *Erotic stories?* she hoped.

He gestured vaguely around. "This whole area. Before I settled in. How you used to picnic here, and all that. Give me a child's-eye view of the North Shore, of West Tisbury, of the Vineyard for year-rounders."

"Really?"

He nodded, twisting the corkscrew in deep. "Absolutely. I want to learn from the natives."

"Mmmm . . . a typical Vineyard childhood is notably lacking in misadventures," she said. "Winter's mostly frozen mud and spring's a lot of thawing mud. That's when skunks come out of hibernation and the ticks start looking for blood meals."

"If you're attempting to disenchant me, you'll have to try harder than that."

He uncorked the bottle and smiled at it approvingly. She thought for a minute about comical misdemeanors but could summon nothing anecdotal. A rural childhood was more romantic in *Charlotte's Web* than in real life, unless she wanted to wax poetical like a particularly soapy "On the Same Page" piece.

"Okay, how about this," she finally offered. "When we were kids, my friend Celia and I biked everywhere, and often on the main roads, in the summer, drivers would stop and ask us for directions. One Memorial Day, a car from off-Island slows down by us on the road—"

"How did you know it was from off-Island?"

"Well, it had New York plates, but if you're from here, you can tell an off-Island car anyhow."

"Really? Very intriguing. How?"

She realized she had no answer. "It's like Justice Stewart from the sixties talking about pornography. I know it when I see it. We all do. The Island gives everything a patina of some kind—oh, shut up," she said without malice, at his mocking laughter.

"Go on with the story," he said, as he went to the larger pantry for a wineglass. "Tell me what happened with the car that was missing a patina." He poured her a glass of wine, then turned the oven off and opened the oven door, from which escaped such a savory new aroma that she was distracted for a moment.

"Ahem," he said. "Patina. Bikes. Girls."

"Right. It's a big car, a fancy car, so automatically we don't like it—"

"I would expect nothing less from you than knee-jerk disdain—"

"—but we mutter to each other and agree that we're nice girls so we're going to be good."

"That's very big of you, since obviously an off-Island driver has no intrinsic right to be treated respectfully."

She glared comically at him. "So it stops, and the driver rolls down the window and asks us how to get to the Chilmark Store. We were near Priester's Pond, where you're sort of equidistant between North Road, South Road, and Middle Road—you can take any of them and end up at Menemsha Crossing. At the same moment, Celia points one way, and I point the other, and we both say, 'That way!'— completely straight-faced because we're both sincere. Then we each realize that the other one is also right, so at the same moment, we each reverse the direction we're pointing in, and say, 'Or that way!' And then we burst out laughing at ourselves. The guy in the car har-rumphs, rolls up his window, and drives off in a huff. We fell over on the side of the road from laughing so hard."

She gave him a *How's that?* look.

He grimaced. "Nah. I expected stories about a seriously darkened youth," he said. "I'm not impressed. Try again."

She could not talk about her private childhood, with failed parents who ceded her to other failed family members until finally she landed with a couple of functional alcoholics—Jen and Hank—who loved her fiercely but were cowed by her aspirations to move off-Island and live among the heathen Manhattanites. She could not reveal the terror that her own grudging attachment to the Island might entrap her like a gnat in honey and keep her as phobic of America as Hank was. She was not going to ruin a dinner date with this attractive, graceful man who did not know there were disassembled jeeps rusting by the chicken coop. Those stories were staying locked in the basement. On the Vineyard, those stories were sadly unoriginal, common as watercress in spring. She would not let them define her.

"How about the morning my high school classmate's dealer came to the bus stop and beat him up, right in front of me?"

"Better. I'd be more impressed if *you* were the dealer."

"My mom did that, it's not really my scene."

He sobered. "Oh. Shit. I'm sorry, Anna."

She shook her head and went for glib. "It's fine. I had a good childhood, grew up with salt-of-the-earth types who made sure I knew how to forage for mushrooms and milk a goat and shuck a scallop. If I'd gone with my mother, I'd have grown up in an off-Island suburb somewhere, spent my time hanging out at a mall or something. Blech."

He laughed, grateful she'd made it a joke. "Your Island snobbery really is *endless*, you know that?" he said, with a cocked eyebrow. He turned to open the oven door all the way and reached for a mitt. "Dinner's ready, but I need another story or you still owe me two hundred bucks."

They talked as if they were kids who had met on the playground, as if there were no looming lawsuit, or at least no newspaper coverage of it. Admitting she'd been stymied in her internet sleuthing, she asked him about his professional life. "I buy things and then I keep them for a while and then I sell them," he said. "It's not worth a conversation, it's the most boring thing about me. Let's talk about *interesting* things." So they discussed books and music and New York nightlife, something Joanna had nearly forgotten existed. They even perused national—not local—politics. He suggested a game of Scrabble, which she agreed to. The Scrabble box he brought out was mahogany, the board of stiffened leather, the tiles hardwood with gold-leaf embossed letters, and the tile racks brass. It probably cost as much as a plane ticket to New York. Or at least a helicopter ride. The game ended in a draw.

He was a perfect gentleman and did not make any kind of move on her. She left before it was indecorously late, needing to get home to check on Hank before lights-out. If she had stayed out as late as she wanted to, and then returned to find him face-planted in the bathroom, she would never have forgiven herself.

IT RAINED HARD overnight, and despite the dazzling blue sky come sunrise, the ground was the sort of mud that tries to suck one's boots off one's feet. The cats would not set paw outside. Hank, up and about for his thirty minutes of morning verticality, was confined to the back porch. His exposed shin was surrounded by its column of slender steel donuts. It looked angry, and cold. She tossed the food scraps out of their ceramic holder into the run, through the window in the chicken wire. Setting the bowl down on a hatchet-scarred oak stump, she went inside the coop, opened the yard door for the hens to go out, and scouted the nesting boxes for eggs. Three hens were hunkered down on nests of wood shavings and straw. Early spring was a broody time of year for them, and the Cochin muttered warningly at Joanna when she reached under the mottled feathers.

"Oh, stop," she muttered back, closing her hand around one warm egg. "If you were raising chicks you wouldn't have time to sunbathe. I know how you like to sunbathe. Really I'm doing you a favor."

As if convinced of the perils of maternity, the hen stood and paraded out of the box with an alto warble. The other two sitting hens, both Silkies, decided to join her, giving Joanna sour looks.

"Don't forget to check under Brunhilde!" Hank called from the porch. Brunhilde was the little red Bantam hen, Hank's favorite. She was cuter than the others. Also, he had decided her petite eggs each only counted as half an egg, which allowed him to ingest more cholesterol than the doctors wanted him to, while convincing himself he was doing no such thing. Joanna had stopped arguing with him about it.

Brunhilde was already outside and the nesting boxes revealed no Banty egg. "Nope," Joanna called back.

"Are you sure?" he said. "She hasn't laid an egg in about three days, that's not normal."

Joanna found it touching that he was concerned about a chicken.

"I'll check again this afternoon," she promised.

"You might as well bring some wood in while you're outside," he said, and pivoted back toward the back door. "Split some kindling while you're at it. Hang on, I'll get the axe."

Her inner child winced in anticipation of an earful. "I left it by the woodpile last time," she said.

He hinged back around on the crutches, leaning against the wall for balance. "Anna! The head's going to rust."

"If you kept it oiled, it wouldn't r—"

"If you brought it inside, I wouldn't have to oil it! You know you're supposed to bring it in, like you have been doing since the age of *five*!"

"If I'd been using an axe to chop kindling when I was five, social workers would have removed me from the property for my own safety," she snapped back. "And since Jen was a social worker, I *seriously* doubt I was using an axe at the age of five."

"Six then! Maybe you were six. Just put the damn thing away. I like that axe, I don't want to have to buy another one just because you were being neglectful." He turned and hobbled back into the house. It was nearly noon, so she guessed he was about to open his first beer.

"Who keeps an axe by the door, anyhow?" she grumbled to the chickens as she closed the coop.

After nesting the eggs in a carton inside the back door, she exited again to the woodpile, chopped an armful's worth of kindling, and brought that—along with the axe—in, as Hank retreated into the recliner to lambast CNN. She went out again, loaded the wheelbarrow with logs. The bark and dead lichen had a mossy stink and left organic grit on her leather work gloves. She thought of how delicate she'd recently been about a smear of grime from a subway turnstile dirtying her city gloves, and laughed at herself. She pushed the wheelbarrow back to the porch. Armful by armful she carried the logs across the room and stacked them in the woodbox, leaving a trail of bark and lichen and sow bugs to commemorate her path of travel. Once she'd emptied the wheelbarrow, she vacuumed the debris with the Dust-Buster.

The house had propane heat as well, but if the wood and the woodstove were on-site, it was a cozier heat, and cheaper. Hank had culled from the undeveloped parts of his property, which had been densely wooded with young oaks when he bought it more than forty years earlier. He had also, over the decades, struck temporary acquaintanceships with the seasonal property owners he otherwise scorned, and proposed that he "open up some vistas for them" in exchange for keeping the wood he felled. Currently there were four or five long, stacked piles of split cordwood within hauling distance of the house, each a different vintage. This winter, they were mostly burning white oak that Hank had felled and split three years ago from the friendly Republicans who had razed the original Hubert's Bakery.

After she'd brought the wood in, she went down to the post office before the lobby closed to pick up the mail. It was soothing to her, when she had occasion to go in there, that nearly always people recognized her, even if not by name. Just the face being familiar enough to warrant the kind of smile and hello that is saved for people you recognize. In the brief walk from the truck to the door to the counter and back out again, on every visit she was likely to encounter a familiar face in the lobby, even after all those years away. The lack of anonymity had been claustrophobic when she was younger. Now it felt soothing, reassuring. Now she needed it. Wondrous, how so small a thing as a neighbor at the post office could set things right again when they felt off. When she had first returned in January, the people who'd recognized her had looked startled at her presence. It had been pleasing to startle people a little. Now it was pleasing to be part of the scenery.

SHE SAW ORION the next day. They went on an impromptu muddy hike through a woody Land Bank property in Chilmark.

The scent of loam was everywhere, permeating everything. Even the moss and the sinuous, tangled roots of beech trees. Last year's pale copper leaves still clung to the twigs, shimmering in the breeze, adding light and texture to the soggy gray woodland. Rarer than beeches was the occasional lone holly tree, usually young, eternally robust and glossy in its muted surroundings. But most of these woods were just gangling oaks with rough bark, boasting barely even any branches but their leafless canopies. Everywhere was thigh-high underbrush of scraggly, leafless huckleberry and blueberry, underlain with the russet carpet of fallen oak leaves. Endless acres of this. The arboreal monotony calmed some part of her like a visual lullaby, soft and familiar from childhood.

They trooped up and down the wooded hills, the paths strewn with a confetti of twigs. The cloudy sky and raw breeze left everything feeling damp. In a streambed, frazil ice protested the rocks. Much of the trails hugged lichen-stained stone walls that were as bland as the oaks and the sky. These marked fields, but also ran throughout woodlands that had been meadows once.

"Those are called lace walls," Joanna said, nodding to a mossy stretch of the one to their left, half-hidden in the heap of dead oak leaves that lay along it.

"Lace, because of all the gaps."

"Yes—the Vineyard's stone walls are unique—"

"Of course they are," said Orion. "Everything about the Vineyard is unique. Everything is special. Nothing is ordinary like on the mainland. You guys are relentless."

"No, seriously, everyone knows this—"

"Everyone who's an Islander, you mean."

"No, even landscape historians and—"

He stopped abruptly and stared at her with a teasing expression. "You're all so desperate to maintain your status quo as the most special place on earth that you have to stoop to calling in landscape historians for backup? What the hell is a landscape historian?"

"See how they're made up of unshaped granite rocks?" she said. This was a recitation from her sixth-grade earth science class. "Not only is there no mortar or cement between the rocks, there's actually deliberate gaps."

"I've always assumed that's because the earlier settlers were too cheap or lazy to build solid stone walls, but now you will tell me that I'm wrong about that."

"You're wrong about that."

"Of course I am. Tell me what an ignorant wash-ashore I am. Tell me why they're so special."

"The Island used to be almost treeless, because the white settlers cut all the trees down for pastureland, and so the gaps are to let the winds rip across the fields unencumbered. The way big banners have holes cut in them so the wind doesn't tear them apart."

He considered this and shrugged agreeably. "That's as good an excuse as any to not bother building a proper wall," he said.

"They've held up for centuries without maintenance—that's unusual for stone walls. And there's a serious craft to building them, because they're all relying on the pressure of their neighbors—you take away one rock and three others fall out of place. It's all interconnected."

He gave her a slightly mocking smile. "Let me guess, that's a metaphor for how the Island community works, and the lace walls are your totem animals?"

"It's an *art form*. Take a good look."

He took a good look. "Okay," he said after a meditative moment. His tone was softer. "I see it." And then in a respectful, solemn tone: "Thank you for admitting me to the cabal of people who cavort with landscape historians."

She'd chosen this trail, so far up-Island, because she wanted to avoid running into anyone she knew who might recognize Orion Smith. He agreed to it because he wanted to survey more of her childhood haunts. Her childhood had more of a romantic patina for him than it did for her.

They walked for an hour under bleak skies, the persistent nothingness of Vineyard spring seeping into their coats and boots and gloves. Each skirted the details of sundry memories and youthful misadventures. He described a relentlessly manicured childhood, including summers in the house he now inhabited. They were about the same age but had never met during those summers, "Because you were busily being trained to be a proper rich kid, right?" she teased.

He laughed once, softly, a smiling *hmph*, and said, "If you insist."

There was a certain confidence that came of knowing how to swing tennis rackets and golf clubs by the age of eight. And that confidence could—in his case, did—extend to a glowing sense of agency and self-regard in other particulars of one's life. She could find no way to express it that wouldn't be rude, but the country-club gloss was his least agreeable quality. He was a handsome man, certainly, and she was taken with his particular charisma, but he would have been immeasurably more compelling were he not so Teflon-coated. She found him more alluring for having learned to bake with his grandmother, and less alluring for having learned to sail simply because that is what his kind of people did. Especially as his grandmother sounded like the most interesting person in his family: she had the public affect of a 1950s housewife, he said, but she was a card shark and smoked clandestine cigars, and generally sounded like somebody Joanna would have sold a kidney to interview, were she still among the living.

By the end of their ramble, it was drizzling hard enough to be called a proper rain, and with noses and fingertips red and nearly numb, they hied themselves back to his house for tea and biscotti to defrost and defog. Once they'd shed their soggy outerwear and the kettle was heating up, Joanna threw a couple of dollars on the smooth granite counter, her gesture of refusing to accept a gift of any size. He grinned at her and then swiped it, shoving the bills into the hip pocket of his jeans. "This friendship is costing you a lot of money," he said. "You must really like me. How about a Scrabble rematch?"

She won. He was impressed.

Then she hurried home to take care of Hank and polish her stories for both papers. The *Journal* needed an update on the proposed moped ban; a profile of a Brazilian business owner; mini-features on the lacrosse and baseball coaches, whose seasons were opening at the high school. Lewis at the *Newes* had asked Joey Dias to write about a study of erosion at Squibnocket Beach and do an "On the Same Page" profile of a newly reinstalled local cop who had returned home after quitting his post with a federal law enforcement agency because he found their treatment of immigrants so hostile. This was on the same page as an article from the earliest years of the *Newes* about the salutatory economic impact of the recent wave of Azorean immigrant seamen.

The cop, she discovered when she interviewed him, was young, lived in Oak Bluffs, and never read either paper, so there was no danger of his realizing who she was.

She got her copy in to both papers by Wednesday afternoon, in time to kibitz during the floating potluck-poker game.

This was the second time it had been at Hank's since the accident, but the first time that he could help prep for it, despite being nearly immobile—something he felt the need to point out twice. She jury-rigged a cutting board so that he could safely keep it on his lap to slice cheese, and he was pleased to be useful. He was allowed up for longer periods now, but still he could only walk with the crutches.

Celia and her soft-spoken boyfriend Ted attended, as did Helen and Paul Javier, and Everett, who had grown up with Hank. Nearly all the conversation was about either Orion Smith or the upcoming Annual Town Meeting.

The rule was always to eat and drink before playing poker, because it was easier to trick people when they were sated and tipsy. Celia set a loaf of warm corn bread on the table, a new recipe she was developing. There was appreciative cooing. The cooing grew in decibels when Ted plunked a gallon of homemade ale beside it, making the old wooden table shudder. Joanna had chowder reheating. Everett had brought signature cheeses from each of the four island dairies. The fire was blazing in the woodstove and Helen was mulling cider in a ceramic pot sitting on it. Gathered around the table, they all looked like the establishing shot for an indie home-for-Christmas-in-New-England movie. With mud outside instead of snow.

"I can never sit through a Town Meeting, because they're four hours long," said Celia, cutting the corn bread. "And Wednesdays are my early mornings. Why the hell are the Town Meetings always Tuesday nights?"

"Same reason Election Day is," said Hank, who always liked to know the answer to things. He was in the recliner, with his leg up on pillows. His beer rested on the battered Scrabble box on the side table. His holding-forth tone suggested she should start to count his empties. "Back in the day, back before cars and paved roads, it gave people time to get to the meeting place, or the polling place, or whatever. You couldn't travel on the Sabbath, right? No, you couldn't.

And this time of year, the thaw is finished but not all the mud and muck has dried up, and travel was a pain in the butt. It took a full day for some people to get to the meeting, and they couldn't start the journey until Monday morning, so that's why it's a Tuesday."

"Nice try, but that doesn't hold up," said Everett. "When my dad was a kid in Chilmark, they had the Town Meeting during the day, and the school kids attended. And it was always on a Monday. In fact, it's still on Mondays."

Hank finished his beer, tossed the can into an open grocery bag near the trash that was collecting the empties, and cheerfully opened another one. "Chilmark is full of rich Jewish folk and they all go to synagogue on Friday nights, so that means they could spend Sunday traveling to Town Meetings, so that's why it could be on Monday," he declared.

They all stared at him. "Hank," Joanna finally said. "Chilmark was not full of rich Jewish folk back before there were cars."

"Obviously," he said. "Before there were cars, most of the Island Jews lived in Vineyard Haven near the Hebrew Center, so they could walk to Friday night services there."

"Probably so," she said. "And that doesn't explain why Chilmark has their Town Meeting on a Monday instead of a Tuesday."

Hank's beer intake was significant enough to propel him to a new conversational track. "Hey, Celia! Your folks took me to the Fish Fry at the PA Club last week, and said they were heading off on a cruise soon. So let me ask you: Are they crazy?"

"No," Celia assured him.

"Yes, they are," Hank corrected her. "How crazy do you have to be to leave a place surrounded by water you're not going to swim in to pay a ton of money so that you can be someplace else completely surrounded by water you're not going to swim in. How is that smart? When did they become people who go on a cruise?"

"I love going on cruises," said Celia.

"Inherited stupidity," said Hank, somehow sounding friendly.

"Ahem," said Helen, "Paul and I are about to go on a cruise around the world."

"That's different," said Hank. "You're going on real boats— freight boats, and schooners, and I dunno, kayaks. Not cruise ships. Cruise ships are ridiculous."

Helen turned her patient gaze from Hank to Joanna. "Speaking of vacations, Anna, do you need one?"

The gentleness almost undid her. Before she could answer, Hank sneered at Helen: "What are you asking *her* for? *I'm* the one who's stuck inside all day, I'm the one who needs a change of pace. She can go out and about whenever she likes, wherever she likes! She's got it easy. Plus she's not in pain! She's not racking up hospital bills! She's not bedridden! Where the fuck, Helen, where the *fuck* do you get off asking Anna if *she* needs a vacation?"

A thick blanket of silence immediately smothered all conversation. Hank did not notice or care. "She's got it easy, she's got a free place to live, people are practically throwing food at us, she uses my truck whenever she wants, and all she's doing for work, if you can even call it work, is showing up every day at the *Journal* so Everett can tell her what gossip to hunt down for the week."

"Hey now!" Everett barked, pulling away from the table. He was too avuncular to get angry at anyone, but he was thrown, almost puzzled, by the sudden outrage. "Hank, jeez, calm down."

"That wasn't kind, Hank," said Helen.

"You don't get to say what's kind and what isn't," Hank bellowed. "You're kowtowing to *Anna* about how hard her life is—her life isn't hard, her life is so fuckin' easy compared to mine! Who's the widowed one? Who's gonna get condescended to in the papers by that rich asshole playboy with the helicopter? Who deserves a vacation? *Me*, that's who." He picked up the Scrabble box and flung it into the corner, just above the television set. It tore open, wooden tiles bursting like kindergarten confetti across the corner of the room. The cats had been napping, curled up together on the couch; they leapt up howling with shock when a tile landed near them, and darted off into the darkness of Hank's bedroom. The board smacked against the wall and then plummeted awkwardly, bent, to the floor.

The silence was so perfect, they could hear one log tumble off another within the woodstove.

"That's true," said Helen, effortlessly gracious. "You're right, Hank, and I'm sorry I didn't think of you. You both deserve vaca—"

"No," he said. "No, that's such bullshit. Anna doesn't need a fucking vacation, Anna is *on* a fucking vacation."

"She's working for me—" Everett began but Hank galloped right over him: "It's a working vacation! She likes to write, she does that in her spare time for fun, so she's doing exactly what she would be doing anyhow except she's managing to get paid for it!" He glowered at Joanna and then turned back to Everett. "As a matter of fact, Everett, there's something you don't know—"

"Hank!" Joanna and Helen both hissed.

"There's a lot of things Everett doesn't know," said Celia with a too-boisterous laugh. "No offense, Everett."

He shrugged. "I'm just the managing editor of the paper. Why should I be in the loop about anything?"

Hank tried again: "You think you have such a loyal little reporter here in Miss Anna Howes—"

"*Ms.* Anna Howes," said Helen. "And by the way, stop talking, Hank. Have some more beer."

"Here's the truth you need to know about your favorite new reporter," Hank sneered to Everett. "She's actually writing—"

"Oh no, don't tell him! It was supposed to be a surprise, Hank. She's actually writing rock songs," said Celia, roaring with laughter. At her beckoning, her quiet boyfriend Ted also began to laugh. Helen joined him, and because Helen laughed, so did Paul.

"Bullshit!" shouted Hank. "That's not what—"

"Well, the lyrics anyhow," said Celia, as if Hank had been correcting her. She assertively made eye contact with Everett and then moved toward the kitchen so that his attention was wrested from Hank. "When Hank was delirious with morphine, she took dictation on whatever he was talking about and now she's trying to turn it into a soundtrack called *The Morphine Variations*. Hey, Hank, lemme pour you some more beer."

"Shut up and listen to me!" Hank shouted, but he looked confused. Celia had distracted him enough that he couldn't remember what he'd been just about to say, so he resorted to a generic complaint: "There is *nothing* about her life that makes her need a vacation. Jesus, you people."

There was a long, horrible silence. Then: "Celia!" said Ted—not the quickest or wittiest one among them, or so Joanna would have said until that moment. "Weren't you going to take Anna out to see a movie?"

"Yeah," said Paul Javier, leaping in a little lamely. "I can help get Hank to bed. You ladies go paint the town red."

"There is no town," Celia said laughing, not getting it. "Or paint, for that matter."

"That's right, Celia," said Helen. "I think there's a late show for that new, um, comedy."

"Right," said Celia, switching gears instantly once she understood. "Of course, how could I forget. Come on, Anna, let's go."

"See!" shouted Hank. "It's that simple for her! She wants to go do something, she just goes to do it! Never mind about me, oh, no!"

"Hank, I said I'd help you turn in tonight," said Paul.

"Good, I hope you do it better than she does," he sneered. "I can't believe what I have to put up with here, I swear to God."

"Come on, kiddo, we're going to miss the previews," said Celia, urgently shrugging herself into her coat. "The previews are the best part." She grabbed Joanna's warmest coat off the hook by the door and tossed it to her. "Let's go, put it on in the car."

THE MOON WAS clouded over and the platinum light was diffuse across the yard and the driveway. It was colder and damper outside

than it would be in New York City. After nearly three months Joanna still hadn't adjusted. The cold slithered into her all the way
to her core. "*Wow*, is he an asshole," Celia said. Mutely, shivering,
Joanna got in the passenger side, holding her coat limp in her hands.
"You know he doesn't mean any of that, right?" Celia said. "He's
just venting, he's ranting, he won't remember any of it tomorrow
and if he does he will feel like such a jerk. You know that, right?"

"I guess," Joanna murmured. She couldn't think where to go that
would feel safe.

"Put your coat on, kiddo. We're not really going to the movies,"
Celia said. "You know that, right? It's after nine on a Wednesday
night in April, so nothing's playing and nothing's open and it's forty
degrees out. We're going to my house to watch *Star Trek* on DVD
and drink homemade beer, how's that?"

So they did that.

Celia's winter rental felt like a college dorm but it was proverbi-
ally warm and cozy. And the beer was excellent. Joanna almost told
Celia she was somewhat dating the town's enemy, but didn't have
the energy to get into it. It was not a theme that would go well with
the preestablished drama of the evening.

A couple of hours later, she was finally completely calm. Ted came
home in Hank's truck, tapping mud off his shoes on the doorjamb.

"He's asleep," he said in a conspiratorial tone, handing her the
truck keys. "And he was really drunk, if that wasn't obvious. He
might not even remember in the morning. But you don't have to
worry about him tonight, we got him tucked in and everything.
You have a lot of work on your hands there, you know that?"

"Thanks," she said. "I guess. But thanks. Especially for putting him to bed."

Once home, and curled up in bed with a cat at her feet, she fantasized that it was summer and all of this had blown over. She tried to send Orion antilitigious energy waves, until she remembered she didn't actually believe in things like "energy waves" (despite finding the idea of them cool and intriguing in junior high), so she was just wasting her time. She finally fell asleep and woke up the next morning feeling miserable.

Although not as miserable as Hank. His hangover—or pretense of one—was so extreme that it prevented even the slightest effort at apology or peacemaking. With a sulky silence between them, she stoked the woodstove embers and added wood, cooked some oatmeal, brewed herself a thermos of tea for the day, made a turkey sandwich for his lunch, and set up both the couch and the recliner with large glasses of water in easy reach. She went to let the chickens out into their run. Coming back inside, she picked up as many of the Scrabble tiles as she could find and put them back in what was left of the torn box. The board was too bent to ever be played on again. She placed it on the table and Hank ignored it. She left for the *Journal* office without either of them having said a thing to each other.

She parked by the boatyard, let the cry of the gulls and the marine smell of the saltwater and diesel fumes wash over her a moment, and then went inside, just in time for the start of the edit meeting. Everett gave her a kindly look but said nothing. After the roundtable, he issued her marching orders, which included covering the Annual Town Meeting, the only thing anyone in West Tisbury wanted to talk about.

And—as always—Lewis Worthington called as the edit meeting was wrapping up. As always, her stomach clenched when she saw his number on her screen; as always, her mind rushed through a dozen possible scenarios that would rip her from her Island livelihood; as always, she forced herself to count slowly to three before answering her phone. As always, she told herself this somehow had to stop immediately, she could not continue hiding in plain sight.

And as always, Lewis was merely pitching an idea for the following week's "On the Same Page" that Joey Dias managed to agree to without letting anyone in the *Journal* offices know what Anna Howes was talking about. This week, it was a profile of the curator of the hospital's art collection on the same page as a story from 1922 about construction of the original hospital.

EXCEPT FOR HER own duplicity, and especially the stress she put herself in because of it, Joanna liked that all this happened. She liked that every Thursday morning there was this meeting, with these people, and it was interrupted by that phone call, with that person. That she'd floundered into such baroque deceit was surreal to her. She could barely contemplate any steps to rectify it; being disingenuous was so alien to her that part of her refused to register

that it was what she was doing daily now. She'd never been a fur-
tive person—indeed she was generally too much of an open book,
and her childhood custody chaos had unfolded so publicly that
she was accustomed to erring on the side of public disclosure. Her
conditioning had taught her secrecy meant shame, and all secrets
should be exposed. So she didn't like that part. But she loved the
regularity and the structure of this life she was building, and above
all, she liked the people themselves. She loved that she woke up in
the morning with the mission to tell these stories about these people
and places. Brian had been right. She wanted a live-in monogamous
relationship with Martha's Vineyard.

Too bad her landlord was being such a ninny.

When she got home, her arms freighted with canvas grocery bags,
Hank was watching CNN and contesting a business-suited woman's claims about single-payer health insurance. He was passionate
and articulate, and could no longer blame his silence toward her on
his hangover.

"Hey," she said.

"Hello," he said, managing to sound ironic. And then he said
nothing else. So neither did she. He eventually resumed his debate
with the television. It was a Thursday evening. If she were in New
York, she'd have just spent the day on household chores and errands,
and would now be about to go out with Roz and Viola, her two clos-

est friends, to dinner and then a movie, or a play, or a concert. Every week a different restaurant somewhere in the city. Every Thursday. She'd forgotten that until this instant, and wondered what it meant that she remembered it now, so soon after confessing to herself that she wanted to set anchor here.

She put the groceries away in the pantry and refrigerator, started a load of laundry in the basement, loaded the woodstove with more logs, and then, with the talking heads of cable news as soundtrack, she fed the chickens and the cats and the birds and the grumpy invalid. She begrudged Hank not one moment of her energy, but the silence—the gruff, embarrassed, cold-shouldering silence that was only made more obvious by the television's blathering—she could not take much more of it. When Orion texted a request for another potluck the next night, she accepted at once, and did not bother to tell Hank where she would be going. It was, she realized, a throwback to teen years under his inconsistent home rule, that she even thought she needed his permission to go out.

DINNER WAS HUMBLER this go-round: clam chowder for Joanna, hamburgers for Orion (from local cows, of course). It felt positively domestic. Following dinner, a Scrabble game on the elegant wooden board. Orion, to his overweening satisfaction, won. There was less flirtatious energy, and Joanna began to wonder if they were over the potential-romance hump, and on their way to a genuinely platonic friendship. She was disappointed at that prospect, even though she'd been in no rush for anything to evolve between them. Her life had felt in limbo and she'd been enjoying limbo with Orion too. As she was leaving, and he was standing in the door to see her off, he held up his hand.

"Before you go, I need to tell you something off the record," he said.

She felt a dull thud in her stomach. He wasn't looking at her.

"I thought by now it was clear everything between us is off the record," she said.

"Everything between us is *irrelevant* to the record," he corrected. "This is not. But it's still got to be off the record. For now. Until you hear it from another source."

That meant she wouldn't want to hear it. "Go on," she said and stepped back inside, pulling the door closed again against the chill.

Orion shifted his weight as if he was uncomfortable, behavior that was alien to him. He continued not looking directly at her. "The ZBA will have received a notice from my lawyer today that I have formally initiated the lawsuit."

She checked her mental calendar. "They meet on Thursdays and today's Friday so they might not know."

"Well, they'll know soon, and Curmudgeon Holmes is going to be hurling abuses on my head, and I know you're covering that beat so you'll hear all about it then. But it felt wrong not telling you myself."

"Thanks," she said. "Um. I can't pretend I don't have an opinion about this."

"I realize that," he said briskly, sounding briefly like a businessman. So this was why he hadn't put any moves on her tonight. "But hopefully this will all get resolved pretty quickly. Then it just won't even be an issue anymore." He gave her a thin, polite smile.

"I wouldn't bet on that," she said.

He shook his head and moved slightly away from her in the vestibule, his energy kinetic and ungrounded for him. "They'll want it all resolved before summer so it doesn't tarnish their appeal to the summer people."

"I wouldn't bet on that either," she said. "Some of them don't care about the summer people. Some of them would actually love to give the summer folks a reason *not* to come."

"Not really," he said. "That's just Yankee bluster. Even Henry Holmes. They want the dollars."

She shrugged, enervated by the conversation.

"Anyhow," he said, heaving a sigh. "I thought you should know."

"Well, thanks," she said. "You know I'm not happy to hear it. And you know why."

"Yes, and I appreciate that you like me despite this reminder that I am the incarnation of everything that is despoiling your beautiful nineteenth-century sensibilities. Given those sensibilities, it's strange you write for the *Journal* and not the *Newes*. But I know you'll stay objective when you have to write about it," he said. "I don't expect preferential treatment because you like me, nor do I expect excoriation because you don't like me."

That last bit sounded rehearsed to her, but she simply nodded. "Agreed. Goodnight, Orion," she said, and opened the door again. "See you after the Annual Town Meeting."

Hank finally spoke to her for real Saturday afternoon. There was no détente or apology. He simply forgot not to speak to her, and asked if she knew where the remote was. From there it was a slippery slope for him. By dinner he had asked what was for dessert, by bedtime he had inquired how much kindling she'd split for the stove, and the next morning he started chatting gruffly at breakfast as if nothing had ever happened. And she was enough of a Yankee, herself, to let it slide. It wasn't worth getting into.

She spent the weekend cranking out a profile about the retiring Menemsha harbormaster. Then she spent Monday morning rewriting it, after she realized she had confused her newspapers, and written it as if it were for the *Newes* rather than the *Journal.*

Tuesday morning, Hank learned about Orion's letter.

She was never clear how this happened, since Hank could not leave the house and would have had no reason to call in to the Town Hall. Unless he was bored. Terribly, oppressively bored. All right then, yes, that would have done it.

She was reading on her bed—*Love in the Time of Cholera,* not for the first time—and the April chill was offset by a small space heater she'd pinched from Hank's workshop in the basement. One of the cats was curled up against her leg.

"That asshole!" she heard him shout over the dull burr of the heater. It was loud enough that even the cat startled. Hank uttered some other colorful things, so she put down García Márquez and went, with the cat, into the main part of the house. She expected to see Hank raging at Anderson Cooper, or perhaps Wolf Blitzer. But he was glaring at a piece of paper.

"What's wrong?" she asked.

"Orion Smith is suing," he said in a voice chalky with bitterness.

"You got the letter already?" she said. "But didn't it—" And then she immediately shut up before she put her foot all the way down her throat.

"What do you mean?" he demanded, looking up at her sharply. "How did you know there's a letter?"

She opened her lips and several generations of the syllable "um" stumbled out, before she could form a coherent thought. "I just meant, you know, the inevitable letter," she said. "You've all known he was planning to sue for weeks, right? Months, even? That's all I meant."

"But why did you say *already*?" pressed Hank. "What did you know about it?"

"Did I say already?" she asked, feeling herself turn pink. "I don't know why I said that. It was just a word that came out of my mouth." She felt as if she were a drone moving smoothly over the person of Joanna Howes, imagining what it might be like to be her—but not quite actually being her. Just listening to her.

Hank decided to accept this. He returned his attention to the letter. "Asshole," he grumbled again. "What does he think is going to happen?" He wasn't talking to her. He wasn't even talking *at* her. He was monologuing. He was pleased to have an audience but he'd have been just as happy to rehearse in solitude, or for the cats. She felt herself return to her body as he boomed ahead: "I mean even if he were to win this lawsuit—which isn't going to happen, it's an absolutely open-and-shut case—but even if he did win it, it would be meaningless because the FAA would probably shut him down. It is a gratuitous waste of taxpayer money."

"Well, at least it gives you something to do with your spare time," she said, hoping she sounded jovial and teasing.

He gave her an incredulous look. "No it doesn't," he said. "I'm not the defense attorney. I'm not on the Board of Selectmen. I'm the ZBA. I'm Exhibit A in the lawsuit. That's all. My job is just to show up and sit in the audience and look stoic, and say *no comment* when the papers ask for details."

"I promise not to ask for details," she said quickly.

"Oh, Jesus, that's right," he said, with an irritated sigh. As if he'd been on the ZBA first, and she'd come along and gratuitously gotten herself assigned to write about him. "Don't ask for details. Of me. Of anyone. He must be doing this to get attention. Don't let him have any. Don't give him any press."

"Not my call," she said.

"Of course it is. Don't abrogate your responsibility of decent journalism. Tell Everett you refuse to write about him because there's nothing of substance to *say*. The *Newes* has got it right this once, not the *Journal*—ignore the bastard. What an ignorant jerk. Why does God put people like that on the planet?"

"To give you something to talk about," she said, in her fading attempt at playfulness. He chuckled wanly, but not the way she'd hoped he would. He often enjoyed getting irate, but he was not enjoying this.

TUESDAY NIGHT WAS the Annual Town Meeting.

Anyone who has never attended an Annual Town Meeting should head to New England and remedy that. If you've ever wondered who We the People really are, they're the ones who show up every year and keep their butts in those industrial stacking chairs for four hours at a go, except for when they stand up to respectfully denigrate each other's intelligence, morals, values, and integrity. It would take an epic poem to describe the world of a Town Meeting.

Joanna had attended every Town Meeting from birth until she went off to college, so she had never voted in one but she knew the superstructure as well as she knew her multiplication tables:

The evening's program was spelled out in a warrant, with articles. A lot of these were rote spending articles. If the Finance Committee vetted and approved it, then generally it would get passed. The Finance Committee was made up of ordinary taxpaying residents, volunteering their time and judgment for a remuneration that would not quite cover the cost of the coffee they drank during Fin-Comm meetings. Anything involving the police or firemen or EMS or school generally passed with minimal debate. Anything involving conservation land or affordable housing was debated ad nauseam, and then generally passed. Grand, finance-free gestures of the town's Progressive Ethos always passed, which the nonprogressive minority found blisteringly smug.

And every year, there was at least one tumultuously important Town Problem that caused a disproportionate amount of debate and angst and immediate family members not speaking to each other for days, and extended family not speaking to each other for weeks. One year the Town Problem was whether or not to allow dogs on the town beach. One year it was whether or not to allow beer and wine to be sold at restaurants. One year it was about solar energy panels being put up on town buildings. One year it was a return to the dogs-on-the-beach issue.

Hank had wanted to come. He'd never missed a meeting, in more than half a century. But Joanna convinced Helen and Paul to scold him with her, and, pouting, he'd agreed to stay home.

Nor, to her disappointment, did she see Orion. She wondered if he'd meant any of that stuff about the thrill of direct democracy in action, or if that was just a good pickup line to use at a political forum.

Hundreds of people crowded through the doors to the school gym, targeted a place to sit in the rows of chairs spread across the hardwood flooring, took off coats, waved to friends, gave political adversaries a cold shoulder, settled in with knitting or sudoku puzzles or cell phones. This was a return to a childhood ritual for her. She was here not as voter but as witness. She was over the discomfort from a few months earlier, of seeing familiar faces and fearing they knew what she was up to; now people were used to her presence, and her note-taking, and her reports. It helped that she wasn't writing features for the *Journal*—that she wasn't editorializing or inserting herself into what she wrote. She gave nobody any reason to feel defensive or self-conscious in her presence. She was here to do her job: report on the meeting for the *Journal*.

And also to do her other job: reporting on it for the *Newes*.

She walked to the side of the gym with her fellow nonvoters, property owners who were registered to vote off-Island but wanted to know where their property taxes were going; a handful of high school students probably here as a project for a civics class; resident aliens, largely Brazilians. The nonvoters numbered, in all, perhaps two dozen, and as a group they were not in the line of sight of the video camera recording the evening's events. But she sat on the top bleacher as far back in the gym as she could, to prevent anyone looking over her shoulder, however innocently, and seeing what she was writing. She pressed her back into the wall as if she would make herself disappear into it, then pulled out her laptop, opened two different Word documents, and sized them both down to fit together in the window. She darted looks at the people closest to her, with a sour expression intended to prevent anyone from coming close, but nobody was paying attention to her. She took an approximate head count for both papers; there were about three hundred people present. That was more than enough to make a quorum, in a town of 2,600 voters.

For the *Journal*, she reviewed the pile of leaflets and brochures she'd been energetically handed by canvassers outside the school doors, and marked which organization was batting for which measures. Everett would take that info and have an intern figure out who was funding what, in case there was a story hiding in plain sight (her guess was there would not be, but he was a newspaperman and hope springs eternal for a scandal).

For the *Newes*, Joey Dias wrote an on-the-fly critique of the town's current poet laureate Bettina Snow's recitation of her poem "Takemmy Hills." Joey Dias gave it a positive review, of course.

Happily, Joanna genuinely liked it, but she'd have given it a glowing review in any case, because she saw Bettina not infrequently at the grocery store and occasionally even walking along the wintry beach. Even if Bettina did not clock her as Joey Dias, she'd have a visceral urge to hide if they crossed paths.

For both papers she jotted down the news of the upcoming Town Picnic, with the *Newes* receiving the lion's share of information about the historical significance of the picnic and the *Journal* emphasizing what people should bring to it. Hippie Richard Burton, aka Moderator Peter Cooke, called the meeting to order, and the rest of the evening was a civic lovefest. It was spirited chaos at times, and at one point a debate about mending the cemetery fences became exasperating ("Dead people don't need to be fenced in unless they become zombies, in which case these fences will not save us," etc.). But compared to the harsh ugliness of politics off-Island, these people were practicing that slippery alchemy called democracy. As had been true since she was old enough to understand what taxes were, Joanna was enthralled by what people could make happen with a simple *aye* or *nay*.

Both papers would hear all about the budget, although the *Journal* readers would hear more about the proposed expansion of the light industrial district while *Newes* readers would get more of the skinny on monies being spent on upkeep—keeping the Ancient Ways cleared and mowed, for example—and the perennial arguments about dredging the Mill Pond.

Before they began the spending articles, Bernie Burt, as chair of the Board of Selectmen, took the floor to advise that the line item for legal services should go up because the town was being sued by Orion Smith of North Road. The town shared a collective hiss at this news—a hiss not worthy of mention in the *Newes*, but certain to be immortalized in the *Journal*. There was debate. The debate consisted mostly of Martin Howes (a relation so distant Joanna could not track it) insisting, despite town counsel assuring him he was mistaken, that if there were no money for a lawyer, the state would assign the town a district attorney, as it would for any other indigent defendant. Therefore, argued Martin (or Mr. Howes, as Anna Howes would report him in the *Journal*; Joey Dias knew the *Newes* would find it uncouth to cover this bit), not only should the town not vote to raise the funds, but it should in fact dissolve and redistribute whatever funds were currently in the legal coffers, to ensure the town would qualify for a DA. He suggested the funds be used instead to buy a new police car, at which point the chief of police stepped up to the audience microphone to politely inform Martin his department was not in need of a new vehicle.

In the end, a motion was grimly made, grimly seconded, grimly voted on, and passed: $100,000 would be raised and appropriated as a war chest for the upcoming legal battle. The town openly loathed Orion Smith. Never mind about the helicopter; now he was costing them money.

Both papers would also hear about the town's vote to donate a thousand dollars to next month's fund-raiser for the Jennifer Holmes Memorial Scholarship, created in honor of the departed wife of the town's own Henry Holmes, who was not present tonight because in trying to prove he was tougher than a nor'easter, he had jumped off his roof and broken every bone in his body, hahahaha. The town formally sends condolences and hopes he is up and about again, causing new trouble, soon.

"Nice coverage," said Everett, glancing over his shoulder when she stuck her head in. He swiveled away from the computer screen tucked in the corner, and stretched his arms up over his head with a yawn as she settled onto the visitor's chair.

"I have to come clean," she said.

He stopped stretching, to give her an arch look. "Something happen with Mr. Smith?" He sounded hopeful, the bastard.

"No," she said, blushing.

"Not *yet*," he corrected her with a jocular leer, and settled back into his chair. "So then, is this about Hank being the new ZBA head again?"

"Sort of," she said. "In part. This has been bothering me for weeks, Everett—"

"Stop beating yourself up," he said gruffly. "You didn't plan any of this, it all happened *to* you. I'm the one choosing to keep you on the story, so it's on me if you stumble. But you won't. You're conscientious. You have integrity."

"No, Everett, I really don't. That's the reason I'm here this morning." She hesitated. If only she could do this by email. Or telepathy. "I have to tell you something you really don't know. And it's the reason you should pull me."

He gave her an encouraging shrug. "All right, lay it on me."

"There's a writer for the *Newes*, you've probably seen the byline a few times without the penny dropping. A new writer. Joey Dias."

"So?"

"Everett. Think about it."

It took him a moment. It was fifteen years since he'd been her boss at the *Newes*. When he realized, he made a face like a fish drowning in oxygen.

"Joanna," he said, slowly. Then: "*Why?*"

"You know why—I needed the money!" she said.

"But the *Newes*? Really? That effete country-club newsletter? The one *you* referred to as the enemy?"

"They're the only other paper here," she said, defensive.

"You've got a successful freelance career in New York. *Surely* you could have gotten an assignment. Which would have paid a hundred times what the *Newes*—"

"I interview people face-to-face, that's what I'm known for, and those are the only gigs I get. The Anna Howes brand, or mystique, or whatever nonsense you want to call it, is all about sharing personal space, so nobody even wants to Skype with me."

"With the fees you get you could certainly fly—"

"Everett, you can't talk me into having done something differently in the past," she said, almost snappy. "I can only change things from this moment going forward, and I think the change should be that I back off of covering this story for you. It's just *wrong*. If I'm working for both papers, I still make enough money to pay my bills, and there's less culpability for you."

He frowned at her. "Who knows about this?"

Sometimes she wasn't certain of that herself. "Hank, who doesn't seem to care. Helen Javier, who says she doesn't care. Celia, who thinks it's hilarious. And my former math teacher who works for the *Newes,* but he won't tell them because he's the one who got me in there. And James Sherman might have figured it out by now, but he's distracted with his new grandchild off-Island somewhere."

Everett sighed with aggravation and impatiently massaged the bridge of his nose. "Okay, so," he said irritably, ". . . are you covering *this* story for them?"

"I covered a couple of Zoning Board meetings for them. You may have noticed, they're not very interested in it."

"That makes you sneaky—as if that wasn't already clear—but if you're not currently covering it for them, then it's not actually a conflict of interest. I've got *nobody* else who can do this."

"What happened to Susan Grant? It's her beat, right? I literally have never *met* her and I've been here nearly three months."

"She had a family crisis off-Island, and I don't know when she'll be back."

"Everyone's leaving the Island to attend to family crises."

"Except you," said Everett. "Your family crisis brought you *back* here." He grimaced. "Look, Anna, you're freelance so you have the right to do features somewhere else. I'm appalled that you didn't tell me, but that's more of a personal offense than a professional one."

"I'm sorry, Everett, it just felt so awkward. I've never been in a position like this before."

"And you've handled it horribly," he said, his brows so knitted they shaded his eyes. "But, like I said, I got nobody. Make this work. If you feel bad, make it up to me by doing what I need now. This is a big story, the *Newes* is avoiding it, you're what I've got. Do it, and do it right, and I'll get over your . . . unfortunate choices."

"I'd be willing to do that but I think it creates a problem for *you*, Everett. Even ignoring the flirtation, I'm writing a story in which one of the major parties is my housemate and closest living relative. It'll make the paper look bad, no matter how impeccably I manage things."

"You and Hank have different last names and you look nothing alike," Everett countered, growing rushed and desperate-sounding, as if his brain were working barely faster than his mouth. "People who don't know you will never catch on, even if they saw you in public together. Not only do you not look related, but I hate to break it to you—you've got that cosmopolitan city thing going on. Someone didn't know you from childhood, they would never guess you grew up here. You pass as someone else now."

"Yes, as someone Orion Smith would want to date," she said, unhappily, under her breath.

"The people who do know you're related, they might call me to gripe," he went on, thinking as he spoke. "I'll explain the situation to them, and invite them to take a crack at finding an alternative. They won't be able to, and they'll say, with a grumble, *Well, okay then*. Most people know they have to be forgiving about these things. And," he said in conclusion, "I am the editor, and have no direct connection to any of your internal connections. So I'm keeping you on it. Just try to keep your budding romance out of sight, okay?"

"Argh," she said.

"And one more thing. If you're writing for both papers, you have money now. Get your own place for a couple of months. Then you're *not* living with the person you're reporting about. There's got to be some empty houses around between now and, say, Memorial Day."

"Everett, do you read the pieces I file? There is no housing anywhere on this Island for somebody in my position."

"Then see if you can house-sit or sublet or something. Not to be indelicate, but after the other night, you and Hank could definitely take a breather. That's an order."

When she drove up the dirt drive that afternoon in the slanting, dappled sunlight, the red Rav4 was parked outside.

"Thank you, Helen," she murmured.

Inside, Hank was on his recliner with a Sam Adams balanced on his lap. Helen Javier was sitting at the table near him, her fingers intertwined around a mug of peppermint tea that delicately mingled with the scent of wood smoke. Over all the years Joanna had known her, the majority of hours she spent in Helen's presence included her hands wrapped around a cup of hot tea.

"Hello, Anna," she said, with a confiding smile. "Hank and I were just having a chat about your domestic situation." Helen glanced at Hank for confirmation; he nodded without looking at her, and definitely not looking anywhere near Joanna.

Joanna knew this, because she'd called Helen and asked her to have that very conversation with Hank. Both women understood him well enough that with very few words exchanged, they both knew how this had to happen.

"Hank, do you want to tell her?" Helen offered, and as they both knew would happen, Hank gruffly presented Joanna's proposal to Joanna:

"It's not like I shouldn't have taken the ZBA position just because you write an occasional piece for the paper," he grumbled. "But since the helipad lawsuit is about to go into high gear, it's awkward that you're writing about it while you're under my roof. I'm not suggesting you shouldn't write about it, but Helen and I have been talking, and we've agreed that while she and Paul are on their round-the-world tour, it would probably be a good idea if you stayed in their house."

"Huh, okay," said the person who had come up with the idea an hour earlier.

"We're renting out the house for the summer, but it's sitting vacant until Memorial Day. Want to stay there? We'd just ask you to cover utilities."

Out of the corner of her eye, she saw Hank glance her way and then away again. She read all the emotions in that understated brief movement: guilt for wanting her out of the house, relief that she had somewhere to go, a little irritation that she was getting a free upgrade while he was now stuck at home without anyone around to do the things he claimed he wanted to do for himself but secretly enjoyed getting treated to.

And—although this was the least of it—he'd miss her.

She'd miss him too. Not his current attitude, but him.

"That sounds wonderful," she said. "If you're sure—"

"Of course she's sure, we wouldn't be talking about it if she wasn't sure," said Hank.

"This way we don't need a caretaker so you're actually saving us money," said Helen. "One thing, though. We planted potatoes, because our renters want to be able to harvest their own potatoes, so you'd need to keep them up."

"Twist my arm," she said.

"Glad to, and thanks," Helen said.

Joanna glanced at Hank. "Thanks for suggesting that, Hank. I think it's a real win-win solution."

He harrumphed, trying to pass as a disgruntled man pretending to be affectionate, but actually an affectionate man pretending to be disgruntled.

>Time for me to take you out to dinner

Not happening<

>We could split the bill

Can't go out in public with you until after the story's closed<

>That's a long time to wait for dinner

Not if you drop the suit<

No reply.

Drat.

Joanna bent her attention back to the edit meeting. Her phone resounded with Django Reinhardt. Lewis always called Joey Dias during the edit meeting.

Everett and Sarah had been talking about an opening game of something—softball?—at the high school. "That's a wrap," said Everett, shooting Joanna a knowing look. "Thanks, everyone." He rose from the table and the rest of the staff began to gather their stenopads and laptops. Joanna abandoned her gear at her chair and scooted for the side door, not bothering about a jacket.

It was calm outside, and sunny, but that deep-rooted chill of maritime spring invaded her bones. The call was not from Lewis, but Orion. He hadn't left a message. She called him back.

"I'd really like to see you, Anna." He spoke with simple affection, devoid of amorous overtones, but that just made it sexier. She leaned against the wall, lightheaded.

"I'd like to see you too. But not in public."

"Well, we're past the potluck phase and I'm done with the Orion-cooks-for-Anna-who-pays-him-for-it options. So if we're not allowed to be seen in public, do you have any suggestions?"

"I'll come over there and whip something up for you," she said.

Another pause. She watched the seagulls squabble over something on the dock.

"That's permissible?" he asked, sounding incredulous. "But that's so . . . cozy."

"I'm not receiving a favor from you, so you're not buying my good regard."

"But you're buying access to me—you're paying for it by making me dinner."

"Good point. See you when the lawsuit's over," she said pleasantly, and hung up.

She stared at her phone. That was the right thing to do. Yes. Okay. She had done the right thing. Good. Good for her. She reached for the handle to the door.

The phone rang again and she jerked away from the door, nestling in by the scraggly forsythia bush, and tried not to grin. "All right," he said. "Run this by your internal ethics committee: you're providing the materials and labor, and I'm providing the tools and location. It's a wash. Nobody is indebted or beholden to anyone else."

"Or we could just put this on hold until after the whole thing has been resolved," she said, gritting her teeth. *Good woman, Anna. What a slightly-less-than-reprehensible journalist you are.*

"Anna, let me ask you something." The tone of his voice had shifted. It was cooler, brisker. "How much money are you going to make covering this story?"

"Wow. That's none of your business."

"Whatever it is, how about I make a gift to you of more than that amount, and you just don't cover the story? Then I can take you to dinner."

A wave of nausea swamped her for a moment and she had to squat down onto her heels, pressing her back against the sun-warmed shingles. But she also felt a rush of adrenaline: his cavalier confidence either enraged or excited her, she wasn't sure which. Maybe both.

"They don't have anyone else to cover the story," she said. "I already begged off and the editor begged me back on. I would be creating a problem for them if I quit."

"But you're a freelancer, so that's not your problem," he argued. "Your problem is money, and I can help you with that."

"I can't tell Everett, 'I know you need me to write about this Smith guy, but I'm not going to write about him because he's paying me not to write about him.' I can't do that."

"Why not?"

"Because it's wrong for you to bribe me, and it would be even more wrong for me to accept! Jesus, Orion."

"It's not a bribe, Anna," he said, sounding taken aback. "I'm trying to help you, in a way that also helps me. I'm not trying to control what's said about me. I don't *care* what's said about me. I don't care if your editor devotes an entire issue to maligning me. But I don't want him preventing my dating you."

"He doesn't need to prevent my dating you, he just needs to be able to trust that I am keeping an even keel. Which, come on, we both know I'm not."

"Are you kidding? You're the most even-keeled journalist in this relationship. So . . . how about you come over and use my kitchen to cook your food and then let me eat some of it in turn, and that's a totally self-contained little ecosystem of obligations and restitutions that has nothing to do with the story."

"If you want to date me, drop the suit." She heard her voice say the words before she'd consciously thought them.

A silence. Then, coolly: "I assume you're speaking not as a journalist, but as a private citizen."

"The very fact we're having this discussion is proof that we are mutually failing to compartmentalize."

"Nonsense. You're speaking as a private citizen. I like you, Anna. For all the usual generic reasons that one person likes another—you're smart and funny and cute—but mostly because you get a rise out of me like no one else, even if I don't let on much, and I enjoy that, I enjoy the sparring."

". . . So do I."

"Good. But here's the thing. I'd really like to please you, but if the only way to please you is by my doing something against my own interest, that makes you a person I'm less interested in pleasing. Do you need to be able to manipulate me that way?"

"No, I—"

"Because that's what you did just now, you just tried to manipulate me."

"I thought of it as a . . . proposition."

"A proposition where you get everything you want but I have to give up half of what I want? No thanks."

She grimaced. "All right," she said. "It wasn't a proposition, it was just wishful thinking. I withdraw the statement. I would like to see you but it doesn't feel right under the circumstance."

"We won't go out in public," he said, immediately warming again. "We won't talk about the story. We won't talk about helicopters or zoning boards or journalism ethics. Promise."

"That doesn't leave much to talk about."

"I'll recite poetry to you," he offered.

"Oh!" she said, failing to think of a retort. She tried standing up, still resting her back against the wall. She was over the nausea, at least. She wasn't sure about the rest of it. "Oh. All right."

The briefest pause. "You disagree with everything I say, so I thought you'd say no to the poetry."

"I didn't say no."

"I noticed. Now I have to actually do it!" In his voice she could hear that guileless smile that had attracted her weeks earlier.

She arrived at Orion's the next evening toting her childhood picnic basket that looked like a small black terrier was about to poke his nose out of it wondering where Kansas went. The viburnum bushes, the outliers of Orion's ex-wife's overwrought garden, were budding, interspersed with cheery yellow forsythias. The yard was strewn with crocus blossoms and emerging daffodils, still many days away from blooming. Spring was cruel to New Englanders, but this garden had a stiff upper lip.

Orion greeted her at the door with a white chef's apron draped neatly over the sleeve of his wool sweater. "Come in and warm up," he said. "Have a drink."

She reached into the basket and retrieved a bottle of hard cider. "I will," she said.

"You really are being ridiculous," he said. "But I respect you for it. Come warm up."

The fireplace in the great room was blazing, small branches snapping and popping. "Pine," she said, pausing, and nodding her head skeptically toward the hearth. "Make sure you keep your chimney clean."

"That's a myth," he said complacently, continuing toward the kitchen. He paused in the entrance and turned back to face her. "Pine resin doesn't cause creosote buildup. I have that from a tree expert. So there."

"It's not the resin," she scolded. "It's the water content. If you burn wood with high water content, it causes creosote. Hardwoods don't burn well when they're still green, but pine does. The danger is in burning unseasoned pine."

"All right, Mom, I promise to burn only seasoned pine."

"*Very* seasoned," she said. "Shame to lose such a nice house." She brushed by him into the kitchen.

"*God,* you're smug," he muttered, following her.

"*I'm* smug? *You're* smug!" she shot back, stopping at the counter. They stared at each other with ill-favored expressions. Then both broke into laughter.

"I didn't know I could be so immature," he said.

"I did."

He offered her the apron. "Want a hand?" he asked, as she tied it on.

"I'm good, thanks," she said. "I'll wear this because I like the aesthetic, but really I just need to heat everything up." She pulled out a small round loaf of honey-colored bread, another bottle of cider, and a lidded Revere-ware pot.

"Hamburger bun? Clam chowder?" He raised the lid and peeked in. "*Oh*," he said in surprise, examining the glop of red stew, densely inhabited with beans, thick wilted greens, and sausage. "Not clam chowder."

"Kale-linguica soup," she said. "Portuguese sweet bread."

"How exotic," he said, happy.

"Peasant grub," she corrected. "I grew up on vats of this in the winter. In the spirit of the evening, I'm commingling it with some more upmarket dishes." From the depths of Toto's basket, she revealed a bundle of asparagus, a lemon, a small package of shredded Parmesan, and a salt-and-pepper container.

He blinked rapidly, as if smacked. "I'm caught between wanting to comment on the absurdity of your bringing your own salt and pepper, and wanting to fixate on the word *commingling*."

She carefully rolled the rubber band off the asparagus. "Meanwhile, you promised me something on the phone, so why don't you get to it."

"Pardon?"

"Poetry. Get on with it, English major."

"Ah," he said. "I was hoping you'd forget about that."

"Tough luck."

"Right. Well, I'm a man of my word. So now I have to recite poetry to an attractive female."

"That's correct," she said, rinsing the asparagus under the faucet.

"I can't wait for this stupid lawsuit to be over so I can do something less harrowing, like bungee-jumping."

"Ground rules: no talking about the stupid lawsuit."

"Which stupid lawsuit?"

"The stupid lawsuit that's in your power to stop."

"Oh, that one," he said, frowning. "I don't think we should talk about it."

"Go find—"

"—find some poetry. Right," he said, somewhat subdued, and shuffled into the great room. "What's your pleasure?" he called out. "Sappho or Dr. Seuss?"

"Six of one," she said. "Host's preference."

"I can recite *The Lorax* by heart," he called back proudly. "But let's see what else I've got here . . . How about excerpts from the *Kama Sutra*?"

"Your maturity is exceeded only by your subtlety," she said. "Have you got a lemon zester?"

Dinner was splendid. And not just the food. Orion had laid out a table far too resplendent for kale-linguica soup. Red linen napkins, fine china, the requisite candles and candlesticks. He had constructed a winter bouquet—sprigs of holly, twigs with pine needles, copper birch leaves, the skeletons of insect-devoured dead oak leaves, dried marsh grasses.

"All of it is local," he boasted, at the end of the meal. "Right here on the property."

It was sweet because he wanted to please her. It was incriminating because of the marsh grass.

"I see you have wetlands," she said, gesturing to the grass. He nodded, happy that she was interested. She gave him a meaningful look, stretching it out to intrigue him. Then: "You can't have a helipad near wetlands; it's very disruptive to the ecosystem."

His eyes had started to widen with frustration before she'd finished. "Oh my God," he said, directing this heavenward. "We agreed not to talk about it." His attention returned to her, with a disbelieving grin. "You are just atrocious at keeping your word, you know that? I think you're sincere in wanting to—you seem sincere—but wow, you are a failure at implementation." As always, he sounded friendly and understanding. "I'm going to fine you the next time you break our agreement. Seriously. Stop grinning. I am actually going to *fine* you."

"What's the fine?" she asked.

"One kiss," he said. Then he blushed so deeply she could see it in the candlelight.

A long pause.

"Is that . . . Sorry, just to clarify, is that supposed to *deter* me from mentioning the lawsuit?"

"You tell me," he said.

"Pretty adroit, putting that on me," she said. Now she was flushed too.

"You are the one who keeps violating the terms of the dining agreement," he said. "Given the intensity of your feelings, I don't imagine you'd *want* to kiss me, therefore *presumably* the fine would work as a deterrent." He dabbed at his mouth with his napkin, although he'd finished eating several minutes earlier. "Let me know if I'm wrong about that."

"The possibility of my wanting a kiss from you exists in a parallel universe from the universe in which I have opinions about your stupid lawsuit."

"Did I mishear you, or did you just mention the thing we agreed not to mention?"

She gave him a knowing look. *All right,* she thought, *we're doing this. We've been balancing on the edge of it for weeks, might as well throw ourselves over and see how we survive.*

"Do you mean the stupid lawsuit?" she said, poker-faced.

"Anna," he said, like a kindergarten teacher warning a truculent toddler.

"Why would I bring up the stupid lawsuit?" she asked.

"I'm seri—"

"I mean, here I am at a romantic candlelit dinner with a smart, attractive, funny man whose only request is that I not refer to his stupid lawsuit—"

"Okay, that's it," he began, getting up from his chair.

"I would have to be such an ass to keep bringing up his stupid lawsuit," she rushed on. He moved toward her. "I mean, *such* an ass that really, why would he ever want to kiss me?"

"I want to kiss you," he said, standing over her now. "I fully intend to kiss you. Am I going to have to gag you first?"

"I'm not really into kink," she said.

"So maybe you could just stop talking for a moment," he suggested. His eyes examined her face. She wondered how much lipstick still clung to her lips, and if her hair was falling the right way, and how insipid it was to think of these things.

"Sure, okay, I can stop talking," she said. "But I'm going to get a crick in my neck if I have to keep looking up at you like this."

"All right then," he said softly. He took one large breath and then, with a smoothness she would never have anticipated, he reached down, scooped one arm under her knees and the other behind her back and lifted her out of her chair—knocking the chair over so that it banged loudly against the granite counter, before ricocheting off and crashing to the floor.

By the time it landed, Orion had carried her straight out of the kitchen and into the great room, where he settled her onto the daybed near the fire. "All right," he said again, as he released her. "Lean back. So your neck doesn't get crimped when I kiss you."

"Oh. Right," she said, stupidly. She leaned back against the cushions of the daybed, face up toward him. "Like this?"

He hovered over her a moment, his eyes sweeping up and down her figure. "Yeah, like that," he said almost absent-mindedly, to her ankles. Slowly his attention moved back up her body to her face.

"Are you comfortable enough that you can lie there for a few minutes without needing to move much? Because I'm about to kiss you and it might take a while."

"I think this will work."

"Good neck support? Your head stable?"

She pressed her head back against the cushions. "Seems pretty good."

"So when I kiss you, if there's, y'know, a certain amount of pressure, maybe a little moving around, you're still good."

She shrugged recumbently. "I can't guarantee anything, but we could give it a shot."

His eyes were slowly scanning her again. "Hm," he said, possibly in reply.

His gaze, suddenly, had an almost physical component to it. She could feel his eyes upon her stomach, moving up her torso—when he reached her breasts, her entire body responded, as if he had reached down and felt her with his hands. She took a sharp, deep breath, tried to be casual, tried to exhale slowly.

He seemed indifferent to her breathing. His eyes lingered over her breasts a moment and then moved up past her collarbone to her exposed neck.

"I'll probably want to kiss there," he said, his studious gaze entirely on a spot under her chin.

"You're being very intrepid."

"Thank you," he said, and finally raised his gaze to look directly at her. "I get that a lot."

"Not surprised," she said.

He sat on the daybed beside her. They stared at each other in the firelight.

Finally they smiled a little.

"You all right with this?" he asked, softly.

She opened her mouth and then hesitated, to create the impression she was thinking about it. ". . . Yes," she concluded.

"That was a fraudulent pause," he said.

". . . Yes."

He grinned. The grin softened into the affectionate smile that was his signature aspect. He leaned in close to her and whispered, "All right, here we go then," and then very gently pressed his lips to hers.

It was delectable, both safe and dangerous at the same time—safe in all the important ways, and dangerous in all the thrilling ones. He stayed there for a long moment and for most of that she could not even think clearly. She was aware of nothing but his touch.

He pulled away and looked at her, the smile tentative but still there. "Well, that was pretty ducky."

She smiled back with a small nod. "Not bad," she said.

"I'm going to kiss you again, but first, that spot on your neck needs some attention."

"Yes," she said. "Yes, it does. I was meaning to mention it to you."

"I'm going to touch you," he said softly. His voice was pleasing. "While I'm kissing your neck, I'm going to run my hand up and down the side of your body as far as I can reach. I'll probably pause on your hip. Then I'll slide it up to near your breast." His voice lowered to a whisper. "I'll nearly touch your breast, but not quite. I will want to, and you'll want me to, but we'll have to wait until next time, because I am a gentleman."

"Does that mean I have to be a lady?" she whispered.

He shook his head. "Please don't feel that you must be." He patted the tip of her nose with his index finger.

He lowered his head to her collarbone and reached under her chin with the tip of his tongue.

They stayed on the daybed for more than an hour.

But he remained a gentleman. A very gentle man. With a joyful smile and happy, kind eyes. So lovely to kiss and be kissed by, embrace and be embraced by.

Hank was long asleep by the time she returned from nuzzling the enemy.

That week, Anna Howes wrote up the news briefs at the *Journal* and did a short feature for the Community section about the opening of a new breakfast café in Edgartown. April seemed a risky month, to Joanna, for starting up a new business. In summer or early autumn, there could be immediate patronage; in the winter dearth, the year-rounders would flock to any new thing for the novelty. But in April, seasonal residents had not arrived; year-rounders with disposable income went south on vacation with their offspring, since the "April = springtime" memo, already half-forgotten throughout coastal New England, perennially failed to cross Vineyard Sound at

all except to some hardy perennials. The couple opening the café—
she a native Edgartonian, he from Brazil—were enthusiastic, newly
married, and quite adorable. The café also featured third graders'
art projects, which one could take home in exchange for a donation
that went toward an animal shelter down the road. The third graders had voted on where they wanted their money to go and settled
on the animal shelter after being informed by the principal that it
would not be sent to help NASA with the International Space Station. This was an easy story and left her smiling for hours after she'd
submitted it.

Meanwhile, for the *Newes*, Joey Dias wrote a lengthy obituary for
Angie Russell, a celebrated Island fishing boat captain who'd fished
out of Menemsha and hadn't been to the down-Island half of the
Vineyard—including, fatally, the hospital—in fifteen years. She'd
retired decades earlier to write and illustrate children's books about
life on the sea, books that were perplexingly romanticized given that
she was writing from her own weather-logged life. The books were
sold exclusively on the Island, and in forty years they'd never gone
out of print. The most popular had been about a little girl awaiting
her father's return from the Great War, and so the obituary was presented on the same page as a story from 1918 about Armistice being
observed on Martha's Vineyard. Joanna was finally in her *Newes*-head
groove and could write "On the Same Page" profiles quickly, with
exactly the right tone to make Lewis and his readers happy. Even
better, though, Angie Russell, although a dedicated reader of both
pages, was no longer alive, and therefore was unavailable to comment on Anna Howes and Joey Dias being the same person.

Of course before she parted from Orion, they'd made plans to meet again. Their hormones were shrieking as if they were in high school, but he declared they must take it slow. She wanted to do whatever he wanted to do, although she wanted to do it sooner than he seemed to. When he asked for another dinner date, she said yes. And this time, she offered to host him, for now she had a place of her own.

Temporarily, of course. Helen and Paul Javier had left on their circumambulation of the planet, and she was in their house until Memorial Day. She'd only settled in the night before, but it was a wondrously fine thing to have a space of her own. Hank was improving, and they had agreed on a routine check-in schedule—he was still on crutches, not weight-bearing, so given the slithery mud in the yard, all chores were still hers, including meal prep. She was also helping his cousin Marie to pull together a display for the fund-raiser the following week, which meant a lot of memorabilia-sleuthing up in the unfinished attic, dodging fiberglass insulation bales. To say she was living at Helen's mostly meant that she'd be sleeping there.

But what a heavenly place to sleep, especially after the musty clutter in her childhood home. The Javiers' house smelled like a greenhouse suffused with sandalwood and cedar. There were skylights and everything was clean and simple, almost Japanese in its aesthetic, compared to Hank's heaps of papers and jumbled gallimaufry of miscellany.

She was still settling into the house. This meant she hadn't sorted out a lot of the electronics yet, as some of them were downright twentieth century. The washer and dryer, in the mudroom, looked like they belonged on the set of *Murder, She Wrote*. The microwave was possibly first generation, afflicted with that peculiar smell she remembered from earliest childhood, as if a morsel of American cheese, including the plastic wrapper, had gotten stuck somewhere out of sight and was doomed to be melted and remelted for eternity. She couldn't fathom the workings of the answering machine or the cable box, which was separate from the modem.

She'd bought makings for paella and pastries for dessert. In the hours before Orion arrived, she began work on the paella while rapping along to the *Hamilton* soundtrack. She lost track of time as she simmered and measured and seasoned and chopped.

By the time Orion arrived, Lin-Manuel Miranda had put her so in the zone that she'd forgotten to dress or comb her hair. No coiffing, no makeup, not even a clean shirt.

It was the first time they'd met up since they'd become on kissing terms. Briefly she wondered what would happen, and then didn't have to wonder because he'd flung himself merrily through the door and taken her in his arms for a warm hug and quick kiss.

"You look terrific," he said, taking in her stained yellow apron and batik-styled pajama top. "I love your hair like that."

"Very funny," she said, trying to smooth it.

"I mean it," he said, nudging her hand away to stroke her wayward ponytail, which had somehow migrated to the side of her head. "You must really trust me if you let me in while you're so disordered. I've been looking forward to this. I was so distracted I could hardly work."

Work on the lawsuit? she wanted to ask, but instead she said, "Me too."

"Really?" He looked surprised, and pleased. Then the scent of simmering mollusks and saffron shanghaied his attention. "That smells amazing," he said, letting his nose guide him toward the cooking area.

"Hopefully it will taste as good as it smells."

"It's a shame our secret courtship is costing you so much money," he said.

"You can take me out to dinner as soon as—well, you know," she said.

He grinned. "Motivation to get it all wrapped up as soon as possible," he said.

"Or motivation to just drop the whole thing," she amended.

"You're a riot," he said, and then glanced around the house. "Nice place. Sort of old-school upscale hippie. You said it's yours on loan? Where do you live the rest of the time?"

"Why don't you just land at the airport?"

He chuckled, and perused the paella. "I don't want to discuss it. So I'm changing the fine. The fine is now that I will *not* kiss you each time you mention the damn helipad."

"Wow, hardball."

"Famous for it." Finding a shrimp, he plucked it from the pan, blew on it, and bit into it. "This is fabulous. We can't discuss the case or suddenly this lovely meal becomes your attempt to buy access to me."

"Yes, I know!" she said. "*I'm* the one who's been banging on about ethics."

"Well, then shut up about the helipad," he said calmly.

They sat and ate. They sipped some lovely rioja. They made witty small talk and reaffirmed that despite their socioeconomic differences, they were aligned on diverse elements of culture such as Wonder Woman, the Grammy Awards, and the death of the American novel.

Dinner finished, they washed and dried the dishes side by side, then opened a bottle of Malbec and settled down next to each other on the couch. Helen lit this part of the house with cascades of tiny white Christmas tree lights.

"You look enchanting in this light," he said. That smile of his always slayed her. So when he said, "Come here to me," she leaned toward him. Let him grab her and pull her closer, so that she was lying on top of him. "Kiss me," he whispered, and she did.

The couch was broad and springy. He began to roll over on top of her, which was gloriously ungraceful because there were also pillows and a throw in the way. After awkward adjustments of body parts, accompanied by giggles, sundry pillows tumbled to the floor, and the throw entwining their ankles, he more or less hovered over her, their weight making the sofa cushions sink languidly into the frame.

"Well, this is elegant," he said, kissing the tip of her nose.

"Is it just exactly as you imagined it?" she asked.

"No, when I was imagining it, the couch was lumpier and there was a draft. Also you had bad breath. This is *much* better."

He relaxed his weight on top of her, and began a kiss.

Then, of course, the phone rang.

It was such an ugly, retro-office sound that they both began laughing. "Can you turn it off?" he said, or something very similar to that while their lips were touching.

"I have no idea how the damn thing works," she said. "Give it a second and it will go to voice mail."

It rang a second time. "Two," he said.

It rang again. "Three," they both said, giggling. And then: "Four."

There were some mechanical clatterings, and then Helen's mellifluous voice saying, as if she had just come from meditating, "Hello, this is the home of Helen and Paul. I'm afraid we can't come to the phone right now. After the tone, please leave a message including your number and we'll call you back as soon as we can."

"Here comes the beep," Orion said somberly.

Beeeep, said the answering machine.

"Hey, are you there? Pick up," said Hank. Oh *crap.* "Anna, pick up. I've gotta talk to you, it's about the fund-raiser tomorrow night, pick up if you're there."

"Who's that?" Orion asked, without moving. "You don't need to answer it, do you?"

"Let me get it just in case," she said, trying not to hyperventilate. "It'll just take a moment."

"He'll have hung up by the time we get disentangled," Orion decided, pressing himself against her.

"He'll call back. He's like that," she said. She pushed gently at his chest; he rose with a lack of urgency.

"Who is it?" he said.

"Okay, well, your cousins want some more memorabilia about Jen that's up in the attic, for decoration," Hank's voice continued, "and obviously I can't get up there, so I need you to go up and get it by tomorrow morning, so come home when you hear this message, okay?"

"Fund-raiser?" asked Orion, cocking an eyebrow.

"Yes, I do have a life outside of cooking you dinner and reporting on your helipad," she said, more sharply than she meant to, sitting up. She had to get to the machine before Hank said something incriminating. Was there a mute button? "It's a fund-raiser for a scholarship in my aunt's memory."

"So that guy's a relative? One of those seventeenth-century-pedigree relatives?" he said, too interested in something she needed him not to be interested in.

"By marriage," she said dismissively.

"I think he's about to hang up," said Orion, and playfully pushed her back down on the couch.

But Hank did not hang up. "There's some photos of us on vacation, that time in Florida, and there's her high school yearbook, and that video we made of her asleep that time, remember? Marie wants all that stuff. Okay, so let me know when you can get here," he said, sounding vaguely plaintive. "I'll be up until nine thirty tonight, and then I'll be up again at seven. But it'll be cold up there in the morning, so come tonight if you can. Okay. Bye." A moment of old-school dial tone and then a clunk, and then silence.

"Okay," said Orion, grinning down at her. "He's done. Let's get back to the good stuff."

Then her cell phone rang. At least that went right to voice mail without them having to listen to it.

Orion gave her a puckish look and reached his hand under her shirt. "May I be a rogue for a few moments?"

"Not for a few moments," she said. "I expect at least an hour of roguish behavior."

"That's sexy. Why is that so sexy?" He put his fingers to her lips. She closed her mouth over his middle finger and sucked gently. He groaned.

The phone rang again. This time, he swore as he laughed.

"Let me get it," she said. "Before he goes off on another monologue."

"Yeah, good idea," he said grudgingly, and struggled with the throw to get off of her.

Hank was already talking by the time she had managed to get upright. "Hi, it's me again. I tried your cell phone and there was no answer," he said. "So I hope you get this. Let me know if the electricity is off or something. I need you to come by before noon because I have to be at the Town Hall before noon for a briefing with the selectmen about the lawsu—"

And then she found the mute button. Half a sentence too late.

"Who *is* that?" Orion demanded, suddenly sitting upright. "That's your uncle? His name is Hank?" He was putting the pieces together faster than his voice could change tone. "Your uncle named Hank has to be at the Town Hall tomorrow for a briefing about a lawsuit?"

"I can explain—" she began. But she couldn't, of course. Anyhow, he didn't wait for her to try.

"Hank Somebody. Who has some connection to a scholarship drive for Jen Somebody." His iPhone had been on an end table, and he grabbed it and said, "Hey, Siri, tell me about the fund-raiser on Martha's Vineyard for Jennifer."

And Siri, that heartless shrew, replied, "Okay, Orion, here's what I've got for Jennifer's fund-raiser on Martha's Vineyard."

He looked at the results. "Article in the *Journal*. Jennifer Holmes," he said, and pressed on the screen. The light of the screen shifted, washing all the humanity from his face. "Memorial Scholarship for student who is interested in pursuing a career in social work . . . named after Jennifer Holmes, social worker and wife of . . ." And here he looked up at her with the sundering of their intimacy deadening his face. "Wife of West Tisbury political figure Henry Holmes." He put his phone down. His expression was angry but his eyes looked more bewildered than anything.

"Your uncle is the chairman of the Zoning Board of Appeals."

"He's actually my second cousin by marriage."

"You grew up in his house?"

". . . Yes."

"You grew up in the house of the man who is in charge of the committee I am suing, and you are writing about all of it for the newspaper."

She took a deep breath and let it out before answering, trying not to sound as miserable as she felt: "That's about the size of it. Yeah."

"That's so outrageous I don't even know what to say about it."

She nodded. "I'm not going to defend myself. It's not like I was trying to screw anyone over. It was just a really unfortunate intersection of work and family and attraction."

"You're defending yourself."

"I'm not defending, I'm explaining."

He shook his head, looking stupefied. "I can't believe this. I mean I literally, actually can't believe this. Please tell me how this isn't what it looks like."

"I wish it wasn't what it looks like. But it is. I want to be better than this. I was just so attracted to you."

"Why didn't you tell me the *truth*?" he demanded.

"At what moment in time should I have done that?" she said. "Think about it, at what moment in this flirtation could I have done that without ending the flirtation?"

"How did you think that was going to work out?!" he demanded, still looking more bewildered than anything.

"I was hoping you'd drop the suit."

"Yes," he said, anger starting to edge out the amazement. "Of course you did. I'm suing the man who raised you. No wonder." A beat. More anger: "And you're writing about it? For the paper? After all your precious scruples about ethical conflicts, you're covering a story about an immediate family member whom you're living with? Are you pulling a fast one on your editor as well?"

"No, he knows the whole situation. It's why he encouraged me to find somewhere else to live until the story wrapped."

He huffed with disbelieving, disgusted laughter. "Is he a lawyer? That's just a slimy technicality. Tell me, where do you get your mail?"

"Post office box?" she offered hurriedly, as if that might exonerate her.

"Who pays your utility bills?" he asked. "Under whose roof would I find your elementary school photos?"

She looked down.

"Jesus," he said. "I completely bought into that bogus nonsense about journalistic ethics. Are you playing me? Have you been playing me this whole time?"

"No!" she said.

"Of course you are; you have a personal interest in my dropping the suit. You have a very personal direct interest in my dropping the suit and you deliberately didn't tell me that. You kept me in the dark. Tell me why."

"I kept you both in the dark—he has no idea I'm seeing you. He'd hit the roof, he'd go *ballistic*, he would feel so betrayed."

"That's a feeling I relate to," he said. "What were you thinking, Anna? What have you been thinking this whole time?"

"I wasn't really thinking," she said, wishing she could curl up under the sagging sofa and quietly suffocate. "I liked what was happening between us so much, I guess it was magical thinking on my part. I just wanted to be around you and banter with you and make out with you—"

"Well, that's over," he said harshly. "That goes without saying, right? You know that. We're done."

"I'm so sorry," she said softly.

"You should be," he said. "You have really fucked up here. I've been duped my fair share over the years—if you have money everyone tries to play you—but I've never—"

"I wasn't trying to play you!" she said. "I haven't accepted anything from you. I don't want anything from you except your company."

"And my compliance," he said bitterly. "You were playing me so I'd be nice to your uncle."

"That's not true!" she said. "A condition of our courtship was that we never even talked about it."

"Total passive-aggressiveness on your part, Anna—it was hanging in the air between us all the time. It was bad enough when we didn't talk about it because of the paper, but *wow*—it's personal, it's been so personal this whole time and you kept that from me. How does that not make you a conniving shithead?"

Maybe she could fit under the couch. This very moment. "I wasn't trying to play you," she said again. "I was stupid and wrong but it's because I wasn't thinking straight because of pheromones."

"Right, blame me," he said, looking for his coat. "We are so done here."

He huffily began to pull on his coat, heading toward the door. Then he stopped, and turned back around to face her. "You're off the story. Tell your editor or else I will. I want confirmation by nine A.M. tomorrow that you are no longer the reporter covering this beat."

"They don't have another—"

"Bullshit," he said, scornfully. "Given the alternative I can threaten them with, they will find somebody. The editor can cover it himself. If I don't get a message by nine that you're off the story, I'm calling the owner of the paper. Got it?"

"Yes," she said, looking down, feeling the shame creeping up the back of her spine, over her skull, and down her front until it landed just below her sternum and began to gnaw on her soul. "I'm so sorry,

I wish there was something I could do to regain your trust or my integrity—"

"That might be the most ridiculous thing anyone has ever said to me," he said, swinging the door open. "Go to hell." He stepped through and slammed it behind him with a billow of cold, damp air.

"Well, that went about as well as could be expected," she said to the answering machine, and then burst into tears.

At eight the next morning, curled up miserably under one of Helen's afghans, she called Everett.

Orion had beaten her to it.

"It's on me," Everett said, chagrined, on the other end of the line. "I knew everything. I let it happen."

She curled up into an even tighter ball. "You trusted me not to mess it up. I messed it up."

"I shouldn't have trusted you."

"You're saying I'm not trustworthy?" she demanded, uncurling slightly.

"I'm saying you're human. That's a mark against you."

"So do I just switch with somebody? I can sit down and go over my beat with whoever you like . . ."

"Already been through my Rolodex." In the middle of the misery, she took a moment to appreciate his using the word *Rolodex*. "Only person I can put on this is Florence, so all I can give you are Florence's pieces."

Florence was a freelancer in her eighties and was mostly interested in things that lived at the intersection of a woman in her eighties and the local hearsay. Since it was spring, this currently meant anything to do with flowers. Since it was spring on the Vineyard, this meant not writing about much, since the Vineyard is relatively underflowered in April compared to the rest of North America, even the rest of New England.

"I can do that. At least until this thing wraps."

"We'll all feel better about this anyhow," he said, trying to find a silver lining.

"I don't see myself feeling better about anything," she said. "Ever again."

"Well," he said, trying to be helpful, "at least you can corner the market on daffodil propagation. And maybe we'll put you back on sports."

She felt like an idiot. She felt like a *bored* idiot. No better a sportswriter than she'd been in January, she covered Little League games with spectacular ineptitude, confusing left field and right field at least a third of the time. Susan Grant returned from her off-Island emergency and therefore to the West Tisbury beat, but Everett kept Joanna on for news briefs. The Martha's Vineyard Museum was preparing to open a new exhibit in late May on the evolving culinary habits of Islanders over the past 150 years; they were seeking old family recipes and kitchen items. The Coast Guard station was ramping up for summer. The piece about the DACA high school valedictorian who was going to Harvard was scrapped for a second time because of concerns about ICE reprisals.

For the *Newes*, Joey Dias wrote a profile of a young chanteuse, a native Islander and recent graduate of the high school, who was establishing herself off Broadway. This would be on the same page as a 1941 article about Katharine Cornell, America's most beloved stage actress and the Vineyard's most beloved wash-ashore. The young singer would be making her professional Vineyard debut in June singing at a private party hosted by old-money clients of her father, a plumber. According to the wife, it was a stunning coincidence that they'd hired their plumber's daughter—really, they'd had no idea! According to the husband, they had hired her *because* she was their plumber's daughter, because that's the kind of leg up "we Vineyarders" give each other. Joey Dias put in both versions and left it to Lewis to decide which to keep, and never bothered to read it when it came out. Anna Howes was too busy researching daffodils.

V

MAY

SHE HAD TO STAY BECAUSE HANK WAS NOT HEALING AS quickly as he should have been. Members of various family branches, and Hank's friends, were good about stepping in and taking care of things in her stead when necessary, but there was a bigger issue, which was that he *wasn't healing*. He was uninterested in discussing this fact in person, so she doubted she could get him to engage with her remotely if she moved back off-Island. Therefore, she was staying put.

Still, after a few weeks of writing news briefs, and penning too many obituaries that could not include the word *heroin* even though everyone knew about it, she fantasized about running away to the big city to spend her days asking rock stars what their favorite breakfast cereal was. Even in early May, the Island felt small, gray, depressed, inbred, unwholesome, and stale. There was a dearth of twenty- and thirty-somethings. Very few of her childhood friends could afford to live here as adults; those who were here had young children and were too busy for friends who didn't also have young children. Plus, they all now tended to treat her, their friend-the-reporter, with the uneasiness one feels about passing a cop on the highway. Even Celia's baking schedule grew suspiciously busy, given it wasn't yet Memorial Day.

She continued to fret about money. She wasn't paying rent, but that was temporary. If she were to move in with Hank again after Memorial Day, when she had to move out of Helen's, they'd probably slay each other. Because of the seasonal Vineyard rental market, she was too late to find a year-round place: landlords with vacancies were already seeking big-money summer tenants. In late September, the price would decrease for the winter, on the condition that the winter tenants vacate again come summer. For generations this had been called the Vineyard Shuffle and it was a topic she'd covered at ZBA and selectmen's meetings. She knew the stats and they were not in her favor. Martha's Vineyard had more houses than it had year-round residents. But most of those were vacation homes and stood empty while thousands of residents scrambled to find proper housing. She could barely keep track of where Celia was living from year to year. So plainly it would make sense to retreat to New York as soon as possible. Until she remembered that she no longer had a place to live there either, since she'd sublet her apartment. But at least in New York there might be options.

But this was moot, because she couldn't leave the Vineyard until she knew what was going on with Hank's health. She stopped by twice a day. As well as carrying out her usual tasks, she perused the trash. Twice she found empty prescription pill bottles, the labels removed with an X-Acto blade, which left stab wounds on the orange plastic bottles. Hank always did that when he tossed out prescription bottles, but she was stymied that he'd not told her what he was on now. Unless there was some other hidden illness, it meant he was still on narcotic pain meds. She would not make plans to leave until she had more information, and trying to get information out of an old Yankee was . . . well, that was its own metaphor, really. It was like trying to get information out of an old Yankee.

All in all, she was in existential limbo once again when Lewis called from the *Newes*.

"Hi, Joey," he said, cheerily. "How's our best profiler?"

This time he had caught her, not in a *Journal* edit meeting as usual, but outside in Hank's vegetable plot. She was kneeling on the damp earth, enjoying the sun's wan attempt to warm her back, weeding around the seedling carrots and peas that Celia had planted for him, while Hank himself was prowling, circumambulating the yard on his crutches, reacquainting himself with the chickens, checking to see how the woodpile, the disassembled Jeeps, and the jury-rigged outdoor shower had all survived the winter.

She'd been listening to Nina Simone on her headphones, so when she took the call she stayed hands-free and continued to weed.

"Can't complain," she said.

"We have a piece I'd love you to do. A new 'On the Same Page.' One of your portrait pieces, maybe a longer one this time since it's a big get."

"All right, I'll bite," she said, as she decided the green fuzz she'd been examining was an excess of carrot seeds germinating together. "Who is it?"

"You already know a little bit about him because you covered a ZBA meeting for us, where he came up. His name is Orion Smith, he's a seasonal—"

She started laughing, trying to turn her mouth away from the earbud mic. "No," she said. "Sorry, I have to recuse myself from that one."

"Why?"

She glanced in the direction Hank had gone, but he was on the far side of the house out of sight.

"Personal reasons. I'm prejudiced. You should ask somebody else."

"I don't have anyone else."

"I could take somebody else's story, then, free them up, and they could do this."

"It's not as if you're all interchangeable, Joey. That's the kind of slapdash amateur attitude they have at the *Journal*. Anyhow, I'm serious, I've got *nobody*. We're not covering any meetings in Aquinnah or Oak Bluffs this week; that's how understaffed I am. Chris has the flu, Rosemary's at a conference, Jane's mother is on her deathbed, and Charles is on personal leave." She had no idea who these people were since she almost never stepped foot in the *Newes* office, but she understood his desperation. "It's on the same page with a piece about building the airport as a naval training base in '42. Can you put your prejudices aside and give him a chance?"

She calmed herself by taking in a slow, deep breath of soil-scented air. "I have to go off-Island for the next couple of weeks. Checking out a job possibility with a New York paper."

"Oh." A pause. "I thought you were going to be staying here." And then, almost sheepishly, Lewis said, "I was planning to offer you a full-time staff position this summer."

She couldn't speak for a moment. Then she realized that wasn't the fantastic offer she thought it was at first. "You mean full-time through the summer, right?"

"No," he said. "I mean full-time, year-round. You'd have to bone up on news reporting, but we get so many compliments on your community coverage, and we should capitalize on that."

"Oh!" she said. And then: "Thank you."

"People want to be profiled by you—I mean high rollers from L.A. and New York who come here to *avoid* media attention. I was at a preseason cocktail party last week and three different people approached me to say, 'Hey, I love that Joey Dias guy. When I'm here this summer, let him know I'd be available for an interview.' They are all names you'd recognize."

"That's classy, how they're suggesting your paper needs their picture in it."

"No, you've got it backward," he said. "It's street cred for them. Everyone wants to talk to you if you're rich and famous . . . except on Martha's Vineyard. Here we only want to talk to you if you *belong* here. In less than three months, Joey Dias's attention has become the high-water mark for belonging here."

"I'm flattered, I really am, but I don't think I'm the right person to do a piece on Mr. Smith," she said, wondering if those other green things in the corner were volunteer potato plants. "Anyhow, I won't be around for the next few weeks." Remembering the pieces she still owed him, she hurried to add, "I'm going to be interviewing the Shelton family and Carol Lee's backup singer by phone, so don't worry about those."

"Well, then you could interview Smith by phone," he said.

She tried to think fast, and she fumbled. Lying by omission, it had turned out, was something she was regrettably adept at. Lying by commission, not so much. "I'm not comfortable taking on new projects, because if I get this job I'm interviewing for, I'll be starting right away. Sorry. It came up suddenly." She glanced around again, making sure Hank was not close enough to hear this invention. He was still out of sight.

A disappointed pause from Lewis. "I didn't realize you were planning to leave the Island."

"I wasn't. But I can't afford to live here as a freelance journalist."

"Oh. Well…" He paused. She realized she had cornered him into something she'd had no intention of cornering him into. "What if I offered you a staff position now? Full-time? Permanent?"

She sat upright, her knees pressing damply into the earth. "Er . . . full-time? Starting right away? With, like, benefits and everything?"

"That's what I meant, yes."

"Wow. Well. Thanks, that's a nice offer." Head spinning. Couldn't think straight. She didn't care if the *Newes* painted the Island with a romantic patina, working on staff there had been her childhood fantasy. Plus: a regular paycheck? Where she could walk the beach every morning? "I don't mean this to sound like I'm working you, but you realize that a big New York glossy is going to offer a lot more than you can."

He must have been expecting that, because his response was immediate: "But *I* can offer you life on the Vineyard. That's a mic drop, I think they call it."

She laughed, mostly from nerves. "Wouldn't expect you to know that lingo."

"Stole it from my daughter," he confessed. "Not even sure I used it correctly. So . . . can we talk about this?"

"Of course. Can we talk numbers?"

They talked numbers, and benefits—it had been years since she'd had benefits. She would not get rich. She could never afford a home in her own hometown. But she could get by, save a little, master the Vineyard Shuffle, and inhabit the place she loved most in the world. Inconveniently, yes, it was the place she loved most in the world.

"I'd *like* to say yes . . ." she said cautiously.

"Wonderful! I'm so pleased. Your first assignment is to profile Orion Smith."

"Lewis," she said. "Please. No."

"You're a reporter, being objective is part of the job. I need it for next week; that's when the court date is expected to be announced. Put the other pieces on hold until then. Thank you, you're terrific."

"Wait, wait, wait," she said, trying to sound calm. "I said I'd *like* to say yes. I didn't say I *am* saying yes. Can I just sleep on it?"

"Sure. Of course. Call me tomorrow, we'll take it from there. Paolo Croce will be thrilled; he asks after you at least once a week."

She sat there for a long moment, noticing birdsong and, distantly, a car downshifting around a bend on Lambert's Cove Road. How ludicrous to be in such a situation, as if she were the heroine of a Shakespeare comedy. Rosalind and Viola would have handled it with panache. All she could think to do was berate herself for being the author of her own misfortune.

A moment later, Hank hobbled into view, clucking to Brunhilde through the chicken wire. Joanna decided she was finished weeding for now and stood up, rolling her shoulders back and brushing the topsoil from her jeans. After kneeling so long in sunlight, it almost felt like spring. She went inside and kicked off her garden boots in the mudroom. In the kitchen she put a low flame under the chowder pot, sliced some bread Celia had dropped by earlier, and dropped it into the toaster.

"How'd it go?" she asked Hank when he entered through the back door.

"Big improvement. This time, I didn't fall and break my ankle," he said with a grin. "Sure takes the wind out of you, though."

"Sit down," she said, gesturing toward his recliner. "I'm getting dinner on for you, but I just got a new work assignment so I've got to head home and deal with things."

"Of course you do," he said. "Me and Wolf Blitzer, we'll manage to survive without you."

She gave him a quick, almost nervous smile. "I'll stop by in the morning," she promised.

BACK AT HELEN'S, as dusk gathered outside the house, Joanna stared stupidly at the tinkling white lights of the living room. They lit the room with a pale, speckled glow that illuminated her just enough that she could see herself, ghostlike, in the plate-glass windows.

Finally, she called Everett at home.

"Now what have you done?" he asked, tired humor in his voice.

"You're the only person I've been absolutely honest with," she said.

"Oh God," he said, the humor evaporating. "What *have* you done?"

"Nothing yet. But I've been given an offer it's hard to turn down. I'm wondering if you can beat it."

"Orion Smith is paying you to relocate to Costa Rica."

"The *Newes* offered to hire Joey Dias as a full-time staffer." She paused. "I didn't ask for it. I didn't see it coming, I swear. But it kind of solves several problems all at once."

A pause. "Aw, crap," he said quietly, as if in self-rebuke.

"I love working with you, Everett, and I'm so grateful to you for putting up with everything, so before I said yes, I just wanted to see if you could, you know . . ."

"I can't," he said at once, funereal. "Especially now, when we have to be careful about what stories we put you on. I suppose you could

just do features, but we're not a features-driven paper like they are."
A brief pause. "Oh, I get it, that's what they want you for? They want
you for the color pieces. Your whole job will just be writing flattering profiles of people."

"Not flattering," she said, bristling a bit. "*Kind*."

"Well, whatever you want to call it, that's your strength, so, you
know . . . go for it. Congratulations. Probably good to take a breather
from us right now anyhow."

"I'll miss you too," she said, stung.

"Sorry," Everett said. "I didn't meant to be . . . to sound . . . Look,
this is coming out of nowhere, I'm just thrown, okay? My inner editor
is trying to figure out how I could have avoided this. I know I didn't
handle things well, but I didn't realize I'd handled them this badly—"

"You didn't, it has nothing to do with any of the messed-up stuff.
I need enough money to live on, and they have it. Orion Smith isn't
even part of that equation." An awkward pause. She stared at her
eerie reflection and realized how metaphorically apt it was: she
needed to be more transparent. "Except for the part about their hir-
ing me to coerce me to write a profile of Orion Smith."

"Oh, for pity's sake," he said. "After all these months of pretending there's no story there, now Lewis wants to celebrate the man
who's wasting taxpayers' money? You recused yourself, of course.
Right? Please tell me—"

"I tried to. Lewis wouldn't take no for an answer."

"I used to not take no for an answer; look where it got us."

"Yes, I know. He seems pretty desperate."

"I wasn't? Oldest trick in the book, an editor telling a writer I'm desperate for you to work with us. He doesn't even get points for originality."

"He wants the piece done before the lawsuit is filed. He wants to give the outsider a human face."

"Well, do your best, whatever happens," he said. "Are you pulling the plug on us right away? You're still working on a few pieces; how do you want to handle that?"

Suddenly she was terrifically tired and didn't want to be a grown-up anymore. "Let me sleep on it," she said. "I think as long as Joey Dias gets Lewis the Orion Smith profile, he'll allow me some wiggle room. I suppose I should come clean to him about being Anna Howes, though."

"If you decide not to, I'll keep your secret."

"You've certainly kept enough of them this winter. Thank you. And again, I'm so sorry for all my bungling."

"Live and learn," he said. "There was no wreckage. Except a punctured romance."

She let out a deep breath. "Thanks, Everett." She waited for him to hang up.

Then she set the phone down. She'd call the *Newes* in the morning. Make it final.

And then try to figure out a way for Joey Dias to interview Mr. Orion Smith.

The *Newes* already had Orion's email address, and before noon the next day they'd set Joey Dias up with an in-house account: jd@mvineyardnewes.org.

> *Dear Mr. Smith,*
>
> *I'm Joey Dias from the* Vineyard Newes. *I'm looking forward to writing about you. Unfortunately I'm traveling for a bit and won't have very good phone or even internet reception, so it looks like we'll have to do this mostly as a Q&A email exchange. I do mean exchange, as I'm sure to have follow-ups to my initial questions. Hope this arrangement works for you. I'll be sending the initial questions later today. Thanks so much, looking forward to it.*
>
> *—JD*

The response came quickly.

> *Hello Joey—*
>
> *Great to (virtually) meet you. I'm a fan of your writing and honored to be worthy of your journalistic attention. I understand that we need to start this as an email, but let's connect in person, or at least by phone, some point soon. I'd love to show you around my property, since my owning it is—at present—what connects me most to the Vineyard. Plus it's a gorgeous place and it would feel exotic to show it off. So let me know when you're back,*

and I'll have you up there for coffee? Give me dates, I can work around them. Thanks! PS: Call me Orion.

Hello Orion,

Thanks for the kind words. I don't think I'll be back on the Island before deadline—the opportunity to interview you came up unexpectedly and I already had plans. Sorry about that. Let's see how the email exchange works. If it proves too difficult, we can either delay the pub date or see if one of my colleagues at the Newes can do a follow-up with you. Best, JD

Hi Joey,

Where are you going to be? In case you haven't heard (ha), I have a helicopter—could come meet you almost anywhere along the northeast corridor. I can even give you an aerial tour of the estate, and get you back to America in time for dinner. Let me know!

-Orion

Dear Orion,

What an extraordinary invitation! Thanks! Unfortunately I'll be in Peru, which is probably out of helicopter
range LOL.

Anyhow, as my editor probably mentioned, a photographer will come out separately to take a photo
of you. So I think we've got all the bases covered even
though we won't get to meet in person. I've done this
before, so I'm confident I can present you to our readers with a credible sense of familiarity. Thanks for understanding the situation.

-JD

Hi Joey-

Well let's start with the email, then. But I feel pretty
strongly that we should have at least a brief meeting in
person. I'm sure you hear this from people a lot, but I'm
enough of an extrovert that it's hard for me to imagine

anyone really grasping my personality without being in the room with me. More than that, though, I'm feeling sensitive around issues of transparency due to recent personal reasons. So call me a diva, but I consider it a necessity—even though I already know and really do admire your work—that we have a chance to connect in person. Ciao. OS

Joey Dias asked Orion Smith, via email, to meet at Hubert's Bakery. It was where he'd first met Joanna one-on-one, so now it could be the last place as well. It was early May, but it wasn't spring. There were some flowers, and maples with fat leaf buds, but it wasn't spring. The air was fresh but still had a nip that no longer plagued the off-Island sections of New England. People still wore jackets. It was the tipping point of the year, when half the Island thought winter would never end, while the other half—caretakers and landscapers and retail or boutique owners—were already overwhelmed by summer's approach.

She drove Hank's truck to the commercial cluster of shops and businesses and parked it where it wasn't visible from the bakery windows. She cut the motor, took a deep breath, pulled the key from the ignition, and tossed it into her canvas bag.

She took another deep breath.

And another one. She realized she was chewing on her lower lip, and made herself stop. Her discomfort moved into her body and her forearms began to itch. She tried to ignore this, pulled the sleeves of her jacket down firmly over the wrists, and opened the door. Placed one foot on the ground. Then pivoted, and placed the other foot down too. She did not want to go into the bakery. If an osprey had flown past offering to carry her away if she would just do him the courtesy of turning into his favorite fish, she would have gone with him. Anything was better than this imminent humiliation. At least, since they'd be in public, there would have to be a limit to his outrage.

Feeling as if she'd swallowed a radioactive ice pick, she willed herself to walk to the door of the bakery. She looked in through the glass panel before she entered. There were only three customers inside, and two young women hovering behind the display cases, prettifying and neatening in the post-rush-hour calm. She could see Orion, relaxing at the larger table, looking about calmly, waiting to meet the writer he already knew he was going to charm.

She took yet another deep breath. Eventually the worst would be over, but it couldn't be over until after it started, so she had better just start it. She reached for the handle. She opened the door.

All heads in the room turned slightly in the direction of the opening door, and then almost immediately all but one head turned away again. She could feel Orion staring at her, without her glancing in his direction. She began to walk toward his table, not able to look up.

As she approached, she could feel the air between them stiffen. "What are you doing? Don't sit here," he said.

She sat, her eyes still nervously averted. She wished she were wearing a broad-brimmed hat to shield her entire face.

"Go away," he said firmly. Calm, but cold. "We have an understanding. Honor it. I'm waiting to speak to someone."

"My name," she said quietly, almost a whisper, "is Joanna. Dias. Howes." Finally she glanced up at him. How awful to see his face without a smile on it.

He stared back with a blank expression, and then a puzzled look puckered his face. His eyes opened a little wider, his brows pulled closer together, and his jaw went slack. It was almost worth it just to see him lose his slick.

"Yeah," she said. "You got it."

He stared. She braced herself for the verbal attack, hoping he would contain himself in public. He just stared.

Then he burst out laughing. He laughed so hard he had to hold his head steady between his hands. Everyone in the bakery stared at him.

"What," she said. She felt almost sucker-punched.

"This is absurd," he said, looking up, containing himself.

"I thought you'd be angry."

"I'm furious. Of course I'm furious. But it's too absurd not to laugh at." His eyes glittered. "Okay, we're going for a walk," he said, and stood up so abruptly his chair squeaked against the floorboards. The onlookers all pretended to stop looking.

"Where are we going?"

"Private conversation. Stand up. Let's go."

He wasn't the sort to hit anyone, but murder might not be out of the question. "Where, though? We're surrounded by parking lot."

He glanced outside, seemed surprised to find that she was right, and sat down again.

"Your ability to disorient me grows exponentially," he said. And continued to stare, until the others in the shop lost interest and stopped paying attention for real. He shook his head slightly, although she wasn't sure if he realized he was doing so. The effect was of somebody contemplating but then rejecting an attack tactic.

"I wouldn't trust you to follow me if I drove somewhere private."

"I don't blame you. I mean, I would follow you, but I don't blame you for doubting me about that."

"Are you evil?" he asked, as if he were asking her astrological sign. "Why are you doing this?"

"I needed the money. I had to write for both papers. But I couldn't openly write for them both."

"You couldn't have gotten a job as a receptionist or something?"

"Do you know what the unemployment rate is like here in the off-season?" she retorted. "And anyhow I'm not qualified to be a receptionist."

"You write features for national magazines, you can manage an optician's front desk, for Pete's sake," he huffed.

She was reassured by this exchange, because it showed he was calm enough to have a conversation. "There's your privilege showing again," she said. "You wouldn't have learned this at your country club, but there is actually a receptionist skill set, and my interviewing rock stars about their favorite breakfast cereal doesn't mean I have that skill set. That's like saying, 'You're a nurse, why not teach kindergarten,' or 'You're a real estate mogul, surely that qualifies you to be leader of the free world.' Anyhow, like I said, the unemployment rate."

"You know that I am going to get you fired," he said, pleasantly, almost giggling. "I can't believe you've put yourself in this position with me. The paper might decide they don't care, but it's now my ambition to personally eradicate your duplicitous tendencies. So please respect my need to make the effort." His eyes continued to bore into hers. "Man, you are a piece of work. It's a shame, because I genuinely liked you."

"I'm very bad at being dishonest," she said. "It's not how I normally roll."

"I'm not even a little interested in that," he said, with a dismissive swat of one hand. "To expect me to care shows how clueless you are. I think that's what smarts the most." He gave her a loaded look, as if he already anticipated her response.

"I don't know what you mean," she said.

"It's not just that I don't know who you really are. It's that—if you're running around being preoccupied by keeping all your falsehoods straight—you're not really seeing who I am either. It's like . . ." He paused, shook his head wonderingly. "I'm at a loss for words, which never happens, so fuck you for that too, by the way . . . It's as if you're playing chicken with me, without telling me. So you don't see me as me, ever. You see me as 'the person you have to not lose the game of chicken to.' I don't merely feel fooled, I feel *unseen*. Which is a *crappy* way to feel after spending weeks getting to know someone." His jaw had been tightening as he spoke and now he leaned back in the bowback chair, nearly gritting his teeth.

She wilted. She had not even considered that, which of course made his point strike home more.

"So," he continued, "why should I want to know anything about you, when you clearly don't have any interest in me?"

"I'm really sorry that it feels that way to you—but we can make up for that, right now, with the interview. You will have my undivided attention and I want nothing more than to see the real you." She thought that was a pretty good recovery.

But he looked appalled. "You're only doing that because you're getting paid for it. You don't actually *want* to do it—you said you tried to get out of it."

She opened her mouth to retort—although she had no idea what she would have said—but he cut her off.

"Here's what needs to happen," he said. He lowered his voice and leaned across the table toward her, gesturing her to mirror him. It unnerved her to have their heads so close together. "You will write up this profile of me," he said, almost directly into her ear. "You'll show it to me. You'll show me that you've made the effort to know me, to see me. That's what I will accept as an apology. Not words, but actions."

"Yes, fine, of course," she said.

"Then," he continued quietly, "we will destroy it, and I will tell the *Newes* I have changed my mind and don't want to be written about. You will not get paid for it. If you're getting paid for it, it's not an apology. You don't have to agree with me, but do you understand me?"

He pulled back slightly so that they could look directly at each other, their faces close enough to kiss. She nodded.

"Good," he said, and then leaned in closer again. "If I like what you write, I won't blow the whistle on you, and you can go ahead and write for the *Newes* for the rest of your life if you like, as long as you never touch a story related to me again."

"Got it," she said.

"I'm not done. If I don't like it, I will blow the whistle and you will never write for either paper about anything."

Now she was the one who pulled back to make eye contact. "So you're ordering me to suck up to you," she said in a flat tone. "I understand you're pissed off, but really? How's that going to make it better—knowing that you can force me to flatter you on paper? I didn't know you were that guy. That bully." He fidgeted in displeasure and she felt her face warm with the heat of righteous indignation. "I'll do it if you want but please own up that that's what you're doing. You held the moral high ground here until you said that."

He looked appalled. "I'm not expecting you to flatter me." He took a breath, let it out slowly. "I don't mean you have to make me look good. I mean you have to show me that you see me. If you examine me and you see warts, write about the warts. But see my warts because you're looking at me, not because you're trying to keep me from seeing your warts. Understand?"

"Yes," she said, wilting again. "Then, what?"

"Then after you write the article, that's it. We're done. Whether or not I reveal you to your boss, after this exercise is carried out, I never want to speak to you again. I wish that I felt otherwise but I can't imagine how I could. I'm sure you understand that."

She nodded, looked down.

"All right, now we've got that out of the way, let's schedule an interview. I think you should come to the house. I have some old photos and letters I can show you."

Joanna held up her backpack. "Why not just talk now and get it over with?" she said. "I already know most of it."

He gave her a dry, disbelieving stare. "Really?" he asked.

ON THE SAME PAGE: ORION SMITH
By Joey Dias

Orion Smith has been in the news lately, due to the legal battle he is preparing to face with the town of West Tisbury. As has been previously reported in these pages, Mr. Smith is in the process of suing the town for the right to fly and land his personal Jet Ranger 505 helicopter on his North Road property overlooking Vineyard Sound.

Mr. Smith has few local friends, and is generally perceived as a wealthy seasonal resident out of touch with the Island way of life. But a closer look reveals a more complicated picture. Mr. Smith was born at the Martha's Vineyard Hospital in Oak Bluffs in the middle of a hurricane, and the circumstances of his life have hardly calmed down since. His youth resembles a novel written collaboratively by Jane Austen and Charlotte Brontë, with perhaps a touch of Dickens.

Mr. Smith's mother, Miranda Pleasance, was the only child of a prosperous family in Ontario County, upstate New York. Her parents were not happy with her choice of spouse: John F. Smith, a man whose background was as unremarkable as his name. Mr. Smith, the son of a deceased mechanic from Rochester, New York, had worked as a handyman on the Pleasance Estate Orchard (Ltd) before he met Ms. Pleasance. An aspiring writer, he would spend his lunch hours with a pencil and notebook in the orchard, seeking inspiration. Here, he noticed Miranda Pleasance walking through the fields with her camera one summer, stalking butterflies and bugs for nature photographs. Fascinated with her stillness, he began to draw her likeness into his notebooks. Soon he was writing poetry about the woman in his drawings ("it was bad poetry," says his son Orion, "but it served its purpose"). Eventually, John Smith got up the nerve to introduce himself.

A courtship developed quickly, but Ms. Pleasance's parents were appalled when they found out. Miranda and John wed in secret in late summer, and by Christmas were expecting a child. By that time they had revealed their marriage, and were living in an outbuilding on her parents' property, which Mr. Pleasance had grudgingly made available to them. They visited Martha's Vineyard the following June, where her mother had grown up summering in a long-held family home off North Road. They were not welcome in that house, but childhood friends of Ms. Pleasance, who found her outlier marriage exotically countercultural, made them welcome in Oak Bluffs. Orion was born at the Martha's Vineyard Hospital in August. That makes him a native Islander.

Unfortunately there were complications from the moment of his birth, and his mother was medevaced to Mass General, but did not survive the journey. His distraught father, trying to cope with the shock and grief, left the newborn with his in-laws. They immediately took legal action to keep primary custody of their infant grandson, fired Mr. Smith from his position, and threatened him with fictitious legal action if he attempted to contact his son. They legally changed his surname to Pleasance.

Until he was twelve, Orion Pleasance lived only with his maternal grandparents, who ensured that during this period he would be raised in a manner that befitted any member of the Pleasance family. His was a country-club upbringing, with golf, tennis, sailing, skiing, and summering on Martha's Vineyard in the North Road house his parents had been denied access to the summer he was born. Ironically, his grandparents were well-known philanthropists in Ontario County, and gave chiefly to social welfare organizations that helped single-parent households. Orion did not even know that John Smith, who had returned to his family home in Rochester, was alive until he was ten; he was able to discover the elder Mr. Smith thanks to his relative fluency with the internet, which his grandparents were literally not plugged into yet. Once he had informed his grandparents that he knew he was not an orphan, he was allowed occasional day visits with his father. By this point his father was working as a helicopter mechanic for Skycroft Aviation in Rochester, supporting his widowed mother, who had recently retired from her job of thirty years as a bakery manager. The hours young Orion spent with her in her kitchen, baking cookies and breads, counted as some of the happiest of his young life.

If all of this sounds extraordinary, it is only the beginning. On the fourth of July after he turned twelve, Orion Pleasance ran away from his grandparents' house during the family's annual Independence Day party, and moved in with his father and grandmother in their small house in Rochester. He was, he explained in a letter to his grandparents, "determined not to ride the wave that would have drowned [his] father, and live a more authentic life among people who truly loved [his] mother, rather than just a romantic re-imagining of who she should have been."

When financial bribery failed to lure their grandson back to them, his maternal grandparents—rather than create a fuss—told curious friends and relatives that they had sent him off to a private school in Europe. They ceased to have anything to do with him personally, but did create a trust fund for his college education. Young Orion began to use his father's family name of Smith and spent his high school years in the working-class neighborhood of Rochester as an apprentice—first informally and then officially—to his father (who, in addition to working as a helicopter mechanic, had continued to write "terribly bad poetry," and instilled in his son a love of literature). A charismatic and smooth-talking teenager, Orion charmed the owner of Skycroft Aviation to teach him how to fly, and earned his private helicopter's license at the age of 17. He skipped his high school graduation ceremony to take the test for his commercial pilot's license.

Orion matriculated at Columbia University, relying on the money from his grandparents. He majored in English, but spent all of his nonacademic time working as a commercial helicopter pilot. With the gift of gab and a disarming demeanor, Orion grew his acquaintanceship with his various corporate passengers into invitations to cocktail parties, and then dinner parties, and—making a comfortable income once he'd graduated and was working full-time—he invested in Skycroft Aviation, until at the age of 26 he bought the company. From then on, he continued to invest, now in real estate and occasionally small businesses.

At 28, he married Lucy Bragg, whom he had briefly dated in college, and they settled in New Haven, Connecticut. At 30, he finally reconnected with his maternal grandparents, who were so astounded by his professional success they attempted to reintegrate him into their social circles in Ontario County, with limited success. He bought their Vineyard vacation home from them—where he had spent his summers—then weatherized and upgraded it. Here he installed both his father and paternal grandmother, who lived there year-round until his grandmother's death three years later. At that point, his father retuned to the mainland, where he now oversees the apple orchard where he met his wife (the apple orchard, too, was purchased by Orion from his grandparents).

Orion's wife was, in his words, "an old-school socialite" who encouraged him to reconnect with his grandparents. Their relationship grew strained beyond repair when, instead of accepting an invitation to spend the summer with his grandparents, he volunteered for a two-month stint with an NGO that operated in the Congo, piloting a helicopter used to deliver humanitarian supplies. Shortly after his return, the couple separated, and eventually divorced.

"He is a magical human being in many ways," Ms.

Bragg acknowledges in a phone interview from her Connecticut home. "Unfortunately, 'magical' and 'good husband' are not phrases that go easily together. I've never wished him anything but the very best, although we came to realize that we had very different ideas about what that meant." Ms. Bragg has since remarried, to Mr. Jacques Lawson-McDonald, an investment banker with Roth-Barnwell.

Orion Smith continues to oversee his various enterprises, chiefly Skycroft Aviation and some real estate projects. Belying his quick wit and conversational abilities, he is loath to speak much about his personal life. Most of the information in this story comes from archival sources, often provided by Mr. Smith himself, but with only the occasional addendum or editorial comment from Mr. Smith's own lips. This is not due to modesty—while gracious, he doesn't pass as modest—but rather from an almost impish desire to see how people will respond to what they do know. "A stranger meeting me at a public forum forms a very different impression of me than would someone I'm dating, for instance," he says breezily. "I'm sure that's true of all of us, I'm just a little more aware of it. It's interesting to see how different people respond to their different impressions of me. I'm sure I seem like a gratuitous jerk to many residents of West Tisbury, not least of them Henry Holmes [the chairman of the Zoning

Board of Appeals, the committee whose rejection of Mr. Smith's helipad permit sparked the lawsuit]. I'm not saying I'm not a jerk, but I'm not a gratuitous one, and I think Mr. Holmes might acknowledge that if he knew the whole truth about me . . ."

It went on for several more paragraphs, mostly describing Orion's property. He read in silence, as she tried to track where he was reading on each page, and what expressions he was trying not to make. Cool jazz was playing quietly from a Bose radio in the pantry. Spring sunshine glared across the granite countertop, uplighting the reader. Outside the sky was blue and colder than it looked from in here.

He lowered the manuscript to the counter. He continued to stare at it for a long moment, almost as if he were too shy to look straight up at her.

"That's not such a bad person you're describing there," he said at last, nodding with his chin to the pages.

"Not at all," she agreed. "Spectacularly interesting. Almost too good to be true, by the standards of . . . well. By my standards," she concluded, blushing.

"Not by mine, though," said Orion. "You left out an important detail."

"I couldn't possibly have included everything," she said. "I already blew through my word count, but there's a limit—"

"It wouldn't take very many words," said Orion. "You just neglected to mention that I'm dropping the lawsuit."

This was so unexpected that it took a moment to land. "Wait. *What?*"

He shrugged. "I maintain that my argument is a valid one," he said. "But there's something to be said for seeing things from the other person's point of view. Context matters a lot. So. In the context of Martha's Vineyard's *Vineyardishness*, I am not contributing to the fabric of the community." He leaned back on his stool, shrugged a little, and said, almost airily, "Mea culpa."

Joanna blinked. "How did you just come to see that now? This article isn't about that at all, it's just about you. Why does this article accomplish what the ZBA, half the Island—and me—couldn't convince you of over the course of months?"

Orion gestured to the manuscript pages lying before him. "There are many ways you could have told my story, but you told it in a way that spoke specifically to your audience. I like the guy in that story. Which, as I figure it, means I must like that audience. Which means I like these people, and what they're made of, and what they value. So I should value it too. And that means reassessing things. A lot of things."

For a moment she could barely breathe. Then relief flooded through her and she sighed. "Thank you," she said. "If that is true, then I feel like slightly less of a loser." A pause. "You won't be reassessing me, though. I mean us."

"Should I be?" he asked. He glanced in her direction briefly, then returned his attention to the manuscript. He'd sounded almost wistful.

"I wouldn't, in your place," she said. "I don't deserve it. I might have helped you to see things in a new light, or whatever, but it doesn't change the past, it doesn't make me not duplicitous."

"True," he said. "On the other hand, if you hadn't been duplicitous, we might never have arrived here, today, at the moment when I decide to drop the lawsuit. This moment is a good place to have ended up."

She wanted to receive this as something positive, but was troubled by it: "You're saying the ends justify the means."

"No," he said peaceably. "I'm just pointing out that you were able to forge something good out of something that wasn't so good. In any case, shut up and be glad about it."

She was a little glad about it. "Does this mean you won't rat me out to my new boss?"

He put a finger to his temple and frowned, a parody of somebody in deep thought. "Hmmm. Nope, I'm not going to rat you out," he declared. And then, the first ghost of a smile since the night of Hank's phone call: "In fact, go ahead and run the story if you like."

"But . . . that's not what we agreed to. The agreement was that I would write this as an exercise—"

"Yes, but you did such a good job, I sort of want to show it off," he said, now with a genuine grin. "Even if I drop the suit, nobody will know what a terrific native Vineyarder I am. Unless the piece runs."

"All right then," she said. "So, we run it, and then . . . that's it."

A pause.

"That's it," he agreed. Their gazes were locked on to each other's like tractor beams.

A pause.

"And we never see each other again. Not deliberately," she said.

A pause.

"That was the agreement," he said.

A pause.

"Feels weird that's the case," she said finally. "Feels strange that once I get up and walk out of this house, I'm never coming back."

He nodded. "It does. Most endings are not so mutually deliberate. We should count ourselves lucky to be so well prepared."

She nodded, feeling sad.

"Of course," he continued, looking away suddenly as his tone of voice changed, "we initially agreed the piece wouldn't run, and then we changed our minds and agreed it will run. So, clearly, we are capable of changing our agreements."

"Meaning?"

"Meaning we could change the agreement about never seeing each other again."

Their eyes sought each other out again. They'd been doing a lot of staring at each other since he'd first realized who she was. A constant sizing up of each other's intentions.

"I think we need to stick with the plan," she said. "At least for now."

He pouted a little. "Why is that?" he asked.

She shrugged. "I feel weird seeing someone I can't tell Hank about," she said. "Not telling him just perpetuates the cycle."

"Why can't you tell him about me? Surely he won't disapprove after reading this, especially once I drop the suit. I mean, I still think he's an ass, but I accept that he's in your life, so I'd like to think that could be mutual."

She shrugged. "Probably eventually. But I'm moving back in with him in a few weeks—nothing's available for rent after Memorial Day, you know that if you've actually been reading the papers—"

"Yes, I know that, Joanna Dias Howes, please give me some credit."

"—and we need to get into a good groove with each other. He's not used to sharing his space anymore and I'm not used to living under someone else's roof. It'll be easier once he's off crutches, but we're going to need some time."

"I understand that. But why does that mean you can't date? I wouldn't be moving in with you."

"There's been a little too much drama around Orion Smith lately to be able to add you back into the mix right now, even as a good guy."

He stared out the window for a moment, assessing something. "So," he ventured, "if I went away for a month and came back in June, maybe I could take him out for a beer."

She grimaced. "Hank doesn't go to bars. He prefers to drink at home, so nobody can accuse him of driving drunk."

"I could bring him home in my helicopter."

"Bit of a logic gap there, Mr. Smith."

He grinned. "Good point. You'll have to invite me over to his place for a beer."

She wouldn't let herself show her pleasure at this. "Don't hold your breath. It's kind of a catch-22. He'd have to decide he wants you in his house before it's okay for me to invite you to his house."

He got up from his stool and walked to the window, gazing out toward Vineyard Sound. "So," he said, musing, "I have to figure out a way for him to realize he wants me in his house."

"Yeah, good luck with that," she said.

"I could tell him I want to get involved in town politics, but I need his advice on how best to do it."

She laughed aloud, from nerves. "That's a bit too hot for a first date, sonny."

He glanced over his shoulder at her. "Got a better suggestion?"

She thought about it. "There are a few things you have in common," she said.

"Other than being duped by you, you mean?" He looked back out the window

"Yes. I'll let you know if I think of anything."

They parted moments later with a handshake, which began without eye contact—deliberately—but then slid into a handshake with eye contact, which led to a brief hug, and then a kiss on the cheek. And that was all. Even the look they were exchanging contained within it the knowledge of how limited it was. Orion watched her, with a slightly forlorn expression darkening his pretty face, as she walked out the antique front door, across the tamped-earth parking area, got into the cab of the pickup, circled slowly and then drove off. In her rearview mirror she watched him, standing in the doorway, head cocked slightly as if he were still trying to make sense of her leaving him when they were no longer enemies. That was not how he had intended to play his turn.

"*You* wrote this," said Hank from his recliner, chucking the paper at the dining table. It slid across the patched oak veneer, knocking over the pepper grinder and half unfolding.

"Yes. You knew that," she said, spooning seafood stew into a series of Tupperware containers she had opened on the counter. The cats were weaving around her ankles, hoping she'd spill some to the floor. The house was almost eerily still without the television on.

"Why don't you write a piece about *me*?" he said.

"Oh my God," she said. "Really? You don't talk about yourself ever. At all. You talk about what you care about, but—"

"That's a part of who I am," he said heartily. He couldn't see her directly without looking over his shoulder toward the kitchen area, but his neck was too tight to manage this in comfort. So he was speaking heartily, in part to make up for lack of eye contact.

"I know that, Hank. I value that about you immensely. It makes you one of the good guys. But you'd have to be willing to talk about all the underbelly stuff. You'd have to be willing to talk about Jen, and your experiences in Vi—"

"I don't have to talk about Jen," he retorted complacently. "I can tell you my opinion about my favorite breakfast cereals. I hear that's the thing to talk about these days."

"Sure, if you're being interviewed for *Impeccable* magazine. If you're being interviewed for the *Vineyard Newes*, not so much, I think."

He paused for a heartbeat, and relaxed back into his chair. Then: "I can talk about Jen to the *Vineyard Newes*," he said.

"You don't even talk about Jen to *me*," she said. "Me as a family member. You're definitely not going to talk to me as a journalist."

"Well, all I'm saying is that it would be nice to be *asked*," he said.

"I'll have Lewis ask you," she offered, setting the soup pot in the sink.

"That elitist asshole," said Hank. "He'd never ask me."

"He asked Helen."

"That's because Helen was retiring from the ZBA."

"Retire from the ZBA and I bet he'll ask me to write about you."

He laughed. "Nice try." A pause. Joanna began to press the tops onto the Tupperware containers of stew. There were six. Four to be frozen, one for dinner tonight, and a smaller one for Hank's lunch tomorrow. She opened the utility drawer to search for a Sharpie.

"So you met this guy, huh?" Hank said into the quiet, possibly just for the sake of saying something.

"Orion Smith? Yes."

"Tell him you were my niece?"

"I did."

"That must have gone over well."

"I didn't tell him at first," she said. "So when I did tell him, it pissed him off that I hadn't told him from the get-go. But he actually had no trouble talking to your niece. In fact . . ." Did she dare go this far? "In fact, I think he'd like to meet you."

He started laughing, and smiled his diagonal-smirk smile. "Oh, now, *that* would be a meeting for the ages. I don't think that would end well."

"Even now that he's dropped the lawsuit?"

"Without apologizing."

"Don't you think his dropping it is its own kind of apology?"

"No," said Hank at once.

"Why not?"

"Because it's not," said Hank. "I'm going to go out and walk around a little." He sat upright so that the recliner folded into a regular chair. "Hand me my crutches."

He was back to wearing a boot, and in general his demeanor was much better than it had been. He still drank more than she wished he did, but that predated the accident and was probably never going to change.

She dropped the Sharpie, grabbed his crutches and handed them to him, then helped him up out of the recliner. As she turned back toward the kitchen, her eye caught movement in the driveway: a UPS truck had left something on the threshold and was pulling away. She went through the mudroom to the front door and saw a rectangular package on the porch about the size of a serving tray, addressed to Henry Holmes, ZBA Chair. There was no return address.

She picked it up and brought it into the house. "Package for you."

He hobbled to the table where she'd set it. "Get me some scissors," he said. When she did, he snipped the packing tape and tore it open.

Wrapped in plastic, with a card attached to it, was a custom-made

Scrabble set. The box was mahogany, and she knew that the board within, which she had played on more than once, was stiffened leather, the tiles hardwood with gold-leaf embossed letters, and the tile racks brass.

The card was linen paper. Hank, staring at the box in wonderment, impressed despite himself, opened the card and read it aloud, at first with a slightly ironic tone that gradually diminished as he realized the writer.

> *Dear Mr. Holmes, I hear you're an expert Scrabble player. I am loaning you my board to enjoy as long as it pleases you. I only ask that if, and when, you are ready for me to retrieve it, we can play together once. Or more. As you see fit. Meanwhile, please give my greetings to your niece. I hope she's not giving you any grief. In case she is, enclosed please find my card. Call or write anytime if you need to grouse about her. Meanwhile, have a lovely spring, I hope your ankle heals soon, and I look forward to that Scrabble game. Most sincerely yours, Orion Smith.*
>
> *P.S. Thank you for your many years of service to this beautiful town.*

Hank looked at Joanna. She was beaming. "Sheesh, you must have charmed the pants off him."

"I wouldn't go that far," she said. "But . . . you know . . . don't you think this counts as an apology? Or at least an olive branch?"

He considered the box. "That is one hell of a Scrabble game. Did you tell him what I did to ours?"

"Of course not. Just mentioned you were a good Scrabble player. Believe me, I'm as surprised by this as you are."

"You've got a grin on your face that suggests otherwise."

She tried to stop grinning. But couldn't. "I'm obviously *happier* about it than you are, but I really am just as surprised."

"Who said I wasn't happy?" Hank said. "It's a nice board." He looked bemused. Trying to make sense of a generous gesture coming from a person he had written off as a selfish ass. "It's sort of a bribe, isn't it?"

"No," she said. "If he'd sent it to you before the ZBA ruled on his helicopter, that'd be different. I think it's just a nice gesture."

He was examining the box without actually touching it. "Maybe," he allowed, a bit grudgingly.

"Want to play?"

He glanced up at her. "You and your word games."

"You always beat me at Scrabble, Hank."

He chewed his lower lip a moment. "You're right," he said. "I do." A pause. "Let's play tonight. You coming by for dinner?"

"Like every night for the past two weeks, yes," she said. "Here's the stew ready, and Celia put aside a loaf for us at Hubert's. I'll figure out something green for veggies."

"Sounds good," he said. "Why don't you come by 'round six."

THE AFTERNOON FELT brief. She drove to Edgartown, which felt a hundred miles away (it was twelve), to finish setting up her desk at the *Newes*, with her own dust-gathering manual typewriter. She organized notes for her next "On the Same Page" interview, which would be with the director of one of the Island conservation groups, on the same page with an article from 1934 about the extinction of the heath hen. On her way back up-Island, she stopped at her favorite consignment store in search of a spring wardrobe, although Celia had offered her some colorful hand-me-downs. Then she drove to Helen's and weeded the young potato plants. She went for a walk on Lambert's Cove Beach, where the eelgrass was scant along the shore now but the bladderwrack kelp was in abundance. The water was azure blue and incredibly clear but still needed a good six weeks of solar gain to be comfortably swimmable.

She walked a mile to Split Rock and then back again. In all that time, she passed a couple in matching corduroy jackets and baseball caps letting their black Labs tear along the sand; a fellow in his sixties dressed in canvas and rubber waders, bass fishing; and a young mother beach-combing with her twin preschoolers, who were squealing over a dead crab. The beach was sandy again, the rocks covered by the caprice of the wind gods, and all was well with the world. In a month there would be parking lot attendants requesting beach passes of all the cars entering the small dirt parking lot, and the dogs would only be welcome in the early morning (per a recent Annual Town Meeting). The water was a pure deep blue, the sky cloudless, there was the slightest verdant mist across the dunes as the leaf buds of beach plums and roses strained close to bursting. In a week, perhaps ten days, there would be green. In a fortnight, it would be impossible to remember that it had ever been winter. That's how spring came to the Vineyard—very late, but very fast.

She walked down the long wooded path from the beach back to the parking lot and drove back to Hank's. He would be able to drive soon, so she'd be yielding up the truck. Hopefully he could manage until she moved back in, come Memorial Day weekend.

As she approached the parking spot beside the house, she saw there was another car there, an old red Jeep that looked vaguely familiar. There was no adornment on it, not even dump or beach stickers, to hint at the owner's identity. A deep thrumming sensation in her stomach warned her she knew who it was, but she brushed the idea away as impossible. She got out of the truck, leaving the keys on the passenger's seat. Walked around the red Jeep to the door. In the mudroom she took off her boots, unzipped her spring jacket, and opened the door to the main part of the house.

"Look who's here!" said Hank, with a jubilance that sounded almost ironic, given his lack of tendency toward jubilation. "It's *Joanna.* You know *Joanna*, don't you?"

Orion smiled politely with a formality she had never seen before. In his left hand he held a Sam Adams, not yet opened, water droplets dewing on the cold glass. He offered her his right hand to shake. "Yes, of course," he said. "It's good to see you."

She took his hand, hoping she was not trembling. "Nice to see you too," she said, looking at his browline rather than his eyes. "That was a good photo they got of you to go with the article."

He dipped his head to the side, almost shyly. "A good photographer can work wonders."

There was a moment of silence. The three of them coexisted in a place of exquisite social awkwardness. *What have I done?* wondered three unspoken voices. *What am I doing here?*

"As I was just telling Mr. Smith here—" Hank finally said, gesturing with unnecessary intensity toward the table, where the Scrabble board sat waiting in its box. "Somebody loaned me this really nice Scrabble board. It seemed a shame not to use it."

"Playing with me wasn't good enough for you?" she asked archly.

"It's not that," said Hank in a mollifying tone as Orion pursed his lips in amusement. "It's just, you know, when two people are always playing the same game together, they kind of fall into patterns, and if you shake it up by bringing in another person, then it's a whole different game, and, you know, anything can happen."

Her eyes darted back and forth between the two of them—two nervous men, each wanting to hold their own space without puffing out their display feathers and riling the other one. "Are you just talking Scrabble, or did the demigod of metaphors spike your beer?"

Hank blinked in confusion. "What?"

"Both, I think," said Orion comfortably. "And if that is an invitation to play, then I accept."

"Okay then," said Hank, and began to hobble toward the table. As he sat, he pushed the crutches in Joanna's direction without looking at her, knowing she would be there to catch them. She leaned them against the back of the couch where he could reach them.

Then she looked at Orion, who was now behind Hank and out of his line of sight. He let his guard down enough for her to see that he was both amused and amazed that this was happening.

"Um. Take a seat," she said, since Hank had forgotten to invite him. Mechanically, she held out her arm, gesturing to the free chair closest to him.

"Thank you," said Orion. He nodded his head, but it looked almost like a stilted bow. She could see his eyes taking in the chaos of the house around him. It made her feel embarrassed for Hank. But there was no malice or mockery on Orion's face. He reached for the chair. "This one?" he asked Hank almost obsequiously, even though it was clearly the one she'd been referring to.

"Yeah, sure," her uncle replied. "Make yourself at home."

Without intending to, she took a deep breath and let it out on a sigh, because she had not been breathing for nearly a minute. Hank didn't notice, but Orion looked at her, concern mixing into all the other emotions he was juggling. "You okay?" he said quietly.

She nodded. Orion sat. Again there was an awkward pause between the three of them. There was a purity to their discomfort, because none of them could pretend that it was anything else.

"I notice you've got some Jeeps out there," said Orion. "I'm guessing you have some mechanical abilities."

"I dabble," said Hank with a shrug.

"I putter about with engines myself," said Orion. "Not as much as I used to. But always nice to meet a fellow gearhead." He smiled.

Hank looked thrown at Orion's placing them in a shared category. "Well, sit down, Anna," he said gruffly. "Let's set up the board."

"I can do that, if you like, Mr. Holmes," said Orion, reaching for the board.

"Don't call me Mr. Holmes," said Hank, as if this should have been obvious. "The name is Hank."

Acknowledgments

It takes an island. And perhaps due to the insularity, several folks I want to heartily acknowledge have asked to remain anonymous. In addition to these Anonymoi, I am grateful to the following Vineyarders and journalists for their wisdom and suggestions: Jamie Kageleiry, Louisa Williams, Bob Drogin, Michael Colaneri, Doug Cabral, Nelson Siegelman, Peter Oberfest, the Gorgeous Group, Janice Haynes, Beckie Scotten Finn, Doug Finn, Geoff Currier, Kate Feiffer, Becky Cournoyer, Caroline Drogin, Dr. David Halsey, Dan Waters, Betty Burton, Geoff Parkhurst, Billy Meleady, and Lauren Martin and Mike Seccombe.

Much gratitude as ever to my early readers: Eowyn Mader, Brian Caspe, Amy Utstein, Marc H. Glick Esq., Kate Feiffer, Jamie Kageleiry, Michele Mortimer, and Lauren Martin.

And how fortunate I am to have Jennifer Brehl, Liz Darhansoff, and Marc H. Glick, Esq., on my team. Not to mention all the other good folk at HarperCollins and in bookstores across the land, who between them transform my manuscript into an attractively published novel that ends up on your nightstand.

About the Author

About the Book

Read On

Insights,
Interviews
& More . . .

Meet N. D. Galland

Maria Thibodeau

N. D. GALLAND is the author of the historical novels *Godiva*; *I, Iago*; *Crossed*; *Revenge of the Rose*; and *The Fool's Tale*, as well as the contemporary romantic comedy *Stepdog* and the near-future thriller *The Rise and Fall of D.O.D.O.* (with Neal Stephenson). She lives on Martha's Vineyard. ∾

When Life Imitates Art: Writing *On the Same Page*

It's remarkable, and true, that the small community of Martha's Vineyard (winter population about 17,000) can sustain two independently owned newspapers. For at least a decade, I imagined writing about the quirky relationship between the two papers (both of which I, and several of my friends, have freelanced for—but never at the same time, since one of the papers really does have a proscription against it).

As a Shakespeare geek, I had the initial impulse to create a romance between writers of rival papers, à la *Romeo and Juliet*. But before I could write that story, I got scooped by reality: a journalist from each paper took a liking to each other and got married. Can't beat that.

So I turned to my favorite Shakespearean comedies, *As You Like It* and *Twelfth Night*. These both feature a woman who must pass as a young man to get by in difficult circumstances. My own novels also feature characters with false faces (most notably *Revenge of the Rose*), so apparently my subconscious finds that theme delicious. I developed the plot of this story accordingly. Because it was about a female writer who grew up on the Vineyard, left, and returned, it was inevitable that art imitated life; I confess to certain autobiographical elements.

Then I reached out to associate publisher Jamie Kageleiry at *Martha's Vineyard Times*. Over the years, I've written some features for Jamie (who used to work at the *Vineyard Gazette*), ▶

3

and I currently write a tongue-in-cheek advice column, "MV Ps and Qs," for the *Vineyard Times*. I was spending my winter in Boston, but I asked her—since I was coming home for the month of March—if I could shadow a "real" journalist at work, or at least hang out around the office, for research.

"Actually, if you have the time," she'd said, "I'd love to hire you to do some reporting for us."

I cautiously said yes, adding, "Kind of funny, this is what happens to my lead character—the editor of the *Times*-like paper sends her to cover West Tisbury."

"Oh, good," said Jamie, "because I'd like you to cover West Tisbury."

So I did. Or tried to, anyhow.

Jamie and others high up on the masthead were patient and generous with me, but I was not a natural. Still, this happy coincidence gave me a great opportunity to research what it felt like to be inept at local political reporting. Thus giving the story an additional soupçon of autobiography. ∾

Have You Read?
More by N. D. Galland
(Writing as Nicole Galland)

THE RISE AND FALL OF D.O.D.O.
(COWRITTEN WITH NEAL STEPHENSON)

When Melisande Stokes, an expert in linguistics and languages, accidentally meets military intelligence operator Tristan Lyons in a hallway at Harvard University, it is the beginning of a chain of events that will alter their lives and human history itself. The young man from a shadowy government entity approaches Mel with an incredible offer. The only condition: she must swear herself to secrecy in return for the rather large sum of money.

Tristan needs Mel to translate some very old documents, which, if authentic, are earth-shattering. They prove that magic actually existed and was practiced for centuries. But the arrival of the Scientific Revolution and the Age of Enlightenment weakened its power and endangered its practitioners. Magic stopped working altogether in 1851 amid the rise of industrial technology and commerce. Something about the modern world "jams" the "frequencies" used by magic, and it's up to Tristan to find out why.

And so the Department of Diachronic Operations—D.O.D.O.—gets cracking on its real mission: to develop a device that can both bring magic back and send Diachronic Operatives back in time to keep it alive . . . and meddle with a little history at the same time. ▶

STEPDOG

Sara Renault fired Rory O'Connor from his part-time job at a Boston art museum, and in response, Rory—an Irish actor secretly nursing a crush on his beautiful boss—threw caution to the wind, leaned over, and kissed her. Now Sara and Rory are madly in love.

When Rory's visa expires on the cusp of his big Hollywood break, Sara insists that he marry her to get a green card. In a matter of weeks, they've gone from being friendly work colleagues to a live-in couple, and it's all grand . . . except for Sara's dog, Cody, who was a gift from Sara's sociopath ex-boyfriend. Sara's overattachment to her dog is the only thing she and Rory fight about.

When Rory scores both his green card *and* the lead role in an upcoming TV pilot, he and Sara (and Cody) prepare to move to Los Angeles. But just before their departure, Cody is kidnapped by Sara's ex—and it is entirely Rory's fault. Sara is furious and brokenhearted. Desperate to get back into Sara's good graces, Rory takes off and tracks Cody and the dog-napper to North Carolina. Can Rory rescue Cody and convince Sara that they belong together—with Cody—as a family? But first they'll need to survive a madcap adventure that takes them all across the heartland of America.

Stepdog is a refreshing and hilarious romantic comedy that asks: What is the difference between puppy love and dogged devotion?

REVENGE OF THE ROSE

An impoverished, idealistic young knight in rural Burgundy, Willem of Dole, greets with astonishment his summons to the court of Konrad, Holy Roman Emperor, whose realm spans half of Europe. Immediately overwhelmed by court affairs, Willem submits to the relentless tutelage of Konrad's minstrel—the mischievous, mysterious Jouglet. With Jouglet's help, Willem quickly rises in the emperor's esteem . . .

. . . But when Willem's sister Lienor becomes a prospect for the role of empress, the sudden elevation of two sibling "nobodies" causes panic in a royal court fueled by gossip, secrets, treachery, and lies. Three desperate men in Konrad's inner circle frantically vie to control the game of politics, yet Jouglet the minstrel is somehow always one step ahead of them.

Astutely reimagining the lush, conniving heart of thirteenth-century Europe's greatest empire, *Revenge of the Rose* is a novel rich in irony and wit that revels in the politics, passions, and peccadilloes of the medieval court.

I, IAGO

From earliest childhood, the precocious boy called Iago had inconvenient tendencies toward honesty—a failing that made him an embarrassment to his family and an outcast in the corrupt culture of glittering Renaissance Venice. Embracing military life as an antidote to the frippery of Venetian society, Iago won the love of the beautiful Emilia and the regard of Venice's revered General Othello. After years of abuse and rejection, Iago was poised to achieve everything he had ever fought for and dreamed of. . . .

But a cascade of unexpected deceptions propels him on a catastrophic quest for righteous vengeance, contorting his moral compass until he has betrayed his closest friends and family and has sealed his own fate as one of the most notorious villains of all time.

Inspired by William Shakespeare's classic tragedy, *Othello*— a timeless tale of friendship and treachery, love and jealousy— Galland's *I, Iago* sheds fascinating new light on a complex soul, and on the conditions and fateful events that helped to create a monster.

THE FOOL'S TALE

Wales, 1198. A time of treachery, passion, and uncertainty. Maelgwyn ap Cadwallon struggles to protect his small kingdom from foes outside and inside his borders. Pressured into a marriage of political convenience, he weds the headstrong young Isabel Mortimer, niece of his powerful English nemesis. Gwirion, the king's oldest and oddest friend, has a particular reason to hate Mortimer, and immediately employs his royally sanctioned mischief to disquiet the new queen.

Through strength of character, Isabel wins her husband's grudging respect, but finds the Welsh court backward and barbaric—especially Gwirion, against whom she engages in a relentless battle of wills. When Gwirion and Isabel's mutual animosity is abruptly transformed, the king finds himself as threatened by loved ones as he is by the many enemies who menace his crown.

A masterful debut by a gifted storyteller, *The Fool's Tale* combines vivid historical fiction, compelling political intrigue, and passionate romance to create an intimate drama of three individuals bound— and undone—by love and loyalty. ▶

Read on

CROSSED: A TALE OF THE FOURTH CRUSADE

In the year 1202, thousands of Crusaders gather in Venice, preparing to embark for Jerusalem to free the Holy City from Muslim rule. Among them is an irreverent British vagabond who has literally lost his way, rescued from damnation by a pious German knight. Despite the vagabond's objections, they set sail with dedicated companions and a beautiful, mysterious Arab "princess."

But the divine light guiding this "righteous" campaign soon darkens as the mission sinks ever deeper into disgrace, moral turpitude, and almost farcical catastrophe. As Catholics murder Catholics in the Adriatic port city of Zara, tragic events are set in motion that will ultimately lead to the shocking and shameful fall of Constantinople.

Impeccably researched and beautifully told, Nicole Galland's *Crossed* is a sly tale of the disastrous Fourth Crusade—and of the hopeful, brave, and driven people who were trapped by a corrupt cause and a furious battle that was beyond their comprehension or control.

GODIVA

Godiva is a crafty retelling of the legend of Lady Godiva.

According to legend, Lady Godiva lifted the unfair taxation of her people by her husband, Leofric, Earl of Mercia, by riding through the streets of Coventry wearing only a smile. It's a story that's kept tongues wagging for nearly a thousand years. But what would drive a lady of the court to take off everything and risk her reputation, her life, even her wardrobe—all for a few peasants' pennies?

In this daringly original, charmingly twisted take on an oft-imagined tale, Nicole Galland exposes a provocative view of Godiva not only in the flesh, but in all her glory. With history exonerating her dear husband, Godiva—helped along by her steadfast companion, the abbess Edgiva—defies the tyranny of a new royal villain. Never before has Countess Godiva's ride into infamy—and into an unexpected adventure of romance, deceit, and naked intrigue—been told quite like this. ∾

Discover great authors, exclusive offers, and more at hc.com.